TOP ELF

TOP ELF

By Caleb Zane Huett

SCHOLASTIC

Scholastic Children's Books
An imprint of Scholastic Ltd
Euston House, 24 Eversholt Street, London, NW1 1DB, UK
Registered office: Westfield Road, Southam, Warwickshire, CV47 0RA
SCHOLASTIC and associated logos are trademarks and/or
registered trademarks of Scholastic Inc.

First published in the US by Scholastic Inc, 2017
First published in the UK by Scholastic Ltd, 2017

ISBN 978 1407 18138 7

A CIP catalogue record for this book
is available from the British Library.

Printed by CPI Group (UK) Ltd, Croydon, CR0 4YY
Papers used by Scholastic Children's Books are made
from wood grown in sustainable forests.

1 3 5 7 9 10 8 6 4 2

www.scholastic.co.uk

For Jack, Willow, Jacy and Rianna

❄ ❄ ❄

Chapter 1

-29° Fahrenheit is the best temperature in the world. I know this *for a fact* because -29° Fahrenheit is the temperature on the most perfect day in the world (Christmas) at the most perfect place in the world (the North Pole).

That's where I live. (At 11 Pipers Piping Drive.)

It's also where I work. (In the Games & Puzzles department of The Workshop.)

AND it's where I eat my dad's homemade ice-cream sundaes. (He's an ice-cream designer, so I try a lot of experimental flavours. Say "yes" to Pine Nut, "no" to Pine-*Sol*, and probably don't try Pining for a Lost Love. It tastes like chocolate, but also like tissues.)

I've got brown hair with a little bit of red, and blue eyes with a little bit of green, so my parents say I've always had a little bit of Christmas in me. My skin would *maybe* be as white as snow if I didn't have so many freckles. Oh, and I'm an elf! Elves come in all shapes, sizes and colours, because elves come from everywhere. Yes, we're a little shorter than humans (OK, about two feet shorter, fine – *why are you so worried about how tall I am?*), but we're just as good at most things and better at some. The only reason we *seem* like we can't get things off of shelves is because humans build their shelves too high. We can get everything off of the shelves *we* make, and you don't see *us* bumping our heads against the ceiling all the time.

Most people don't know this, but Christmas really starts on July 2nd, the middlest day of the year. On that day, the current Santa Claus gives a speech to all the elves and Clauses living at the North Pole. Before the speech, everyone spends their time inventing and planning. Santa Claus designs new suits and sleighs, maps out new Christmas routes to make sure he gets to all the new babies, and updates our Naughty/Nice database. Mrs Claus does the business planning and keeps the whole town running by doing maintenance and repairs on the Wish Generator. The elves—

OK, I'm just going to get this out of the way: SOME ELVES ARE DENTISTS. Of course they are. Every place needs dentists. At the North Pole, that job, like most jobs, falls to us. We cook all the food. We build all the houses. We even test all the video games. (It's work! Really!) The only humans that even know about the North Pole are members of the Claus family.

I've lived here since I was born. Like most elves from around here, I learned mapomatics, toyology, list-erature and Santa Studies in The Workshop from an early age. This year, when I turned eleven, I started work in Games & Puzzles (or G&P, as we like to call it). I'm still learning every day, but it's about the things I *want* to learn about, like how much glitter makes a fairy doll's wings sparkle just right. (Two handfuls, and then a third handful to put in your own hair.)

At G&P, I spend the first half of the year coming up with ideas and submitting them for approval. (The only reason you don't have a catapult that launches sprinkles is because the Elf Council said we'd get grumpy letters from parents, even though I *told them* that was *exactly* the point.) After July 2nd, I work together with my friends in the department to build our best ideas in time for delivery on Christmas.

On this particular July 2nd, as we waited for Santa's First Big Speech, everything seemed normal. Everyone at the North Pole crammed into Peppermint Square, just like they always did. Claus Castle's balcony was decorated with the usual bright, colourful flags and a candy-striped carpet just for the occasion.

There was only one big difference this year:

Santa was *late*.

I was pretty sure this was a HUGE PROBLEM.

"Santa's *never* late," I panicked to my best friend, Celia. "Something's wrong!"

"You're just being paranoid," Celia told me. "This isn't Christmas Day, Ollie. He's allowed to be late."

Celia's the best inventor at G&P, even though she's my age. One time we were stuck in a house with nothing but a pad of paper and a pencil, and in just two hours, she came up with *five* different board game ideas that got made into presents that year. There was DITTO!, where you sat in a circle with your friends and yelled words at each other until two people yelled the same word and won. There was M4Z3M3NT, where somebody played as a computer that tried to trap players in an endless puzzle maze – this was Celia's favourite because she never lost. My own favourite was FOR GOODNESS SAKE, which had you team up with your friends on a quest around the board doing good deeds until a unicorn in the centre of the board decided you were worthy and opened its mouth to blow confetti all over you. (While Celia was coming up with all these games, I drew a really great picture of a reindeer on a surfboard wearing sunglasses that ended up on my mum's fridge, so I don't think I did too badly myself.)

Celia was usually on top of any game. But this wasn't any game – this was SERIOUS CHRISTMAS BUSINESS.

"What if Santa fell asleep at the computer and switched all the naughty and nice kids?" I asked her. "What if his beard got stuck in a door? *What if every nice kid is on the naughty list AND his beard is stuck in a door?*"

Celia looked at me like my noggin was full of eggnog.

"Maybe he overslept." She reached up and adjusted her safety goggles, which were often holding her big cloud of curly black hair away from her brown forehead. "You always get nervous about the first speech."

"I'm only nervous because I love Christmas SO MUCH! How can you *not* be nervous?"

"Because it's our job. Christmas always happens the same way every year." She yelled so I could hear her over everyone talking at once. "There's nothing to worry about. It'll be just like always!"

I tried to believe her, and bounced on my toes while I stared at the balcony. It was hard. (The believing part. I'm one of the top three bouncers of all time, easy.)

"Saying Christmas is always the same is like saying chocolate tastes the same way every time!" I protested. "Or that puppies are always cute! Or that rocket ships are always awesome! Or that dinosaurs are always a little bit too scary for me—"

"All those things are true," Celia pointed out.

"Yes, but it *doesn't make them less perfect*." I crossed my arms and looked down my nose at her. (Well, she's a little taller than me, so I looked *up* my nose at her.)

She poked my nose with her finger, and I sneezed.

"Bless you," an old elf woman yelled over the noise. I said thanks, then went on.

"You know how exciting it is – you've been seeing it your whole life! We're gonna get more letters from kids! We're gonna get to sing carols! And we're gonna be busy all the time! I know you love making stuff, too."

Celia grinned. "I do love making stuff."

I pointed to the balcony. "Look!"

I felt like I was going to blow into a million pieces of confetti, and then all those pieces were going to fly in to the wind and spell out *I LOVE SANTA*. You know that first second of warmth right after your whole body has been cold from head to toe? Seeing Santa feels like that. He's better than a rock star. Better than getting out of school early. And the *best* part was that I got to see him like this every year.

Two elves in formal clothes (reds, greens, little bells on the ends of their shoes and hats) marched out on to the balcony of Claus Castle and played trumpets to signal the arrival of the Clauses. I loved this part of the tradition, when we got to see the whole family waving to us from the Castle, starting with the children and ending with Mrs Claus and Santa.

Klaus came first. He was fourteen, the oldest of the Clauses' four children. We all knew he would inherit the title of Santa one day – he always dressed in red-and-white suits to make sure we never forgot. He sometimes seemed harsh when you first met him and didn't make much time for fun because he was busy working as hard as he could – although in his case, "work" involved making demands, not toys. A lot of people said he walked around like he was wearing peppermint underpants. And then there was his name, which even ordinarily nice people laughed at. I mean, *Klaus Claus*? (He never had a hair out of place or a wrinkle in his suits, though, which I found very impressive.)

Sally Claus was next in the line. She was a year younger than Klaus, and walked on to the Castle balcony without looking up from her book – *Will You Merry Me?: An Introduction to Cheer Theory*. I knew Sally a little better than I knew the other Claus kids because she was always sneaking over to G&P to tinker with toys and grapple with gift wrap. Klaus didn't like to get his hands glittery, but Sally wasn't afraid to have a little tinsel under her fingernails. She also wore really big, goofy glasses even though she probably didn't have to.

Kurt, the third of the Clauses, was a year younger than Sally, only a year older than me, and you could always recognize him because he always had the end of a candy cane dangling out of his mouth. He wore a leather jacket (on top of his two or three regular ones – it was super cold) and snowboarded everywhere he could – including now, on to the Castle stage! We couldn't help but laugh at this entrance, and he acknowledged our laughter with a tiny bow. Almost everything he did was a kind of joke . . . although I wasn't sure that Santa and Mrs Claus found him as funny as I did. Or Klaus – as Kurt strutted into place, cool as an ice sculpture, Klaus's glare was up to Heatmiser standards. If being a Claus was a career for Klaus, it was the most extra of extracurricular activities for Kurt. (Most of the older elves had nicknamed him "The Escape Claus.")

Bertrand was the youngest of all the Clauses, two years younger than me. He had a tendency to get lost in snow drifts and to sneeze at the worst possible times. (Like when he was wrapping kids' presents, which could make unwrapping them *really messy*.) But he had a great attitude and an *awesome* brain; he usually stayed happy even when his big brothers were picking on him, and was good at finding clever ways around problems. I once saw him make shoes with retractable platforms that extended so he could reach a cookie jar on the top shelf. Plus, he always wore little butterscotch bow ties, so I couldn't help but like him.

After the Claus kids were all assembled on the Castle balcony, they split into pairs. Klaus had to guide Sally to her spot, since she refused to look up from her book until the chapter was completed; Kurt kept stealing Bertrand's hat and holding it too high for him to reach, but Bertrand was laughing and having fun jumping for it. Not long after they found their places on either side of the balcony, Santa and Mrs Claus came out to a louder blare of trumpets.

Mrs Claus was thin and covered in soot – she had just come back from working on the Wish Generator and hadn't even changed out of her yellow jumpsuit. Her hair was tied back in netting to keep it from falling everywhere, but she smiled really big, like she didn't even notice she was dirty. She always seemed more at home that way.

Santa looked just like everyone thinks he does: big white beard, long white hair, huge red suit with white trim. The hat resting on his head was sleepy and perfect, tilted just so. His cheeks were cheery and red, his smile was wide, and you could feel his jolly all the way across Peppermint Square.

"HO, HO, HO!" A microphone in one of Santa's buttons

boomed his voice all across the square. All the elves went dead silent, waiting for what came next: "MERRY CHRISTMAS!"

The whole square erupted into cheers and applause. Celia and I started chanting "Santa! Santa! Santa!" and soon the whole crowd was chanting, too. Santa made a motion with his hands to bring the volume down, and everyone got quiet again. He cleared his throat.

"I know you're excited for this year. I've got a little feeling this is going to be the best Christmas ever!" We all cheered again. He said this every year, and it never stopped being true. "But today, I've got a special announcement." His face changed to something more serious, and Mrs Claus patted him on the back, still smiling. The children looked surprised. They were glancing at each other and shrugging; Sally even looked up from her book.

"I wonder what this is about," Celia whispered to me, scrunching up her eyebrows and frowning. "Maybe you were right to be nervous."

That was not what I wanted to hear. My heart started to beat louder than reindeer hooves on a metal roof.

"I don't want to be right!" I told her.

I looked forward again . . . and couldn't believe my eyes.

There was a faint hiss, and the front of Santa's suit split open from the side, swinging around until it was two half suits holding hands with each other. Inside was a mess of wires, blinking lights, toys sticking out of pockets . . . and a skinny man in a red-and-white-pinstriped suit.

I had never seen Santa out of the Santa suit before. Based on the gasps of the elves around me, they hadn't, either.

Without his Big Red Suit on, he didn't look nearly as jolly. Underneath was a business suit: all crisp lines and sharp angles. His puffy cheeks and gentle smile looked out of place on top of a thin body making quick, nervous gestures.

Celia looked at me with wide eyes, and I returned the look with an even wider mouth.

Santa reached around and popped the microphone button off the front of the Big Red Suit. He held it up to his mouth.

"Is this working?" The speakers made a loud screechy noise, and everyone cringed and covered their ears. He shifted the way he was holding it, and the noise went away. "How about now? Is that better?" Some of the elves in the front gave him a thumbs-up.

"As you all know, this is my twentieth Christmas as Santa." Some of the adult elves around mumbled about how surprised they were it had been that long. (Adults are always surprised that they're old, and the older they are, the more surprised they seem to get.) "Before that it was my father before me, and his father before him, all the way back to the original Kris Kringle Claus, who gave us this." From his pocket, he pulled out a glowing blue snow globe without a base. Or at least I thought it was a snow globe. The gasps were even louder this time.

"That's the Quantum Kringle!" Celia whispered to me. "The engine for his sleigh." She handed me her binoculars so I could get a closer look. It was a sphere just like a snow globe, but the snow inside was swirling on its own in the shape of a beautiful white galaxy. Even far away, through the binoculars, I almost felt like I could fall into it. It was so beautiful, so big, but held safely in something so tiny.

"I didn't know it was really real," I whispered. No one but the Santas had ever seen it, as far as I knew. Not even his family knew where he kept it on the 364 days that weren't Christmas. It was the North Pole's most guarded secret.

Hubbub and shock rippled throughout the crowd, and Suddenly Serious Santa went on with his Super Surprise Speech. "With this magical device, my ancestors have delivered presents to children all around the world. It can push a sleigh faster than any other engine ever invented, and to this day, we don't know how to make another one. It's a lot of power for one person to hold." Santa juggled it back and forth in his hands. One hand slipped, and he made a face as it fell toward the ground. Then he caught it smoothly and grinned at us: It was a joke. Celia laughed, nervous. I was having palpitations – I wasn't sure how much of this my elf-sized heart could take.

"Why is he showing it to us?" I asked Celia.

Celia shrugged. "I dunno. But it's got to be a good reason."

Santa continued, "My wife and I have decided that keeping this power in our family is unfair to you, unfair to the world, and unfair to Christmas." The crowd's mumblings grew louder. The Claus children continued to seem as surprised as the rest of us, and Klaus looked especially distressed. "So this year, we will be having a competition. You are all invited to participate. The winner will be trained personally by me and will inherit the Kringle when I retire."

"What?!" I didn't mean to say it out loud, and clapped my hands over my mouth right after saying it. The crowd had suddenly got very quiet, so my one word travelled pretty far. I saw some people shake their heads in amazement.

Klaus was angry. He ran back inside the Castle, shoving one of the trumpet elves out of his way. Kurt had the opposite reaction, laughing loud, as if this was suddenly the best day of his life. Sally looked terrified. Bertrand was hard to read because I could only see his eyebrows over the banister. Mrs Claus gathered the three remaining Claus children together to listen until the end.

Santa, meanwhile, smiled down at us.

It was his Delivering Presents face. So it was like he was delivering *us* a present.

I wasn't sure it was a present. *Could* anyone be Santa? It seemed crazy. But Santa was saying it, and he didn't look crazy. He looked calm, like he had thought about this for a while. I wasn't sure what to think, but I trusted him.

"Sign-up will be outside The Workshop," he announced. "Any elf or member of the Claus family may enter, from anywhere in the world. Those brave enough will undergo a series of rigorous, dangerous, and one-hundred-percent-Christmas-y challenges until we narrow down a single winner to inherit the Quantum Kringle." He raised it above his head again, with a flourish. "You must be sixteen years or younger to enter. Terms and conditions may apply. Thank you, and merry Christmas." Santa turned to walk away, and his suit closed and walked itself inside after him. After a moment, his family shuffled in, too.

The moment Santa was out of sight, all the elves went bonkers. Nobody – I mean *nobody* – could believe it.

"What next? Is he going to move Christmas to February?" one elf grumped.

"I'm no good at tests!" another cried. "This is so unfair."

"I'll bet it's rigged so his kid will win," a third elf complained. "How's an elf supposed to fit in the sleigh?"

"They could make another sleigh. An elf-sized one," Celia said to her.

The elf scoffed. "But then where would you put all the presents?"

I pulled Celia away before she could get into a fight about how Santa's Bag worked.

Elves were shouting for answers. A dozen elves climbed on to each other's shoulders to try to reach the balcony. The chorus of old elves who always sang after the July 2nd speech started yelling carols, nervous and off-key. Someone bumped the elf handling the fireworks, so they started to go off in the shapes of snowmen and tree angels too close above the crowd. Some hats were set on fire and quickly put out by snowballs. As the crowd started pushing out of the square, Celia and I had to grab hands to stay together.

"Why is this happening now?" I yelled to her over the noise of the crowd. She kept her eyes forward, dodging through the green-and-red sea, pulling me along.

"I don't know!" she yelled back. The sound of bells jingling on toes and hats was deafening. "Let's get back to The Workshop!"

I agreed. I thought that going back to The Workshop would bring back at least a little piece of normal.

Instead, I found the world had gone all topsy-turvy there, too.

Chapter 2

The Workshop towers above the North Pole even more than Claus Castle. The older elves tell stories their parents told them about when The Workshop was just one little building where a few elves and Santa worked together to make presents for the few nice children who knew to ask for them. That's hard to imagine now, though, because it's become the heart of all elven life.

There are toy factories, sure, but there are also basketball courts and restaurants and cobblers. If you need a quick eggnog to get you through the day, you go to Nog Your Head in The Workshop. If you need a place to hold a meeting to discuss the extra paper needed to produce nine-hundred-page fantasy novels for the kids who read them, you reserve a conference room in The Workshop. And if you're not sure about the instructions you've written on how to assemble a Smelligator (a toy that's half alligator and half dustbin), you go to The Instructionarium so the proof elves can make sure you have the right steps in the right order. Really, anything you could ever need you can find at The Workshop. Most adult elves live in the apartments there, too.

As Celia and I got closer to The Workshop, we saw a crowd forming at its front.

"What're all those people doing?" I asked.

Celia lifted up her binoculars, then reported, "Looks like they've already put up the sign-up sheet for the Santa contest. Klaus, Sally and Bertrand have already signed it, along with a couple of elves."

"Who?" I asked.

Celia shook her head. "You're not going to like it."

"Tell me!" I insisted.

"Buzz, for one."

I grimaced. Buzz was the only elf in the whole North Pole I didn't like. He was bigger than everybody and thought he could do whatever he wanted, and mostly what he wanted to do was pick on everybody else. When he felt like working at all, the toys he designed were too dangerous. Last Christmas, we caught him sneaking a bunch of swords into presents for little babies. (Luckily we found them all.)

If he became Santa, we'd all be in trouble.

"Other than Buzz, it looks like Gadzooks, the triplets . . . and some out-of-towners who must have already called in," Celia continued. "No Kurt, though. I wouldn't be surprised if he skips it."

I got distracted by a cloud of snow spraying up the hill nearby.

"I think that's him. Let's go see!" I tugged Celia along behind me. Kurt didn't slow down as he approached the crowd, so they parted to let him slide in on his snowboard. He shifted his weight for a hard stop, spraying snow all over the elves in the crowd. The board unclipped from his feet on its own, and he flicked a piece of candy cane from his mouth and crunched it into powder with his toe. Then he pulled another candy cane from a small box folded into his sleeve, stuck it into his mouth, and held out his hand to one of the elves nearby.

The elf, a little girl with black hair twisted into plaits, placed a pen in his palm. He winked at her, then whipped around and signed *KURT* on the sheet and added a little skull with two candy canes crossed underneath it. He tossed the pen back to the girl, who stared at it with wide eyes.

"Excuse me, Kurt! Kurt Claus!" An adult elf with long, wavy hair and a microphone came up to him, a camerawoman from NPNN close behind. "I'm Maria Duende, North Pole News Network. You've stated on several occasions, quote, 'Who would even want to be Santa, anyway? What a dumb job. As if I would even want it. Not in a million years.' What's made you change your mind?"

Kurt snorted and moved the candy stick to the other side of his mouth.

"I don't want Klaus to win. Duh." He jumped up into the air and slammed both feet down on the snowboard, where they clicked into place. A vibrating sound rose from the board. Suddenly two little rocket jets turned on, whooshing him back up the hill. We were all covered in the snow he left behind, but I didn't mind. *Kurt is so cool.*

"You heard it here first, folks!" Maria Duende said to the camera. "The Claus family rivalries have already begun!"

Celia rolled her eyes. She was not the biggest Maria Duende fan. (I knew this because Celia's game AVOID THE REPORTER WHATEVER YOU DO, NO, SERIOUSLY, SHE'S THE WORST was one of our top sellers, especially within the Duende family.)

"Can you believe that?" Celia said to me now. "What a jerk."

"Maria Duende?"

"No – *Kurt.*"

"I dunno," I said. "I think he's kind of funny." Celia looked at me like I had four arms, so I added, "What? I do!" She shrugged and started walking toward one of The Workshop's side entrances. I jogged to catch up to her and asked, "Don't you want to try out?"

"Of course I don't. I like working in G&P," she replied, holding the door open so we could both slip inside. I punched a button to call an elevator. Celia continued, "And I don't want to compete with everyone. Did you see how all those elves were climbing over each other to sign their names after Kurt's? This is going to be a total pile-on. And I don't want be there when the pile-on topples over and everyone gets bruised." The elevator opened. We climbed in and hit three buttons so the elevator would know how far up, sideways, and forward to go. The elevator dinged, and the door started to close . . . until a bright piece of metal was shoved between them. The elevator dinged again, and the doors opened back up.

"Hey, pipsqueaks." A huge elf, bigger than me and Celia combined, pulled his enormous axe back from between the doors and propped it up on his shoulders.

"Axes aren't allowed in The Workshop, Buzz." Celia held out her hand to stop him from entering. She pointed at a sign in the hallway. It was a picture of an axe with a red X over it that said *No Weapons!*

"S'not an axe. It's a toy." The edge of the blade was so sharp I could feel it from feet away.

"A toy?" Celia challenged. "For what kind of kid?"

"A cool one." Buzz ignored Celia and walked in, pushing past her without even acknowledging she was in the way. He ran his hand across all the buttons, lighting them all up.

I groaned. Then I leaned my head back and yelled at the ceiling, "Come *onnnnn*!"

"Whoops." Buzz was smiling, but it was a rude smile. A mean one.

"Let's just get the next elevator," Celia told me. We tried to move around Buzz, but he blocked the door.

"Seriously?" Celia said. "Buzz, just let us—"

"Let you *what*?" he said in a perfectly innocent voice. "I'm not doing anything!"

"Get out of the way!" I tried to push him, but he was too strong. He didn't budge even a little.

"Only if you sign up for the Santa Trials," he said.

That surprised me.

"Why?" I asked. "We don't want to be Santa."

Even as I said it, I wasn't sure it was true.

"I don't care if you enter, Dollie. But I'm tired of everyone acting like Celia's the best thing since cookies and milk. I want a chance to show them who's *really* number one."

Celia raised an eyebrow. "That doesn't sound like my problem."

Buzz shrugged. "Then I guess we'll stay in this elevator for ever."

Celia clenched her teeth and blew air out her nose. "Fine." She spat the word and then moved with such purpose that even Buzz shifted out of her way. "We'll see you at the competition, Buzz." He started to follow us, but she snapped her head around to glare at him, and he froze in place. "Have fun on the elevator." The elevator dinged and closed. We could hear the quiet rumble as it started moving.

"Are you really going to sign up?" I asked.

"No. I just wanted him to leave us alone." She pushed the button to call another elevator. I frowned. If this Santa test had anything to do with brute strength and brute thinking, then Buzz actually had a chance of winning. And if Buzz became Santa, I'd have to do something really drastic, like move to Florida.

Have you ever tried to build a decent snowman in *Florida*?!

Which meant I had to get Celia to join the competition. If anyone could wrangle the Kringle out of Buzz's hands, it was her.

"I think you can do it," I told her. "I think we could at least make sure Buzz doesn't win."

"He's not going to win." She said this like Buzz had as much of a chance as a snowman would have making it a whole day in Florida. (I was very worried about this.)

"You don't know that!" I argued. "We have no idea what the test is like. What if it's . . . axe battles?"

"It's not axe battles."

"But what if it is?!"

"Then we'd lose anyway."

I crossed my arms and shook my head. Celia was my best friend, but she could be SO FRUSTRATING sometimes. I knew I couldn't change her mind.

But I could feel my own mind changing.

Did I want to stop Buzz?

Yes.

Did I think I could?

No.

What if it was a really big snowman?

No. Even if it survived the Florida heat, an alligator would probably eat it. Stop being so worried about this!

Did I want to be Santa?

No.

Or . . . maybe.

Maybe sort of yes?

Mostly maybe with a strong hint of yes.

Sure, me, but consider this: How about definitely yes?

Alright. "Yes" it is.

I had made some stupid decisions in my life. I'd tasted my dad's bogey-flavoured ice cream. I'd stuck my tongue to the North Pole (the actual pole, in the centre of town). I'd even once tried to be *friends* with that huge jerk *Buzz.*

But more than those, this could have been my stupidest decision ever.

And yet, I found myself saying to Celia, "You don't have to sign up . . . but I'm gonna." Without looking back, I walked all the way around the building to the front, where the crowd around the sign-up sheet had thinned significantly. I pulled a pen out of my pocket and added my name to the bottom of the list:

Ollie Gnome.

Another pen slipped around me and signed under my name, in tight cursive: *Celia Pixie.* I turned around and grinned at her. She narrowed her eyes at me.

"I just want to make sure Buzz doesn't kill you in an axe battle," she said.

I hugged her all the way around her arms.

"I knew you would." I squeezed.

She laughed. "Or maybe so *I* can kill you in an axe battle."

I laughed, too, but I couldn't shake a little nervous worm in my brain:

What if it isn't axe battles?

What if it's way worse?

Chapter 3

Over the next month, I could feel the whole town waiting for Santa to announce the first challenge. Members of the extended Claus family flew in from all over the country to enter the competition and were all living together in The Workshop's Ho-Ho-Hotel. I'd never seen the North Pole so busy and full this early!

According to the gossip, Klaus had begged Santa and Mrs Claus to take back their decision, but they weren't budging. Now he was spending all of his free time in the library studying the techniques and skills of past Santas. The other three Claus children didn't put much energy into preparation: Bertrand maintained machinery around town with Mrs Claus, Sally worked on designs with us in The Workshop, and Kurt was . . . well, somewhere. He had a habit of disappearing.

When the sign-up sheet was finally taken down, there weren't as many elves on it as I thought there might be. A lot of kids didn't want to be Santa, or their parents thought it would be dangerous, or they didn't really believe an elf *could* run the North Pole. My parents didn't seem too worried.

"If that's what you want to do, then I guess you should do it," my mum said through pins she held between her teeth. (My mum is The Workshop's top clothing designer; she always has pins and wires in her teeth and hair.)

"Can I go now?" my little sister, Polly, whined. She was always having to model for our mum's kid clothes. "Ow! You poked me!"

"I didn't poke you." My mum winked at me. Polly was always making things up to get out of doing her job. "Just be careful, Ollie. OK?"

I nodded. "OK."

My dad stuck his head out from the kitchen, and ice cream dripped out of his red hair into a puddle on the floor.

"Looks like the competition's pretty fierce, Ollie Pop. You sure you're going to be alright?"

"I'm sure," I said, even though I wasn't. "Celia's going with me."

He brightened. "Oh! You'll be fine, then."

I hoped he was right.

❄ ❄ ❄

The letter inviting us to the first challenge told us to wear armour.

"Looks like there *will* be axe battles," I moaned to Celia. In the list of the top two-thousand things I was able to do, I didn't think you'd find either the word *axe* or the word *battle* – and definitely not the two of them together. Maybe *slam poetry battle*, if I was given a lot of time to prepare. Or if *axe* was used in a pun, like rel-*axe*-ation. I could maybe win at rel-*axe*-ation.

Plus, I didn't own any armour.

"It doesn't say *armour*; it says *protective clothing*," Celia corrected. We were in our personal office in The Workshop. While I read the letter out loud, she was tweaking the code for a rocking horse that gave advice while you rode it. "*Protective clothing* probably means, like, goggles and long sleeves."

"How are goggles and long sleeves going to stop an axe?!?!?"

"The contest is in the mailroom, not a coliseum."

"So they want to make sure we don't . . . get paper cuts?"

"Maybe. Didn't you work in the mailroom for a while?"

"Just for a class project. It was pretty boring, cooped up all day sorting thousands of letters." A thought struck me. "Actually, Klaus was in the mailroom the same year I was. I think they make all Santas start there."

Celia nodded. "That's what I was thinking. We'll probably be sorting – " She was interrupted by a beep.

"A HORSE A DAY KEEPS THE DOCTOR AWAY," the rocking horse whinnied. I laughed.

Celia did not look pleased. "I'm still working on that," she said while tightening the bolts and holding down the horse's silver mane.

"I thought it was funny," I told her.

"You think *everything* is funny."

I frowned. "That's not true!" (For example, I didn't think going axe-versus-axe against Buzz was funny *at all*.)

The horse beeped again. "THE JOURNEY OF A THOUSAND HORSES BEGINS WITH A SINGLE HORSE."

I couldn't help it: I laughed more.

"See?" Celia said. (I guess I saw.) "It's supposed to listen to your conversation and give good advice, but it just speaks up whenever it wants. Plus, there's this bug where it keeps adding the word *horse* to everything. I think I'm going to wipe it and start over."

I gasped and hugged it around its neck. "You can't!" I looked at Celia with my best puppy-dog eyes. "That's not a bug. That's her personality!"

Celia frowned at me, her finger hovering above the controls. "It doesn't have a personality. It's a messed-up robot."

Beep. "HORSE IS NOT MEASURED BY THE HORSES YOU TAKE, BUT BY THE HORSES THAT HORSE YOUR HORSE A-HORSE."

Celia and I stared at each other, trying to keep a straight face. After a second, her lip trembled and we both burst out laughing.

Now it was my turn to say, "See? She's not a messed-up robot. Her name is Horse, and she's perfect."

"OK! You win. If you think kids will like her, I'll submit her as a prototype." She unplugged Horse, who powered down with a soft, grateful neigh. "I should be working on new games, anyway. She's just something I've been messing with in my spare time."

"That's why you'd be a good Santa," I pointed out. "You've got so many ideas about everything!"

Celia shook her head. "I almost gave up! You saw that she could be lovable. You'd make a better Santa than I would."

"I'm not sure that lovability is something you need protective gear for," I told her, which was my way of saying that even though I was laughing I was still FREAKING OUT.

"You're going to look great in goggles," Celia replied. Which was her way of saying STOP FREAKING OUT.

"Aw, shucks." I helped her carry Horse to the side of the room. "I guess we're just going to have to win!"

Her face lit up like she just remembered something.

"I just remembered something!" she cried. (Told you.) "We've got some reject bodysuits from when we made those impenetrable superhero costumes. They got printed with the wrong pictures, but they should protect us from anything – they were built to withstand fire, ice, gum-in-hair, and other natural disasters." Celia thought for a second, then pressed a few buttons on a keypad on the wall. A clunking noise climbed up from the floor, and a panel in the wall swished aside, revealing a cardboard box in a cubbyhole. She pulled out the box.

"How did you know which storage unit they were in?" I was amazed.

Celia shrugged. "I've got a really good memory." She paused. "Oh, wow."

"What?" I asked.

She held up one of the suits. My mouth fell open.

"Oh, *wow*."

"That's what I'm saying." She sighed. "It's the best we've got, though."

We had to be at the mailroom long before our usual wake-up time the next morning. I braced myself for laughter as we walked toward the small crowd of contestants gathered around the doors, but it was so dark no one could see our suits from far away. The doors were still locked, apparently, so the other Santa hopefuls were doing last-minute stretches or talking nervously among themselves. On the outside, the mailroom warehouse was pretty boring:

a huge grey rectangle. On the inside, it would be an ocean of stamps and children's handwriting.

"Nice outfits." Kurt, leaning against a candy-striped street light away from the crowd, was the first to see us. He was wearing a full-body brown jumpsuit under a new leather jacket, a bright red one with *CHRISTMAS CHRIMINAL* stitched into the back. He laughed – or at least I thought it was a laugh. Whatever you'd call a *tch* noise released through a sneer.

"Thanks, Kurt!" I yelled, too loud. I was determined to stay positive.

Bright lights came on around the entrance of the mailroom. Kurt ran a comb through his coiffed black hair and kicked off of the pole.

"Guess it's time to go," he mumbled. He took the piece of candy cane out of his mouth and rubbed the saliva off in the palm of his hand. Then he tucked the cane into the box in his breast pocket. "You comin', kittens?"

I followed him. Celia's eyes were staring hard at the ground. If she had stayed there longer, I'm pretty sure her glare would have melted snow. She hurried to catch up with us.

As we approached the crowd, more than a few people turned and sniggered at us. Under the powerful lights in front of the mail-room, our outfits were uncomfortably obvious: I was wearing a skintight superhero suit *covered* in pictures of babies cuddling with puppies, and Celia's was covered with kittens wearing bows on their heads. And then, of course, we both had big goggles on our foreheads.

"Check out the superdorks!" Buzz called from somewhere in the middle of the crowd. Laughter bubbled up from the elves.

Stay positive. Stay positive. Stay positive, part of me thought.

I am positive that I want to destroy Buzz and turn him into death glitter, the other part of me thought.

What colour is death glitter? a third part was wondering.

Probably like red, black and a dark purple, the first part suggested.

I ended up shouting, "At least we're prepared!"

The big elf shrugged. He was wearing a denim waistcoat and shorts. That was it. He was ignoring the letter's advice on purpose, *of course.* I also saw he was wearing a belt with two big holsters, one on either side, but I couldn't make out what was in them.

I looked around the crowd while they blinked and rubbed their eyes under the light. Klaus, Sally and Bertrand were off to the side, away from the crowd, in matching outfits that looked like the sort of thing you'd wear at a boot camp. Bertrand's was too big, and the long sleeves hung over his hands. Sally was reading *The Merry Mailroom Manual*, her eyes flitting quickly across the last few pages before she ran out of time. Klaus paced and lectured the other two about strategy.

"The mailroom is a key part of the Christmas process," Klaus explained. "The Wish Generator only picks up *verbal* wishes, so the mailroom—"

"Helps us get power from *all* wishes, even the ones kids are embarrassed to say out loud." Sally waved the book at him. "I know. I read. And Bertrand knows more about the Wish Generator than you do, Klaus."

Bertrand nodded. "I've input thousands of letters into it myself!"

"Yes, but *I'm* the only one of us who has worked in the mailroom before, which means *I'll* be the leader. It's more difficult than you think. For example, it's not actually in *perfect* alphabetical order, and . . ."

I moved away and stopped listening. Several other humans stuck out above the crowd of elves, all extended Claus family. I had seen some of them around town the past few days, but Maria Duende was flitting about and asking them to identify themselves like they had just arrived. She shoved right past us – the camerawoman nearly knocked us over – and stuck her microphone in the face of . . . well, definitely the strangest sixteen-year-old I'd ever seen.

"Ah, yes, I'm Ramp Claus," this very strange human explained. He stroked a long white beard that reached down to his knees. His back was stooped over with a hunch. He had very baggy trousers sagging slightly off his hips, and when he shifted his legs they looked very, very skinny. On top of his head, a dark black toupee rested awkwardly between his ears. He was also wearing sunglasses even though it was hardly bright out.

"Nice to meet you, Ramp!" Maria Duende had on her biggest, brightest, reporteriest smile. "The contest rules state that you must be sixteen or younger to enter. How old are you?"

Ramp leaned in to the microphone and cleared his throat. "I'm, hm, well, I'm sixteen." There was no hint of a joke on his face. "Just had my birthday last week." The reporter's smile faltered for a second. Then she returned, bright as ever.

"That's a very long white beard for a sixteen-year-old!"

"It runs in the Claus family, you know. As luck would have it, I've got my birth certificate right here." He pulled a rolled-up piece of parchment out of his pocket and handed it to Maria Duende. She opened it. "And also an extensive, illustrated family tree that explains exactly how I'm related to the Claus family." He pulled out another, larger scroll and handed it to her. "And moreover, I have numerous anecdotes about how well I know the family. Why, one time—"

"That won't be necessary." She glanced over his paperwork. "This does seem to be in order. Do you mind if I ask: Why the sunglasses?"

Ramp grinned. He was missing several teeth.

"Why, because they are hip and cool! I am always fly, as the kids – uh, as . . . *we* say. You know – kids like me. Just like me. A kid. In fact, just the other day, someone pointed right at me and said, *Look at that kid!*"

Celia raised her eyebrows at me. "Can you believe that guy?" she whispered.

I wasn't sure what to say. He definitely didn't look like a kid to me – but then again, if he *was* a kid, you had to feel sorry for him, looking like that. And also – I squinted at his face – something about him looked *familiar*.

"Maria Duende said his birth certificate looked real, so . . ." I trailed off. Celia shrugged. The front doors opened, and a tall, broad reindeer sauntered out with a sour expression in his eyes and a tired tilt to his antlers. He wore a military-style hat covered in medals that signified his service in many, many Christmases. He also had a red nose.

As we all hushed and watched, Rudolph snorted, and the reindeer-language translator around his neck piped a monotone robotic voice across the crowd.

"What a sorry bunch of Santa wannabes," the voice droned. "I've seen all sorts of Santas in my time, and they all looked more capable the day they were born than any of you lot."

"Why is he being so mean?" I whispered to Celia, and then immediately knew I shouldn't have.

Rudolph's ears swivelled toward me before his head did. "Did I sound like I was done talking, wannabe?" he shouted by raising the volume level of the voice. Otherwise, it stayed monotone.

I shook my head vigorously. His hooves started clopping toward me, and the crowd parted so he could bring his snout right up to my face.

"Well? Did I?"

"Uh, no. No, sir. No, Rudolph, sir."

His nostrils flared, and his nose grew bright.

"What's your name, wannabe?" The robot voice got quieter as he approached, which actually made it scarier.

"Ollie, sir. Ollie Gnome."

"Gnome. I see." He turned his body around – a slow process for an old creature with four legs – and the volume of his voice rose again. "Well, thanks to Gnome, you're all running a lap around the mailroom. Now."

Klaus, who was standing at the front of the crowd with Sally and Bertrand, bristled.

"Before the test?" he protested. "That's almost two miles!"

Rudolph bobbed his head in a nod. "Thank you, Klaus, for reminding me." He shifted his head, a gleam in his eye. "Make that TWO laps! NOW! Everybody MOVE!"

We all took off running. Several other competitors pushed me, mumbling something about ruining their morning. Celia patted me on the back.

"Don't worry about it," she said. "He would have made us do this no matter what."

I wasn't sure anybody else thought so. An elf in a light-up waistcoat ran ahead of me, and the lights on the back spelled out *THANKS FOR NOTHING, JERK*. He was even shorter than I was, and the waistcoat was tiny, so it took a while for all the words to scroll past. Afterwards, he turned around and ran backwards.

"Did you see what it said?" he asked.

I sighed. "Yes, Luther. I saw it."

"I meant it!" He stuck his little tongue out at me and then ran ahead. Luther's kind of rude, but he's mostly harmless. I thought about saying something back, but a snowball smacked me in the side of the head.

"Nice one, Dollie," Buzz jeered. I pushed to run ahead of him, but he caught up easily and tripped me with his foot. I stumbled into Ramp, who pushed me up.

Ramp shook his head as I regained my balance. "Bunch of whiners, if you ask me," he said. "In *my day*, I had to run all the way to and from the candy store, full sack of candy on my back, uphill both ways. Never broke a sweat!"

Celia narrowed her eyes at him. "When was *your day*?" she asked.

"Wednesday," he responded immediately. "My day was last Wednesday. I'm in the best shape of my young life! Bring on the running, I say. Don't worry about upsetting the nose-beast, kiddo."

"Uh, thanks," I said. "I think?"

We weren't the quickest (we were competing against humans, whose legs were, you know, longer) and we weren't the slowest (we were competing against humans, who spend more time thinking about running than actually running), but we slowed down when we realized Ramp was falling way behind.

"Are you OK?" Celia was able to walk alongside his jog. He was wheezing pretty badly.

"Never better!" He barely finished the words before he was coughing. Celia and I exchanged a look, then set ourselves up on either side of him, giving him some support. It made us a lot slower, but made him a lot faster. We carried most of his weight around the rest of the way . . . and ended up the very last three to cross at the end.

"Thank you," Ramp mumbled between ragged breaths while we turned the final corner. "You're the best friends a sixteen-year-old boy could hope for."

Rudolph shot us a look that made it clear we had taken too long.

"Well," the reindeer said, "it looks like we have our last team."

"Team?" I looked around. Other contestants had sorted themselves into groups of three.

"You three are all that's left. You'll be braving the mailroom together. Gather around!" The teams tightened up into a circle around Rudolph. As he spoke, he paced around the inside of the circle.

"As you may know, all Santas start in the mailroom. Normally you have several years working here to prove you can handle the pressure, but since Santa has decided to throw everything out of whack this year, we've had to find ways to speed up the process."

While he explained the challenge to us, I glanced around at the other teams. Klaus, Sally and Bertrand had joined together – one of the older two had probably carried Bertrand. Buzz was on a team with Kurt and one of the Claus cousins, a very pale girl with short red hair and freckles. I recognized, also, a team of three elves who had been working the mailroom since before I was there: Goldie, Frank and Myrle. They were triplets, two boys and a girl, and always wore the same clothes, so you could never tell who was who. Today, they were wearing the typical mailroom uniform, a light blue jumpsuit.

An older elf was walking around the outside of the circle with a huge stocking, handing out hats that looked just like Santa's. Another was passing out something small to each team.

Rudolph went on: "Once you're in there, your goal is to sort as much mail as possible. To aid in keeping score, you each have a different stamp to label the letters you sort." I tested the stamp on my hand – it was a picture of Santa on a beach, lounging under an umbrella and drinking something cold through a straw.

Celia whispered to me, "The mailroom uses traditional stamps with a wooden handle, but there's a mechanism inside releasing ink to make sure it never dries out. I did some research when I found out we were coming here."

"I understand a few of you have worked the mailroom before," Rudolph acknowledged. Klaus looked especially smug at this. The triplets smiled, glancing at each other. "Well, you can forget what you think you know. *This* mailroom is nothing like what you're used to. So don't get too comfortable." Klaus's face fell. I honestly felt bad for him; it must have been rough, to suddenly be competing for a title you thought you'd already won. "And that's not all!"

The door opened again. A big wheel squeaked over the floor inside, then crunched the snow as it rolled out in front of us. Atop the wheel was a giant human child – or at least something that was maybe trying to *look like* a human child. It had the one big wheel instead of legs, thin metal arms, and hands that looked like one of those grabber-claw toys. It had a huge steel head with a bright, smiling face painted on it. Its mouth was flat and opened like a ventriloquist dummy's.

Everyone looked immediately creeped out by this monster . . . except for Rudolph. He continued, "In the field, Santa has to be able to avoid detection at all costs. Even a brief encounter with a human child can throw off his finely tuned delivery schedule."

The elf that had been passing out hats changed into a big yellow suit that covered his whole body. He placed the Santa hat on top of his head, over the suit, and the child-bot instantly noticed him.

"*Is that you, Santa?*" it asked without moving its mouth. Its voice was quiet and sweet, like a little girl's. "*Santa, it is you!*"

The child-bot's mouth dropped open, and flames poured out of it, enveloping the elf. After a moment, the child-bot stopped. Instead of a hat, there was a small pile of soot on top of the elf's suit. The elf unzipped it, stepped out, and gave a thumbs-up. He was sweaty but fine.

I was suddenly very glad we had worn the super-suits. As long as we didn't get blasted in the head, we'd be OK. I glanced at Buzz. He didn't look nervous at all, the jerk. Kurt, too, was smirking. They were the only ones in the whole crowd who didn't look surprised. Even their third teammate looked uncomfortable.

"That's the game," Rudolph finished. "Stamp it, sort it, don't get caught. Only half of you will make it forward according to how much mail you sort. You can leave at any time, but you *have to* leave in two hours. Starting in three . . . two . . ." He paused. All the teams got even tenser than they'd been before. "Almost forgot. Lose your hat and you're out. Even if your team wins. Hats on!"

There was a quiet shuffling as everyone put on their Santa hats. *"One."*

Chapter 4

The doors scraped against the ground as they swung open. We were one of the last teams to rush inside, since Ramp couldn't really move at much more than a hobble.

"Sorting mail?" Ramp croaked as we neared the door. "Why, if that's all it takes to be Santa, I'll be holding that Kringle in no time!"

Celia and I exchanged a look. He had no idea what the mailroom was like.

"The mailroom is way bigger than—" I started, but Celia cut me off with a look that said, *Let him see for himself.* When we stepped through the door, he did. We all did.

The mailroom was dark. *Very* dark. This was the first immediate difference from normal. From what we could see, there were overhead lights hanging from the ceiling at equal intervals all the way up and down the warehouse that left big patches of darkness between spots that were very brightly lit. We could hear the squeak of the child-bot wheels moving around, but none of those awful machines were visible to us at the entrance.

We couldn't see very far into the room because there were

thick walls, probably around fifteen feet tall, forming three different paths into the mailroom. To our left and right were mountains of mail with mailbags lying in a heap between them. Some teams were still scooping mail into their bags, lagging behind others who had already run into the maze.

I checked the perimeter walls: The mail slots were still there, so at least that was normal. There were slots up and down the mailroom's tall walls all the way back. Each was connected to a tube that sucked the letters underground and then redistributed them to the proper departments at The Workshop, Wish Generator or Claus Castle. On the far wall of the mailroom were slots for every individual citizen of the North Pole as well; the tubes would take mail directly to our houses or apartments.

There was a lot of mail here.

A LOT of mail.

And not a lot of time.

Celia took charge. "We'll have to open the letters and figure out where they go as quickly as possible. Ollie, you should do that, since you've done it before. I studied the mail-slot organization last night, so I can make sure we get to the right departments quickly." Celia kept her voice down, to avoid attracting child-bots. She looked to Ramp, who was scooping letters into a bag. "Ramp, we have to keep from getting burned, so you're on child watch."

"I'm on what?" Ramp couldn't hear her, and he spoke so loudly we both jumped.

"Shh! Child watch."

He still couldn't understand. "I can't hear you. What?"

I glanced around, nervous.

"Child watch!" Celia yelled. "We need you to make sure the children don't find us!" There was a faint squeak from the path on the far right.

"Is that you, Santa?" a sickly sweet voice called. The only other team that was still by the entrance took off running.

"You shouldn't yell, Celia," Ramp chastised, as if her yelling hadn't been his fault in the first place. "We're supposed to be *sneaking* around those automatons."

Celia looked like she was about to start yelling *at him*, but I grabbed their hands before she had the chance and pulled us down the middle path.

"Santa, that is *you!"*

I heard the child's voice as we slipped between the maze's walls, followed by the crackling sound of fire. I hoped the robot hadn't set the whole pile of mail ablaze.

We found a quiet spot after a few sharp turns in the maze. We passed several more piles of mail, so at least we'd be able to fill our bag up on the go. I opened our bag and pulled out a letter from Eliot McAvoy:

Deer Santa:

    This Christmas, what I want more than ANYthing is for a dinosuar toy with yellow—

"Workshop. Animals division." I stamped it and passed it to Celia, who looked around to orient herself. Ramp peeked around the corner, keeping a lookout for more child-bots. I hoped his eyesight was good enough to be helpful.

"Animals is back by the entrance." She grabbed the letter and took off running. We followed after her, and I opened another letter while we ran, from Nora Carter:

Dear Santa,

This year, I want only one thing for Christmas: my sister to stop stealing my hairbrush and getting her gross hair all over—

"This one's Workshop. Beauty." I figured getting a hairbrush for her sister was probably the best solution.

"Watch out!" Ramp yelled. I reached out and grabbed the back of Celia's suit, tugging her back from a corner as flames shot out from the other side.

"Santa, where did you go?" The girl's voice echoed around us. We hid against the wall, in the dark, while the child-bot rolled around the corner. This one had hit its face on something, leaving the paint scraped off where one of its eyes should have been. The mangled metal baby-doll face rotated around the hallway while we held our breath. *"Santa, I miss you!"* We pressed our bodies against the wall and pulled each other slowly around the corner. We sighed with relief when the bot moved out of sight, which was nice because I had completely forgotten about breathing.

Celia led us back to the entrance of the mailroom and then right back into the maze on the far left. Sure enough, before the first turn there was a slot in the wall that said *WS: ANIMALS*. She brought the letter close, and the pipes sucked it in and away.

"Peanut brittle!" she swore.

"What's wrong?"

"Beauty is right next to it, but the maze is in the way." She was right; since the departments were in alphabetical order, Beauty would be just a little bit farther down the wall. Unfortunately, because of the shape of the maze, we'd have to turn and go deeper into the centre to find our way back. "Open another one and see if it's closer."

I found one from Abraham Danton:

Dear Santa Claus,

My favourite colour is pink. For Christmas, I would like something pink. I don't like purple, so it can't be purple at all, and my mum says I can't ask for anything too big, because our apartment is not very big. I also do not want anything that is an animal, because for the last few years all my toys have been animals. I don't want to sound ungrateful, because I like animals, but-

"What's taking so long?" Ramp was sweating, and it made his whole body smell like mothballs. I heard the whoosh of fire and someone screaming deeper in the maze.

"Abraham Danton won't get to the point!"

Celia rubbed her temples. "Let's just send it to G&P – I'll find something for him later." I nodded and went to stamp it, but suddenly it was knocked out of my hands.

"Sorry, superdorks. Looks like I got that one first."

Buzz holstered a stamp gun back on his belt and sauntered

over to us. He picked the letter off the ground – it was stamped with a picture of Santa Claus playing the marimba.

"That's not fair, Buzz." Celia frowned at him. *How did he know to bring a stamp gun? How did he know to* make *a stamp gun?* "That letter was ours!"

"And now it's mine. You said G&P, right? Thanks for reading it for me." Buzz took off running, but stopped suddenly at an intersection. He counted with his fingers – three, two, one – and a child-bot rolled past the corner. He waited for it to pass and ran down the hall where it had come from.

How did he know it was going to be there?

"What a jerk." I split open another letter, this one from Mindy Ratchford:

Dear Mr Claus,

I wish for a cannon for Christmas so that I can—

"Wish Generator." We aren't supposed to make weapons, but her wish could at least provide a little bit of energy for the city. "She wants a cannon."

Ramp shook his head. "Kids these days, all violent." He looked dangerously on the verge of a much longer complaint. "It's those video games, I tell you. Turning their – uh, *our* brains to mush. Because I *love* those video games. Mush my brain right up, I say!" He did a motion with his hands like he was squishing brains between them.

Celia and I stared at him. Then Celia said, "OK, well, the

Wish Generator slot is in the back of the room, on the other side. I guess we're just going to have to try to get through the maze."

I said, "I heard this thing where, if you put your hand on the left side of the wall and follow it, you'll eventually get everywhere in the—"

"I don't have time for this!" Ramp cut me off and leaned over to pull off his shoes. I held my nose. His trousers were so baggy and low that I couldn't see his feet, but he looked very relieved, and wobbled back and forth for a second. "Give me the letter." I handed it to him warily.

Ramp tilted his head to look up at the top of the wall, like he was measuring the distance. He bent his knees a little, then suddenly sprang up from the floor and landed on the top, balancing perfectly. Celia and I gasped, startled.

"I'll be right back," he said, and took off running along the tops of the walls, bounding across the maze. Within a few seconds, he was back standing above us.

"How did you do that?" I examined his shoes to see if they had any special tricks inside them. They seemed normal.

"We don't have time for stupid questions. What's the next one?"

I ripped open another letter – *I want to be Bigfoot* – and said, "Workshop. Costumes."

Celia thought for a moment and told him where to go, and he bounded off in that direction again. We must not have been the only team to have this idea; I saw the triplets tossing each other across the walls above us while we were waiting for him.

Our plan seemed to be working pretty well: I figured out where the letters should go, Celia remembered where the slot was, and Ramp jumped over the walls to get there. We had to keep moving almost constantly to avoid the child-bots, but it was still way faster than doing everything as a group.

We only ran into the team of Claus children once – Klaus was barking orders to Sally and Bertrand the whole time. Bertrand had a little mechanical penguin on his shoulder scanning and sorting letters quickly, and Sally made a toy that threw her voice and distracted the child-bots.

I saw Kurt a few more times; he and the redheaded girl were roller-skating through the maze like they'd done it a hundred times before. Buzz wasn't with them, probably because he was off stealing letters on his own.

I saw one team get in a fight over which one of them was being lazier, and all three yanked off each other's hats and threw them right into a child-bot's mouth. It quickly grabbed them in its pincer hands and dragged them outside while they kicked and screamed.

Luther got caught because his waistcoat glitched and stuck on maximum brightness. He shone the word *JERK* like a beacon for the child-bots, but at least he was so short that the fire didn't even hit his body, just burnt the hat right off his head. So he was out.

When the ten-minute warning sounded (Rudolph's translated voice blaring across the whole warehouse), Celia, Ramp and I were all exhausted. Ramp landed on the ground next to us, and I handed him his shoes, which he took a long time to put back on – I think he stuffed them with something from his pockets. As he was bent over tying them, I started to panic.

"Uh-oh, uh, guys, um—" I stammered. Celia and Ramp both looked at me while I danced back and forth on my feet and pointed at Ramp's head. I've never been very good at getting my words out in high-pressure situations. "His – the, um—" I pointed to my own head and jumped up and down.

"What, elf? Spit it out," Ramp grumbled, "and stop dancing. I'm tired enough without seeing you put on this shameless display!"

"Oh no." Celia's eyes widened as she realized what I was trying to say. "Your hat! You lost your hat somewhere."

Ramp reached up and patted the top of his toupee. His hat was definitely gone.

"Peppermint bark!" he swore. "I must have dropped it while I was delivering letters."

We only had ten minutes to search the whole maze – and before we could even try, one of the child-bot's voices rose from around the corner.

Celia's eyes widened. "Holy jingle bells!" she started off yelling, then pulled her voice back down to a whisper. Suddenly a huge smile broke out on her face. "I get it!"

"Get what?" I asked. Celia pulled us back into the shadows while the child-bot passed by.

"Did you eat your milk and cookies, Santa?" it asked. The voice sounded scarier and scarier every time.

"The pattern. They're following the same paths, over and over!" Celia said. I thought about Buzz and how he knew to wait for one of the child-bots to pass by. "Ramp, I know you had your hat when you sent that letter to the Jawbreaker Department, because you said it was 'ugly and annoying and no one with any sense would ever wear it.' Do you remember anything after that?"

Ramp thought for a second. "Oh, *yeah*. I took the hat off and threw it on the ground because I hated it so much while I was delivering the personal letter for Gary Goblin."

"You *what*?!" Celia yelled.

"Personal letter!" I tried to keep us focused. "That means the back of the maze, right?" *As far back as we could possibly go.*

Celia nodded. "Follow me."

Ramp groaned. "I can't keep doing this. I'm too tired."

I patted him on the shoulder. "That's OK. You helped us a lot today!" I tried to give him my biggest, most supportive smile, even though inside I was kind of upset with him, too. "If you want, we can get it and meet you back at the entrance."

"You'd better." He started walking away without as much as a thank you. "I'm not losing this challenge because you couldn't find a hat!" He kept grumbling as he got farther away.

Celia frowned.

"We wouldn't even have had a chance of winning without him," I reminded her. "Plus, he's old. I think."

"Yeah, what's up with that?"

I shrugged, so Celia shrugged, and then we both shrugged at each other again and laughed.

"Focus, you goofball!" she chided.

"*You're* the goofball!" I replied. She stuck her tongue out at me, then signalled which way to go with her head and started running through the maze. I followed as close behind her as I could and paused when she signalled. The difference was amazing; now that she had figured out the pattern, we hardly ever even saw a child-bot. We also didn't see anyone else, so I guess most people had found their way out by then.

I kept my eyes on the ground but never saw the hat. I was starting to give up hope – maybe someone had grabbed Ramp's hat because their own had been burned – when I heard a quiet flapping noise.

We were all the way up against the back wall, and the ball of Ramp's Santa hat was stuck in one of the mail slots. *Goblin, Gary.* Just like he'd said. The pipe was too small to suck the hat all the way in, so the air current was making it flap up and down. Celia and I grabbed it together and yanked it free.

Suddenly, a siren started playing. Rudolph's voice came over the loudspeaker: "Five minutes left, wannabes. And I've got a surprise for you punks who think it's a good idea to cut it this close."

Celia put her face in her hands. "I don't want to know," she groaned. We were as far from the front door as it was possible to be. The sirens stopped, and the squeaking of wheels we had been hearing for the past two hours doubled in speed.

"Santaisthatyou?" Even the voice of the child-bot had sped up and turned high and unnatural. It whipped around the corner at lightning speed, barrelling toward us on its one wheel with terrifying purpose. It was the bot with the missing eye . . . *back for vengeance!!!!!!!*

"RUN!" I yelled. Celia and I bolted back into the maze, the child-bot on our tail. Every once in a while it would shoot flames at our heels just to remind us it was there. About a quarter of the way back, another bot spotted us and joined it. A few turns later, a third and fourth.

"SANTAITISYOU!" they screeched in chorus. I saw Celia's foot get caught in a blast of flame, but other than a little singe on

the face of a kitten, the suit protected her. We barrelled to the front door, where Ramp was huddled in a corner.

"I don't like these automatons," he babbled as I threw him his hat. He tugged it on, and Celia shoved open the door for him to run through. "Not one bit!" I let Celia go out ahead of me, then glanced back. A one-eyed giant child face was inches away from my face; I was staring directly into its scary, painted-on mouth. The flamethrower's hatch fell open.

"DIDYOUEATYOURMILKANDCOOKIESSANTA?"

I leapt backwards out the door and slammed it behind me. I fell on my butt while flames licked out from the cracks in the door. Celia was bent over, hands on her knees, panting. Ramp was looking grumpy as ever.

"Well" – Ramp looked around at the tired, sweaty crowd with a sour expression – "I suppose we didn't do terribly."

I saw Goldie, one of the triplets, roll his eyes. "Ya hear that, Frank?" He elbowed his sister in the ribs.

Frank punched him back in the shoulder. "Yeah, Goldie, I heard that. Ya hear that, Myrle?" She smacked her brother in the back.

Myrle hit her in the stomach. "I heard 'em. They think they did good! Whatta bunch of twerps." All three of the triplets laughed in exactly the same way. Celia and I pretended not to hear them.

Rudolph trotted through the crowd to us as a group of elves with clipboards sifted through to mark which contestants lost their hats. He passed Kurt, Buzz and the redheaded girl, who all still had theirs. The Claus sibling team was safe, too, and Klaus looked confident. (He always looked confident, though. Maybe that's just his face.)

When Rudolph arrived at our team, he lit his nose up as bright as I had ever seen it – we couldn't look directly at him. Everything, especially the snow, was bright red.

"You got lucky this time, wannabes. Looks like enough hats got burnt that you're barely scraping through."

Celia and I beamed at each other. *We made it!* I saw the triplets shrug in the corner of my eye.

Rudolph turned back to the group, and his nose blinked on and off like a strobe light.

"You'd better watch out," he called loudly over us all. "You'd better not cry. You'd better not pout—"

"Why?" an elf in pigtails interrupted.

Rudolph glared down at her and snorted. "I'm telling you why." He returned his focus back to the crowd. Falling snow gently piled on his antlers. His nose stopped blinking, and he tapped a hoof on the ground twice, roughly. *"The Santa Trials have only just begun."*

Chapter 5

The next month went by *really* slowly. It felt strange to go back to my regular Games & Puzzles work after so much deadly excitement. Santa never gave us a clue about when the next trial would start, so the only choice was to keep moving. The Workshop wasn't boring – there is *nothing* boring about Christmas – but it felt like when you cry during a really great movie and then realize, when you walk out into the sun, that everyone else was just having a regular day. The contestants in the Santa Trials had been through a once-in-a-lifetime experience, but we still had to make sandwiches and go to the bathroom. Celia said she was relieved for a break from the excitement, but I'd never seen her working harder.

"How many new blueprints have you turned in today?" I asked as she slipped another rolled-up piece of paper into the air tube on our office wall.

She counted in her head. "Eight. No, nine. Wait, are you counting today as starting at midnight, or business hours? Because at two a.m. I sent in plans for a dustbin that sings when you throw things away."

"I think that already exists." I was programming the paint in a dollhouse to change colours when no one was looking and had already coded the furniture to move around when everyone left the room. It was actually one of Sally's designs: a truly haunted doll mansion.

Celia shrugged. "Well, I made a better one."

I got the hint that she didn't feel like talking. When I was through painting, I powered my paintbrush down, waved goodbye, and slipped out of our office into the hallway.

Hallways in The Workshop are busier than streets, especially around lunchtime, so I let the flow of the crowd pull me along toward the grand staircase. An elf woman with blond hair in a big, neat tower on top of her head was leading two children along by the hand so quickly their feet were coming off the ground.

"Oh, yeah. We brought the whole family to watch the rest of the Trials. This is history, you know. These guys" – she lifted her kids high off the ground and wagged them in front of her friend – "are a little too young to compete, but the memories will last a *lifetime.* Won't they, boys?"

"Yes, ma'am," the kids chimed together. They looked a little overwhelmed. Their mother's friend, a skinny man in a long, fuzzy robe, nodded.

"I feel bad for his son Klaus." The man spread his arms out wide and shrugged. "He's a hard worker who deserves to be Santa. This must have come as a terrible surprise."

"*I* think an elf should win. Wouldn't that be a nice change?" The woman apparently grew tired of leading the kids by the hand and set one of them on each of her muscular shoulders. They held on to her hair tower to keep from falling off.

I missed the man's response because they turned off down another hallway and I was pushed ahead toward the staircase. I had to quickly slip around other elves to get to the edge of the crowd and almost tripped down the stairs when I finally pushed free of the current. I clung to the handrail and looked down.

The grand staircase was the most beautiful part of The Workshop. Two intertwined spirals wrapped around each other in a double helix, like DNA, with a slide along the edge of both staircases that you could ride all the way down from the top to the bottom. (Most people didn't, because it was *very fast* and *very scary*.) The spirals had thin, flat bridges connecting them to every floor across the wide-open space between the hallways and the stairs. Huge decorations and giant glowing Christmas ornaments hung suspended in the air all the way down, and it was easy to get distracted staring at them since they were redesigned and replaced every month.

Today, I didn't have a chance to get distracted. The Workshop was even more crowded than usual because of all the visitors here to see the Trials, and the crowd was pushing me down the stairs so fast I would have fallen if we hadn't been packed together so tightly.

When I got to the cafeteria, I slipped around the crowds to get in line for my favourite restaurant (Oh Bring Us Something Other Than Figgy Pudding) and started scanning through the menu even though I already knew I was going to buy the reindeer nuggets (chicken nuggets *shaped* like reindeer, not *made of* reindeer, obviously). Somebody shoved me forward into the human in front of me, but I caught myself on their back and pushed back up. They pretended they didn't notice, and when I turned around, I realized it was Buzz's crew. *Of course.*

"I'm pretty much the reason we got first place." Buzz was bragging to the group of elves who were always tagging along after him. I couldn't believe he was *still* talking about the first trial. "I convinced Kurt to sneak in early with me, and we scoped out the mailroom. We got lucky and even saw them testing the robots. Figured it all out before the trial even started." His crew laughed in a gross, mean way, and my face turned bright red. They CHEATED. *Not that I should be surprised.*

I ordered my food from an elf with an eye patch and a bionic hand that could change into any kitchen utensil. He had worked in the cafeteria so long that everyone just called him Chef.

"I'll have the reindeer nuggets," I said.

He nodded. "Good choice, kid. But be careful – they're spicy." That's what he always said. Everyone was "kid," and everything was always spicy, even when it wasn't.

"Just how I like 'em," I said. He giggled his high, tinny laugh and pushed on some nuggets with his spatula hand. The slats widened, shifting the spatula to form a little grill. The bars grew bright red to cook the nuggets on top, too.

There weren't any open tables near the edge, so I wandered deep into the centre.

"You don't under*stand,* Sally," I heard Klaus grumble. I jerked my head around and realized I was only a few feet from their table. I quickly lowered my head. I knew I shouldn't eavesdrop, but . . . I found a seat very close so I could hear the conversation.

"You three were never going to be Santa. Dad did this because he doesn't think I can handle it." Klaus didn't sound sad, like I expected. He sounded *excited.* "These contests are the perfect way to prove that I *can.* And I will. Obviously."

I took a bite of my reindeer nugget. It wasn't spicy.

"I don't know about *obviously,*" Sally replied. I heard her book slam shut, which she only did when she was irritated. "I've never seen Kurt be bad at anything he actually tries to do well."

"Yeah, but when was the last time you saw him try? He's only competing for some sort of stupid joke. He'll get bored eventually."

"Maybe. Or maybe the joke is that he's going to win. Either way, Bertrand is a better mechanic than any of us."

Klaus paused. "Yeah, I guess Bertrand has a shot, too," he said. But he didn't sound like he believed it.

I heard a small voice groan. "You're only saying that because you don't want to hurt my feelings." I hadn't realized Bertrand was at the table, but his voice was unmistakable. "I have just as much of a chance as any of you."

"That's what I said." Klaus sounded like he was talking to a little kid, which just made Bertrand angrier.

"You don't *mean* that."

"I do." There was a moment of tense silence, because everyone knew he didn't.

"Fine!" Bertrand said. "Treat me like a baby if you want. I'm not helping you in any more challenges. Even if there are teams."

"That's stupid." Klaus was still dismissing him. "We know each other best. It makes sense to stick together when we can."

"No, you only know *yourself* best." I heard Bertrand push angry air out of his nose. "And I don't care. If you want to be Santa, you can do it on your own. I'm going to prove that I'm a better Santa than all of you." I heard Bertrand's heavy footsteps as he walked away – he was stomping – and the pages of Sally's book flipping back open in the silence that followed.

"What about you?" Klaus asked after a while.

"What *about* me?"

"You think Kurt and Bertrand could beat me. What about you?"

There was a short pause before Sally answered. When she spoke, she sounded like she was choosing her words carefully: "I'm not worried about winning."

"You don't want to be Santa?"

"I didn't say that. But Bertrand's right; it's better if we don't team up any more."

I heard the dishes on Klaus's tray clatter as he jerked it off the table.

"Great. Glad you both want to abandon me."

"We're not *abandoning* you, drama king. And if we were, it would be because you act like this."

I was already trying not to cry and was relieved when I heard Klaus breathe heavy out of his nose (I guess it was a Claus thing) and walk away. I *hated* seeing them angry with each other. They were the Clauses! They were supposed to represent the joy of Christmas for all of us!

I stood up and stepped over to the table where Sally was reading by herself. I set my tray down next to her and looked at her with big eyes. I didn't see her glance away from her book, but she pushed up her glasses and frowned.

"Are you going to cry?" she asked.

"No," I said, but in a shaky way that really meant *probably, yes.*

She smiled a little. "Good. Don't. You should be happy. Klaus needs to learn what to do when there's no one to boss around." She looked up at me for a second. "It's Ollie, right?"

I nodded.

"Can I tell you a secret?"

I nodded again.

"You have to promise not to cry."

"OK."

"I *don't* want to be Santa. But I can't tell anyone else, obviously. A Claus dropping out of the competition is just another story for the news." Sally flipped to the next page of her book. (*How is she reading and talking at the same time?* I wondered.) "And my dad keeps telling me how *amazing* he thinks I would be at the job. I think he wants me to try even more than Klaus. It would break his heart."

One little tear rolled down my cheek.

"You promised!" She flipped a page in her book and smiled.

"I'm sorry! I'm trying very hard not to cry, I mean it." I started smiling before I even finished. "I think it was a leftover tear from earlier."

"Thanks for listening. I gotta go. Do you want my extra reindeer nuggets?" Sally pushed her tray over to me, and I grabbed the ones that were left. "See you la—"

But before she could finish, everyone in the cafeteria started yelling and pointing at their phones.

The next competition was announced!

Chapter 6

"'You have one week to build the best sleigh you can, using any materials available at The Workshop,'" Celia read out loud from the official email. Ramp, who had come to our office without asking, was listening with his eyes closed and maybe – *definitely* – snoring just a little bit.

"'This includes, of course, assembling a team of reindeer,'" Celia continued. "Uh-oh. That means we have to convince them to join us, doesn't it? I can make a sleigh, sure, but talking to those snooty-snouts is going to be a disaster."

"What's so hard about grabbing some reindeer?" Ramp snapped without opening his eyes. I guess he wasn't sleeping. "They're just animals."

Celia laughed. "Yeah, and so are we, to them."

"Don't you know about the reindeer, Ramp?" I asked. "Aren't you a Claus?"

Ramp shook his head. "I haven't taken animal husbandry yet, since I am sixteen, and am only in . . ." He looked at me like I was going to tell him, and paused for too long. "Fourth grade?"

"High school," I said. "I think you mean high school."

"Ah, yes. I have completed every one of the low schools."

"Well, here's what they didn't teach you." Celia flipped over a nearby whiteboard and pulled the cap off a red marker with a satisfying pop. She drew a simple picture of Santa Claus, but young and with a red beard. He was holding a little blue snow globe. The whiteboard hummed a little as it turned on, and the little Santa drawing yawned and stretched. "Kris Kringle Claus was the greatest Christmas scientist in history. He made the Quantum Kringle—"

"Ah, yes, tell me more about that!" Ramp interrupted. "For example, where does the current Santa keep it? Asking for a friend."

Celia paused and looked at him with suspicion. "You already know what it does. And nobody knows where he keeps it. That's not part of the story."

Ramp scribbled down some notes on a piece of paper. "*Nobody . . . knows . . . where . . . he keeps it.* Got it. Thanks."

"But he also raised unique reindeer who can completely ignore gravity." She doodled a few reindeer; they flipped and twirled around the board. "He started with just a few – eight, obviously – and they passed it on to their kids, who passed it on to their kids, and now all the reindeer in this part of the world can fly. It also sometimes leads to other genetic mutations, like Rudolph's glowing nose and exceptionally long life-span." A little doodle Rudolph, hat and all, grumpily corralled the whirling reindeer into two lines. The Santa doodle connected them to a sleigh and then placed the Quantum Kringle into the centre console.

"They help the sleigh get off the ground, but also keep it from running into things while it's going at light speed. That's why you need at least eight of them for a sleigh with the Kringle – it's impossible for a human to think that fast alone. Since we're just making regular engines, we'll probably only need three, max."

"Each?" I asked.

Celia nodded. "The letter says this is a solo contest. We each have to make our own sleighs."

Ramp frowned. "I still don't understand what you're worried about."

"Well, the thing is, they know they're special." Celia powered down the whiteboard and all the drawings froze in place. "And they know we need them. So they demand a lot."

"Plus, they *really like flying*," I added. "So it can be hard to get them to sit still and listen. I would like flying, too, though, so I get it."

"Yes, yes, we all like flying," Ramp grumbled. He stood up slowly and started shuffling out of our office. "I guess I'd better get started. All by myself. Just me, alone."

"OK, bye." Celia was already sketching a sleigh on a blueprint. Ramp sighed heavily. I huffed out air, to tell Celia that she should look back up at me. She did.

I mouthed, *I feel bad.*

She mouthed, *About what?*

I pointed at Ramp. She looked at him, then looked back at me. *You can help him if you want,* she mouthed.

But should we help him? I started mouthing words faster so I could finish before Ramp got to the door. *He doesn't seem like he's necessarily a nice guy. Plus, I'm pretty sure he's not sixteen at all. If we don't help him, though, are we jerks? I don't want to be a jerk. He's all by himself, you know? Where is he even going to build his sleigh if he can't use our office? His hotel room? I bet his hotel room is too small to build a sleigh! He'd have to get rid of his bed! IF HE IS REALLY AN OLD MAN, HE HAS TO HAVE A BED, CELIA. WHAT ARE WE GOING TO DO???*

Celia stared at me for a second. *What?* she mouthed. I threw my hands up in the air.

"Hey, Ramp?" I called out to him, interrupting the slow-motion lift of his hand to the doorknob.

"Hm? What? Yes?" Ramp turned around, suddenly very quick.

"You can build your sleigh in here with us, if you want." I smiled at him. He kept frowning, but nodded.

"Only if you promise to clean up this mess," he said, jogging over to us in a tenth of the time it took for him to get to the door. He looked over Celia's shoulder at the blueprint she was working on. "Where do we start?"

"I'm not making your sleigh for you." Celia didn't look up from her drawing. "So don't even try."

Ramp looked at me expectantly. I tried to avoid eye contact.

"Uh, I guess . . . well, I guess you start with the engine." *And I guess I'm going to have to walk you through the whole challenge. Again.*

"Great!" Ramp clapped his hands together and grinned. It was the first smile I had seen from him in a while, which made all the work I had coming feel worth it. "Let's get to work."

❄ ❄ ❄

I woke up the next morning in a plush seat with a wrench in my hand. I rubbed my eyes and looked around, slowly realizing I'd fallen asleep while working on my sleigh. Celia was already awake and had already showered and changed clothes. She had a welder's mask on and was welding together spokes for her wheels.

I heard a growl from under me and leapt out of my seat.

Celia's torch clicked off. She lifted her mask up and wiped the sweat off her face, flicking it to the ground. The next growl was even louder without the fire buzzing from the torch.

"It's Ramp," she said, laughing a little at the scared face I was making. "He's snoring under your sleigh."

I peeked under the sleigh's body, currently held up by cinder blocks. There he was, curled up into a tiny ball. His toupee was sliding off centre a little, but something was holding it in place. I glanced down at his baggy jeans and big shoes and remembered how he'd jumped during the first challenge. *There's gotta be something up with his legs*, I thought. *Now's my chance to find out.*

I flattened myself down on to the floor and slowly dragged myself under the sleigh as quietly as I could. I stretched my hand out . . . and closed my fingers around a bit of his jeans at the ankle . . . and started lifting up . . .

"What are you doing?" Ramp snapped. I let go immediately and moved my pinched fingers to the ground.

"UH . . . AHA!" I said too loudly, and lifted a hair I'd found on the ground. "I WAS WONDERING WHERE THIS WENT."

"You were looking for that hair?"

"INDEED I WAS."

"Well, look quieter." He turned over and went back to sleep. I pulled myself out from under the car, where Celia was looking at me with a look that said, *What was that all about?* I tried to look back at her in a way that would explain what I had wanted to do, but I couldn't think of one, so I just waggled my eyebrows up and down.

"I had an idea," Celia said quietly, setting down her welding gear. She fluffed out her dark curls that had been squished by the helmet. "I'll help both of you with your sleighs, and Ollie can help us with the reindeer. You're way more patient with them, and I can build the sleighs twice as fast."

"Twice as fast?" I frowned. "I don't know about that. I'm actually very—"

She gestured to her sleigh. Its body was basically finished . . . and basically perfect.

"I'm not saying you can't do it, Ollie. It just might be a better use of our time."

I nodded. She was right. Still, it meant I'd have to wrangle some reindeer . . . *alone.*

❅ ❅ ❅

The Stable was really more a palace than a stable. A huge glass dome rivalling the size of the mailroom shone sparkling and beautiful, even with a light dusting of snow. I could see plants inside, but the snow kept me from really making them out. Four clear glass towers spiralled up into the sky on every side, with large open windows on top for the reindeer to fly into. It was big, extravagant, beautiful, and it had no doors.

Not *one* door.

Anyone who couldn't fly had to climb up a very old rope ladder hanging from one of the tower windows. I took a deep breath, grabbed the first rung, and started to climb.

After two minutes, I was totally scared. The wind got stronger as I climbed, and the rope ladder started swinging just enough to feel like it was going to snap. I wasn't even a quarter of the way up yet, and I was ready to give up and go back down. *Get some peppermint tea, try again later.*

The rope ladder swung away from the tower, suspended me in the air for a second, and then swung back into the tower, slapping me against the glass. *Actually, you know, maybe I shouldn't be in this competition after all. Who needs that kind of responsibility, anyway? I'll just let Buzz be Santa.*

Oh, really? You're just going to let Buzz be Santa? I argued back at myself. *And we'll all just walk around with axes for hands for the rest of our lives?*

He's not going to make us replace our hands with axes. I'm pretty positive about that, and I'm surprised you would be worried about something so silly, I responded.

I shook my head and climbed up another rung. *Either way, we can't let him win. One foot in front of the other, right?*

About halfway up, something big and brown slammed into the window next to me, then scrabbled its hooves against the window and kicked back off, floating behind me with a dazed look on its face. A reindeer. She was young – only a little bigger than me, with little stubby horns. Strapped around her head were big flight goggles. They looked *adorable*.

"Hi!" the reindeer's voice box chirped. She was using a more modern voice box than Rudolph's, with an actual voice that could express things like exclamation points. "Whatcha doin'?"

"Climbin'," I said, and kept climbing.

She turned her body sideways and rested her hooves on the tower. With a *clop-clop-clop*, she trotted alongside me like it was the ground. "Looks borin'," she said.

I shook my head. "Not boring. Scary."

After a few minutes of her watching me struggle, she tilted her head and observed, "You sure aren't talkin' much."

"*Very* scary."

"Oh! Well, here!" She kicked off of the tower and did a loop-de-loop. I felt her bump up against my legs. "I'll take you the rest of the way, no sweat."

"Really? Thanks!" I carefully swung one leg around and gently sat down on her back. I also saw how far I was from the ground and almost threw up. "Let me just – OH, OK, I GUESS WE'RE GOING, WHY ARE WE GOING SO FAST WHERE ARE YOU TAKING ME???" I yelled as she rocketed away from the tower at full speed.

"Oh, yeah! I didn't tell you." She craned her neck around to yell at me over the sound of the wind. "My name's Crasher!"

"MAYBE YOU SHOULD LOOK WHERE YOU'RE GOING?" I yelled. "I MEAN, YOU KNOW MORE ABOUT FLYING THAN I DO, I GUESS."

Crasher laughed with her real voice instead of her voice box. Have you ever heard a reindeer laugh before? It's mostly a string of loud snorts. She did another loop-de-loop that left me dangling from her neck. I was *maximum* scared.

"Fun, right?!" She snort-laughed again. "WOO-HOO!" She sped toward the tower so fast I thought we would slam into it. Right at the last second, when I could see myself reflected in the glass, she pulled up. When we got to the top, she braked suddenly and whipped us into the opening. I flew off her back and into the tower, landed on some wooden planks, and rolled to a stop. She tumbled in not long after, snorting and rolling.

"So whatcha doin' in the Stable?" she asked, prodding my arm with one of her hooves. I didn't move from my facedown position.

"Nothing, ever again," I said. "I'm done doing things. I've done all the things I need to do, I think." My heart was still beating so fast I could feel it in my fingernails. Crasher pushed at me with her snout. I rolled over and narrowed my eyes at her. "You scared me on purpose."

"Well, yeah," she said. "Duh." Her big eyes lit up. "Oh! Are you competin' in that Santa thing? You need a team, right?"

"Uh, well . . ." I tried to find a way out of saying yes.

"*Sweet.* Then I'll be on your team." She rubbed her head against a peg sticking out of the wall and popped the goggles off. "I'm fast. Even faster than most adults. I'm not so good at landin's, so I guess it's pretty good that landin's aren't important."

"I think, maybe, that landings are very important, from a certain perspective—" I tried to argue, but she wasn't listening.

"Great! You gotta go see Dreamer to get the rest of your team. I can take you, if you want."

She was right. I *did* have to get permission from Dreamer. And I wasn't just here for my team, I was here for Celia's and Ramp's teams, too. Having her on my side was at least better than navigating the Stable on my own.

"Thanks. I'm Ollie." I stuck out my hand to shake, and then

realized that was silly. Crasher wasn't bothered, though, and stuck out her hoof. We shook.

"Nice ta meetcha. Dreamer'll be in his grove." She started trotting down the tight spiral staircase, and I followed. "Did you bring any gifts?"

"Uh, I . . . no? Is it bad that I didn't?"

"Don't worry too much," Crasher said, lifting off the ground and looking at me while she floated down the stairs. "He's probably not going to like you anyway."

"He *has* to like me," I insisted. "I need nine reindeer!"

"Eight," she corrected.

"Eight, I guess, if you're totally sure you want to help me—"

"I'm sure."

"Eight."

These stairs sure did take a while.

"Did you know Dreamer's never touched the ground?" Crasher flicked one ear and spun around, landing gingerly back on to the steps. "He even sleeps in the air. And he doesn't leave the Stable any more. Not at all."

"Why is he in charge, anyway?" I asked. "If he never leaves and he's so hard to talk to."

"Biggest antlers."

"Seriously?"

Crasher rolled her shoulders in a way that might have been a shrug.

"It's an old-school reindeer thing. Some stuff never changes."

We finally reached the bottom of the stairs, and my wobbly legs were thankful. Crasher reared up on her hind legs and pushed on two double doors that opened out into a lush, warm garden. I took a deep breath and even the air felt greener.

And there were so many reindeer, all with different antlers and coats and heights above the ground. Reindeer splashed in the stream or flew to the tops of trees to pick fruit. They rolled around in flowers or duelled antler-to-antler in the air. Crasher hopped around me in a circle.

"Welcome to the Stable!" she said. "I can tell it's your first time."

"It's so *beautiful*!" I whispered. "And *warm*." She laughed with a barrage of snorts. I took off one of my coats and wrapped it over my arm.

"C'mon." Crasher grabbed my sleeve between her teeth and tugged. I let her pull me deeper into the dome.

We passed a miniature forest, where a reindeer was pruning a hedge into the shape of a reindeer wearing a wig and posing dramatically on a boat. He was surrounded by a bunch of little hedge elves and humans, all huddled up and rowing.

"That's Snipper. He's been doin' famous paintings this year. I think that one's George Washington," Crasher said. I nodded even though I didn't know what a George Washington was.

A few reindeer glanced at me in a way that didn't feel very welcoming, but no one came close enough to bother us until I, distracted by a butterfly, walked directly into a human and fell over backwards. The human, of course, was fine. When I got my bearings, I recognized the red-haired girl from the first challenge. She grinned and jingled a whole handful of dog tags in front of me.

"You're here to build a team, too?" She reached a hand down and helped me up.

I nodded and brushed myself off. Crasher was sniffing at an empty burlap sack she was holding in her other hand.

"What's that?" I asked.

She glanced down at the sack. "Oh, I live on an apple orchard back home. I figured we'd have to do something like this, so I brought some apples you can't find around here. Dreamer loved them. Didn't you bring a gift?"

I shook my head.

"Yikes." She must have seen my face fall, because she knelt down and put a hand on my shoulder.

"Here's a secret: I heard he likes corny jokes. So, if you can think of any . . ." She patted my shoulder a few times and stood up.

"I'm Ollie!" I exclaimed. "I just realized I don't know your name. And you're being so nice to me."

There was a look on her face for a brief flash where she seemed uncomfortable, like maybe a bug bit her or something. She smiled.

"Andrea. Good luck." Andrea waved two fingers in a little salute and tossed her red hair over her shoulder as she walked away. I looked at Crasher, who had been unusually quiet the whole time.

"You OK?" I asked.

Crasher turned to me with a dreamy look in her eyes. "Just thinkin' about apples."

A few feet ahead was an archway of branches, the only opening in a thicket of trees. I stepped into the shade.

"Is this it?" I asked.

Crasher nodded but didn't step forward. "I'm not goin' in there, though. I gotta go get my tag for you."

"What? You have to go with me! I don't know what to do on my own—"

"I'm not scared, if that's what you're askin'."

"Uh, I didn't say you were scared, but I'm pretty sure *I* am!"

"You'll be fine. Maybe. Goodluckseeyoulaterbye!"

I turned and headed deeper into the tree tunnel. The entrance had been made of entirely normal trees, but as I got deeper, they started looking stranger: Some trees had glowing leaves, some had bark that shone like metal, and others were growing fruit that looked like Christmas ornaments right from the branch.

I heard a soft, repeating crunch, like someone marching on glass. I creeped slowly to the end of the tunnel and caught a glimpse of a snout above huge reindeer teeth, chowing down on one of the ornament fruits. Inside it was juicy and green, but the skin made a sound just like glass. I hoped it didn't *feel* like glass.

As I turned the corner, Dreamer's huge green eyes swivelled around to stare at me.

"Another? Already?" A gentle, calm voice came from all sides. I whipped around, surprised, and saw speakers hanging from branches among the ornament fruit. Dreamer must not like to wear a voice box. "And an *elf*, no less." Dreamer's voice remained quiet and smooth, but I got the impression he wasn't happy. I turned around and looked him over for real.

The first thing I noticed was *antlers*. He had huge antlers, bigger in spread than his body, jutting out from his head and forming a great web. The antlers were decorated with several pieces of hanging ornament fruit, and beautiful red birds tweeted from a nest among them. The reindeer's body was slender and small for a reindeer, and his thin legs ended in unusually little hooves. His coat was shiny, flawless and gold; all this framed by perfect sunlight streaming into the grove through a skylight in the trees.

He lost interest in looking at me and floated around, occasionally twirling upside down – his ornaments remained hanging in place, aligned with his individual gravity.

"Well?" his voice projected, and then the speaker yawned even though his body didn't. "What have you brought for me?"

OK. Andrea said he likes jokes. Gotta give him a good joke.

"What kind of camera does Santa have?"

"You came here to ask me this?"

"A North Pole-aroid!" I faked a big smile and shook my hands festively.

"Excuse me?" Dreamer scratched his back against a tree.

That joke must not have been good enough. "What's Santa's favourite garden tool?"

"Why are you asking questions to which you already know the answer?"

"A hoe, hoe, hoe!!!" I think I sounded more frantic than funny. Dreamer hovered forward and stared at me again, confused, but he still wasn't laughing. I took a deep breath.

"What do gingerbread ghosts wear?????" I was sweating, hard.

"Must I ask you to leave?"

"COOKIE SHEETS!!!!!!!!!!!" I punched the air with every syllable and then spread my arms wide and wiggled my fingers. Dreamer began herding me with his antlers back to the archway.

"I am unsure why you have come here to act like a fool," he went on, "but I have no more patience for this. Goodbye."

"Wait! Please!" I fell down on my knees and stopped backing away from his antlers. He froze, too, maybe because he didn't want to touch me. "I didn't bring anything. I'm sorry. Someone told me you liked jokes, so I was trying to be funny."

"So those were 'jokes.'" Dreamer turned his eyes toward the sky and looked thoughtful. "I hated them. This 'someone' gave you inaccurate information."

"She must have been confused. I don't think she meant to lie to me, or, uh – waste your time, uh, Your . . . Highness?"

At that, Dreamer laughed lightly from the speakers. "Fine." He floated up and did a little twirl in the air. "I'll take your shoes, then."

"My shoes?" I looked down at my warm red boots. "I don't think you're a size four."

"I didn't ask for your *thoughts*. I asked for your shoes."

I took them off and set them neatly beside each other on the edge of the tree line. Dreamer rolled his neck around, stretching.

"With a little stuffing, it is easy for hooves to fit into your two-leg shoes. And I look best in red."

I decided not to waste any more time. "I'm Ollie, sir, an elf competing in the Trials—"

"No, no," he interrupted.

"No?"

"Here, we are named for what we do, not who we think we are." He pushed off of a tree and floated over to the other side of the grove, where he pushed off a different tree. "And right now, you are Beggar."

"Well, OK, but I need a team of reindeer for me and my two friends—"

"No, no."

"Still no?"

"Introduce yourself again."

I resisted the urge to groan and thought for a second.

"I'm, uh, I guess I'm Beggar—"

"Very good."

"And I'm competing in the Santa Trials. I'm supposed to ask you to assign reindeer to me and my friends."

"Who are these friends?"

"Celia Pixie and Ramp Claus."

"No, no." Dreamer sounded frustrated.

This time I caught on faster. "Uh, I mean, Thinker. And . . . Complainer."

"Why do they not come before me?"

"We thought it would be better this way, so we wouldn't waste your time . . . Your Highness." This seemed to make him happy again.

"How many?"

"Uh, eight. Three for each of them, and two for me."

"Only two? You believe we are less necessary?"

"No! Of course not! I love all of you. Reindeer are amazing, and perfect, and I wish I had been born one instead of an elf, probably! But Crasher already said she'd help me."

"You dare to seek my reindeer without my approval?"

"She didn't really give me a choice."

"I see." Dreamer floated up to a tree in the back of his grove with dog tags hanging off every branch. He used a branch of his right antler to pull a tag from the tree. He circled around the tree a few times, inspecting tags and choosing specific ones. Eventually, he dumped eight on the ground in front of me.

"I picked the perfect reindeer for you." His voice sounded pleased, maybe even excited. I was so glad we were ending on good terms. "They'll meet you when the competition starts, like all the others. Bring these tags to claim them."

I nodded and put them all around my neck so I wouldn't lose them. Dreamer snorted and kicked his little legs, floating away and spinning like a wheel.

"Thank you, sir, uh, Dreamer, sir."

"Farewell, Beggar. Break a leg, as they say."

I looked down at my socks and wiggled my toes. "Thanks."

* * *

"He called you WHAT?!" Celia started yelling as soon as I finished my story. "I should've gone. I would have knocked those antlers right off his stuck-up head."

"That's exactly why I had to go." I finished my piece of protein peanut brittle. "Because you totally would have. And then he'd have no antlers and we'd have no reindeer team."

Her frown cracked into a smile. "True." Then her smile grew into a wide grin. "Do you want to see what I made?"

"Is it our sleighs?" I asked, even though I knew the answer.

"It is absolutely our sleighs." We high-fived, low-fived, and then behind-the-back-fived. I glanced down at my hands, and they were covered in black grease.

"Oh, sorry." Celia handed me a towel. "I forgot to clean up. Engines, you know?"

"Where's Ramp?" I asked as I dried my fingers. "Is he asleep again?"

"I think he's at the cafeteria. Speaking of which . . ." She tossed the tarp off of the first of three sleighs with a flourish that looked *very cool*. The sleigh was black and red, with a bunch of computer screens in front of the plush seat. "I was planning to not try very hard on his, but it turns out I can only make things that are *super awesome*. It's a curse."

I laughed, and looked around the sleigh while she explained it.

"So, I focused on the fact that he's totally super old." Celia paused. "He's one thousand percent super old, right?"

"For sure."

"Yeah. So I put all these big screens in front that will tell him everything he needs to know while he's driving in big letters, so he can read them. The whole sleigh pretty much drives itself, but the autopilot takes so much power that I couldn't make it very fast. If he gets into any really dangerous situations, he can push that red button."

I sat in the seat and pushed the red button. A bright green bubble wrapped all the way around the sleigh, lifting it off the ground. Right as the bubble started to roll sideways, I hit the button again, and the sleigh *thunk*ed back to the ground.

"The engines don't work at all when the force field is on, but he can press it on and off to maintain momentum and protect himself. There's an automatic setting for when you think multiple projectiles are about to hit, especially since this tech doesn't leave room for a strong engine." She saw me inching sideways over to the next tarp. "That one's yours. I get to take the tarp off, though."

I made a pouty face.

"We can do it together," she offered.

"OK, but only if I get to wear it like a cape afterwards." I grabbed hold of one corner, she grabbed another, and we counted down from three and whipped off the tarp. It rippled in the air so beautifully I forgot to look at the sleigh.

"That looks very silly," she said as I tied the tarp around my neck like a cape. "And I wish it had been my idea."

"Tell me about my sleigh!" I commanded, feeling like a king. She rolled her eyes and stepped up to it.

My sleigh was mint green with shiny metal trim (*cute*), but compared to Ramp's, it looked pretty simple.

"For yours I focused on making everything *really good*." She ran her hand along the top. "Comfy seats, sleek design. I made it out of very light material so it can propel itself pretty quickly. Here up front there's a monitor that can show you everything that's happening in all directions, thanks to little cameras I hid in the sides. Plus, there's a headset to keep you connected with your reindeer and any sleighs you want to talk to, like mine. Hopefully the reindeer can handle most of the steering, but if you need it, there's a pretty effective manual option. And the best part . . ." She clicked a button, and a hatch opened on the front of the sleigh. A metal horse head slid out of the front and clicked into place. Its eyes lit up green, and it rotated around to look at me.

"HELLO, OLLIE. A PLEASURE TO HORSE YOUR ACQUAINTANCE."

"No way!" I put my hands on either side of horse's head and kissed her on the nose. "I missed you, Horse."

"Actually, now, she's H.O.R.S.E.," Celia said. "She's completely connected to every part of the sleigh and can answer any questions you have while you're flying. She's got protocols to protect you if things get really dangerous. There are a few other features, too, which you probably won't ever have to use. She'll tell you about them if they come up."

"I AM PROGRAMMED FOR OVER HORSE MILLION POTENTIAL HIGH-PRESSURE SITUATIONS," H.O.R.S.E. whinnied.

Celia leaned against her sleigh, tugging on the tarp a little. I suddenly realized her sleigh looked a *lot* bigger than mine. Like twice the size.

"The engine's the best part."

"You said H.O.R.S.E. was the best part."

"I lied." She whipped the tarp off of her sleigh (before I had the chance to argue) and tied it around her neck like a cape. "*I'm* the engine."

Her sleigh was the opposite of mine in every way. Instead of small, sleek and cute, it was huge and unpainted with pipes and gears sticking out all over the place. The seat in front was barely a seat, and there was an opening where an elf could crawl directly into the sleigh and mess with the engine from the inside.

"Your sleigh has slots on the side I can hook my sleigh into. Yours has its own engine, of course, but most of your energy is devoted to being a good command centre. My reindeer and I will be completely connected to you all the time, but I'll mostly be doing active maintenance on this absolutely *nutso and bonkers* engine I've built. It's very powerful, and very awesome, but unstable."

"That sounds dangerous. Why use it?"

"Because it's crazy amazing and the coolest thing I've ever made, no contest. You'll see when it's running."

"Are they gonna let us link up like that?"

"Nothing in the letter said that two racers who *happen* to have parts that link up couldn't *accidentally* become one perfect sleigh. The letter also doesn't go on to say we can't have all of our reindeer on one radio channel just in case something that crazy and impossible happened."

Crazy and impossible . . . that sounded about right.

Chapter 7

"Please speak into the microphone." Maria Duende had her smile plastered on big, and it looked even bigger on the big screen. "They can't hear you if you don't speak into the microphone."

The camera switched over to Buzz, who was standing in front of his sleigh and trying to figure out what to do with his hands. For now he had settled for putting one on his hip and one behind his head, like he was posing for a magazine.

"Is that, uh, is that this thing they put on my shirt?" Buzz glanced between Maria and the camera, obviously uncomfortable.

"Yes." Maria had very white teeth.

"I think her smile actually gets bigger when she's unhappy," Celia whispered to me. When we realized Maria was looking for interviews, we decided to hide in the crowd to watch them on the big screen instead of being forced to talk about ourselves. A kid in a beige sweater turned around to shush us. He looked familiar, but I couldn't place from where.

"I'm, uh, Buzz Brownie." Buzz was now forcing his chin down

into a weird position, to try to talk as directly into the microphone as possible. "Is this better?"

Maria gave one quick, sharp laugh. "It isn't worse. Tell us about your sleigh."

"Sure thing." The camera panned out to show that he was standing in front of a big metal machine at least twice his height. Buzz took the hand from behind his head and reached back to touch the sleigh but was farther away from it than he realized and tripped. He caught himself on the sleigh and patted it twice like it was what he'd meant to do.

"My baby's got a fifteen reindeer-power engine, carbon fibre interior, suspension for days – you know about suspension?"

"No, please explain."

"It's super important, and I have a lot of it."

I thought I saw Maria's eye twitch. "And could you tell me about these?" She gestured to four huge wheels under his sleigh.

"These are circular treads of my own design, so it can cover more ground. And here on the back . . ." The camera followed him as he ran his hand along the side to four big rocket boosters on the back. "These'll get you off the ground in seconds. You've never seen a sleigh like this one, I can promise you that. I'm gonna win this competition, and none of those dorks are gonna stand in my way." He winked at the camera.

"That's great. Could you introduce us to your reindeer?"

Buzz frowned, breaking the pose he had been holding. "Oh, I thought we were done."

"You'll know we're done when the red light turns off." Maria was already leading the camera to the front of the sleigh. A few members of the crowd laughed.

"I've got two reindeer." Buzz pointed to the front of his car, where two big reindeer dummies with painted-on smiles were being held above the ground by wires connected to its grille. "Their names are, uh, Pull . . . er and Sleigh-er."

"Slayer?"

"Yep. Puller and Slayer. You got it." He patted one on the head, and it bounced up and down on its wire, limply. "Good strong names, for strong reindeer. I'm gonna win this competition, and none of those dorks are gonna stand in my way." He winked at the camera again.

"Still not done. Mr Brownie, I'm going to cut right to the chase." Maria made the face she always did when she was about to crack a story wide open. Celia groaned because she *hates* that face. "How do you respond to comments that your 'sleigh' is, in fact, a car?"

Buzz stared at her blankly. "I don't understand."

"An anonymous expert recently said, quote, 'It's got four wheels, a steering wheel, its own gas-powered engine, and the reindeer are fake. It even looks a lot like a Jeep.' How do you respond?"

"I don't have to say anything, because it's a lie. They're not wheels, they're *circular sleigh treads*." One of the reindeer's ears split at the seam. Some stuffing fell out. "See, you hurt Slayer's feelings." Buzz pushed at the camera that had come in really close to his face. "I'm here to win, not to answer dumb questions." He ripped his microphone off and threw it on the ground. Maria quickly started saying something to the camera, but Buzz pushed her out of the way and grabbed *her* microphone. "Red light OUT!" He winked again at the camera, which didn't stop rolling for another few seconds.

"These identify your starting positions." When we arrived at the corner specified in our emails, most of the other contestants were already huddled around a table. Mrs Claus was speaking very quietly, like always, to force anyone listening into complete silence. "You will bring your sleighs from the warehouse to that spot and await the starting signal. Your reindeer are already waiting. Santa will—"

"Wait, starting signal? Is this a race?" It was Andrea, the girl who told me that Dreamer liked jokes. I needed to warn her that whoever told her lied! "I thought we were just being judged on our sleigh design. I didn't prepare for a race!"

Mrs Claus gently smiled at her without opening her mouth, somehow looking very sweet and also definitely telling her she shouldn't have interrupted. "If your design is sound, it shouldn't be a problem. Speaking of design, it's time to talk about your *next* challenge." She raised her voice and turned her head to the side. "Bring the car around, please."

A limousine pulled up on the road behind us, and all the doors opened at once. Ten elves in very stylish suits and sunglasses stepped out and lined up in a neat row. Mrs Claus parted the crowd and walked in front of them.

"These are the ten top-ranked clothing designers at the North Pole. Only the top ten of you will continue past this competition, and each will be assigned a designer based on your place. That designer will help you with your next challenge: making your own Big Red Suit."

"YES!" I yelled loudly – and I was the only one. Celia stifled a giggle, and everyone else turned and looked at me. "Uh, sorry, I . . . uh . . ." The more they stared at me, the more nervous I got. I ran out of words, and just finished with a very quiet *"!!!"*

Celia leaned over and whispered, "Well, now we *have* to win," because she was the only one who understood why I was so excited.

The designer at the end of the line pushed down her sunglasses and winked at me. I recognized those eyes. I recognized that suit. I knew that pin she had between her teeth.

The North Pole's number one clothing designer. Or, as I like to call her:

Mum.

My nerves calmed down a lot even though my heart was pounding. *We're gonna win now*, I thought. *It's meant to be.*

Mrs Claus dismissed us, and the crowd started spreading. I left Celia for a second to catch up to Andrea.

"Hey, Andrea!" She turned around and smiled at me.

"Oddie, right? Hi."

"Close!" I did a little fake laugh but was too nervous and focused to correct her. "Hi. I just wanted to tell you: Someone lied to you about the jokes. Dreamer hated them! He almost made me leave right away." I put both hands on my cheeks to show how surprised I was then. She put both hands on her cheeks to show how surprised she was right now.

"Oh my gosh." She knelt down and pulled me into a big hug. I patted her on the back a couple of times because I wasn't sure what to do. "I am *so* sorry. I didn't know – I can't believe that they – this is a huge surprise that I could never have predicted, but it is my fault, and I am so sorry."

"It wasn't *that* big of a deal, but thank you—"

"No, no, it's a *huge* deal. I can't believe it! I could never forgive myself if I didn't make it up to you. Here." Andrea took her backpack off her shoulder and stuck her hand in one of the pockets. A second later, she was clipping a button on to my shirt. It was bright yellow with a smiley face on it. "This is for good luck at the race. My grandma back on the apple orchards always used to tell me, 'Best way to make sure you have good luck in a race is to wear a button someone else gave you,' so this *definitely* makes up for it."

I was confused. "I've never heard that saying before. I don't think—"

"It's *very* real, and I probably shouldn't even give it to you, because now you're going to win." She zipped up her backpack and put it back on. Before I could say anything else, she was jogging away. "See you later, Oldie! It was great talking to you! Don't take that button off no matter what!"

I walked back over to Celia, who was having a very energetic conversation with Bertrand.

"—but how is that *possible*?" she was asking him. "The Wish Generator works as well as it does because it's stuck in one place. How would the wishes even know where to *go*?"

"It actually works the other way around – as long as you know, in general, where the wishes are coming *from*, you can tune the sensor to pick up from that area. Kris Kringle just found a way to have it find the wishes on its own." Bertrand looked really proud of himself. Celia obviously couldn't believe what he was saying; I still couldn't understand it.

Bertrand nodded at me, and adjusted his bow tie. "Hello, Ollie! I was just telling Celia about the engine I built for my sleigh."

"He replicated the Wish Generator, Ollie. And made it *portable*!" Celia was bubbling over with excitement.

"As long as the driver is consistently making wishes, it should move at a pretty good speed." Bertrand fidgeted with his hands, which made him look unsure. "But I thought this would be more about *building* than *racing*. It's a prototype, you see, and—"

"Who cares about *winning*?!" Celia yelled, loud enough that others in the crowd looked up. She lowered her voice back down. "You've done something no one else has ever done, Bertrand. You reverse-engineered a Kringle device. Your family has been working to make this happen for *centuries*."

"Well, they can keep trying. This is *mine*."

After he walked away, Celia lay down on the concrete. "If it was my choice, he'd win Santa right now. That's amazing."

"It's not your choice, though, and we should go get ready!" I grabbed her hand to pull her up, but she acted like deadweight.

"I can't . . . I'm too . . . science . . ."

I hooked my arms underneath her arms and heaved her up. "We have a race to win." I started pulling her in the direction we were headed, dragging her heels along the ground.

Five minutes later, she said, "I can't even believe how science I am right now."

But I didn't need her to be science.

I needed her to *drive*.

* ❄ *

Celia and I split to our assigned starting positions and made a plan to meet up on the track as soon as possible. I could see Buzz to my right taking a nap while loud music blared out of his not-sleigh, and Bertrand to my left scribbling on a notepad. I couldn't see Celia at all, which made me nervous, but since our sleighs were linked by radio, I knew I'd be able to find her.

I was trying to decide which direction Celia was in when I was hit in the chest by antlers.

"How's it goin', Ollie?" Crasher's voice piped out of the reindeer's voice box. She sniffed at my shirt. "I already told 'em all about how I'm in charge of the team, so ya don't have to worry. I'm the fastest, I told 'em, and they said, 'That's right!' Well, Snoozer just snored, but he snored in a way that meant 'That's right!'"

"Snoozer?" I asked. Crasher nodded.

"That's Snoozer, and that's Truther." She pointed her antlers at the two reindeer already hitched up to my sleigh, one of whom was definitely asleep on his feet. The other had a hat made of tinfoil stuck in between her antlers.

"Christmas was invented by aliens," her voice box chimed. I figured that was Truther.

"Snoozer, wake up!" Crasher yelled. Snoozer flew a few inches into the air and snorted loudly.

"Telephones are a lie." Truther didn't seem to be talking to anyone in particular, but she was staring directly at me without blinking.

I definitely hadn't expected Crasher to be the reindeer I was *least* nervous about. *The perfect reindeer*, Dreamer had said. Maybe he did have a sense of humour. I took a deep breath and looked out at the track. As far as I could see, the blinking green lights that lit up the snow and pointed out the path kept me separate from Bertrand and Buzz; it was just a straight line forward until it hit a hole in a huge block of ice jutting out from the ground. There was a hole for every contestant, from what I could tell, with no sign of what happened after you got inside.

"Hey, Ollie, can you hear me?" Celia's voice came into my earpiece.

Loud and clear! I thought, and then remembered I needed to talk out loud. "Loud and clear!"

"Great. Hopefully the track will let us link up after we get through whatever's going on with that iceberg. Do you remember that ever being there before?"

"No, and I feel like we would have noticed an ice mountain."

"It's never been there before," Crasher interjected on her headset. "Musta been set up last night."

"Right. Let's be careful. Do you see my sleigh popping up on your map?"

I looked at all the screens but didn't see Celia's sleigh anywhere. "No. I don't think my screens are working."

"Your screens aren't working?"

"Celia, I don't think my screens are working is the sleigh broken what do I do?!"

"Try turning the sleigh off and turning it back on."

I was suddenly very embarrassed. "Oh. That would . . . be hard."

"Why?"

"Because I haven't turned it on yet." I pushed the power button, and the screens started glowing. The map screen blinked with an *O* for *Ollie* and, a little ways away from that, a *C* for *Celia*. The hatch in the front opened and H.O.R.S.E. popped her head out.

"HORSE MORNING," she said as she powered up.

"Horse morning!" I replied, grinning.

"Horse morning." A loud BANG came over Celia's microphone. "Cinnamon sticks!" she swore. "I've gotta fix this. The countdown could start any second, so make sure you know how to use the sleigh. H.O.R.S.E. can help you if you have questions."

Trumpets blared, loud, all around us. Snoozer flew awake again and slammed into Truther, who pushed him back and mumbled something about how cats were going to take over the world. The trumpets stopped, and Santa's voice boomed around us.

"Contestants ready?"

I panicked. I hadn't realized it would be *this soon.* Celia probably hadn't, either. Could she hear him? Was her sleigh ready?

"Set!"

OK, *that's the steering wheel and that's the accelerator and that's the – what is that?*

"H.O.R.S.E., what is this thing?"

"THAT IS THE HORSE."

I suddenly realized a fatal flaw in her design.

"Wait, H.O.R.S.E., I need a helmet!"

The seat next to me flung itself open to reveal a helmet inside. I stuck it on and started tightening the strap.

"GO!"

Chapter 8

Sleighs started flying forward, but I couldn't get the helmet strap to click.

"Uh, Captain, I think we should—"

"Safety first, Crasher!"

"No one is safe," said Truther, not helping.

I finally clicked the strap into place and slammed on the gas. Crasher yelled out loud and flew ahead, tilting left and right to keep us steady between the blinking lights. My steering wheel could suggest movement, but the reindeer had the last call.

"I got started late!" I yelled into my headset over the wind.

I heard Celia laugh on the other end. "That's OK," she said. "I got started early! They held me back for a second." She sounded *incredibly pumped up*. The engine she was working on started whistling. "I gotta fix this. Do you mind steering my sleigh?"

"What?!" I looked up at Crasher, who was pulling us along toward the ice mountain. H.O.R.S.E. neighed, and turned to point her glowing eyes at me. "WOULD YOU LIKE TO HORSE YOUR STEERING TO CELIA'S HORSE?"

"How do I know what to do?! I can't see her sleigh." Suddenly, one of my screens that had been blank blinked on. I could see snow rushing by, the ice mountain up ahead, and three reindeer that I didn't recognize. The leader had lightning bolts shaved all over her fur, and her antlers were two more huge lightning bolts jolting out of her head. The other two had dyed their fur a bright red and a bright blue. "Uh, Celia's reindeer, can you hear me?"

The lightning-bolt reindeer flicked her ear. "Loud and clear." Her voice sounded tough and like she really needed to cough. She also had apparently chosen an English accent.

"What's your name?"

"You sure this is the time?"

"I feel bad telling you what to do if I don't know your name."

"My name's Rocker, this is Slammer and Jammer, and we're about to go off the rails."

Celia butted in. "The engine's too powerful for them to steer on their own, Ollie. You can rotate the jets themselves to keep us focused forward."

"The jets?" Nobody had said anything about jets.

"I'm so excited for you to see this thing." There was a harsh crack. "If we make it that long. Gotta go!"

I told H.O.R.S.E. to hook my steering up to Celia's sleigh and told Crasher to keep us heading toward the ice wall. She yelled at Snoozer to wake up, and Truther babbled something that I one-hundred-percent ignored and *I am not sorry about it*.

I grabbed the steering wheel with both hands, and the screens shifted around on their own so that Celia's camera was right in front of me.

This is just like a video game. It is basically exactly like a video game. Except for where we could get really hurt if we mess up.

Don't focus on that!! I yelled in my mind at the part of me that was being negative. *Don't you dare focus on that because you are too busy winning this video game.*

I could tell the sleigh was shifting too far to the right, so I steered it to the left and jerked the sleigh so hard the reindeer got yanked by their harnesses.

"Watch it!" all three reindeer yelled in unison. The other two had English accents, too.

"Sorry." I made a mental note that the engine was *way more powerful* than I expected it to be. I could only safely use gentle movements.

"We're comin' up on the mountain, Captain!" Crasher yelled. I glanced up from the screen and saw that our sleigh was much closer than Celia's, somehow. I set hers to as close to straight as I could and asked H.O.R.S.E. to shift my steering back to me.

"Can you see anythin', Captain?" Crasher yelled. I squinted at the hole, but it was totally dark inside.

"*!!!*" I tried to say, but realized I had hit too nervous to talk. This was the most high-pressure of high-pressure situations.

"Captain?" she yelled again. I swallowed on a heavy lump in my throat.

And suddenly we were coming up on the hole in the ice mountain.

And suddenly we were in total dark, with only the screens lighting up my face.

And suddenly Celia was coming up on the hole in the ice mountain.

"Captain, I can't see!" Crasher yelled. "Should we slow down?"

Celia was in total dark, and her camera couldn't show me anything.

"Boss?" Rocker rasped at me. I swallowed, fighting the heavy lump again.

"WOULD YOU LIKE TO HORSE THE LIGHTS ON?" H.O.R.S.E. whinnied.

"Ollie. It's me." Celia came over the intercom, speaking quietly. "You can do this. Both of our sleighs have headlights. You just have to tell H.O.R.S.E. to turn them on."

I wanted to say, *Why don't you do it?* I wanted to say, *You picked the wrong job for me. I can't talk when I'm nervous, and you knew that! Why did you do this when you knew that? Why didn't I mention this before it got out of control?*

I looked at the map, which was now covered in a bunch of big, useless question marks and a note that said, WHERE DID THIS ICE MOUNTAIN COME FROM? NO DATA ON THIS ICE MOUNTAIN, OBVIOUSLY, BECAUSE THERE'S NO REASON IT SHOULD BE HERE. BET IT'S DARK IN THERE, HUH? SORRY ABOUT THAT. WISH I COULD HELP. SHOULD HAVE TOLD ME, YOUR MAP, ABOUT THIS ICE MOUNTAIN. MAYBE YOU'LL THINK ABOUT THAT NEXT TIME.

"Captain, if we hit a turn like this, we're gonna crash. And not the good kind of crash."

"HEADLIGHTS!" I yelled. H.O.R.S.E.'s head whipped around, and her glowing eyes grew incredibly bright, illuminating an ice cave ahead of us. The screen that showed me Celia's reindeer lit up, too. She had caught up, even got a little ahead of me, and we were both heading for a sharp turn.

"CELIA STEERING!" I yelled, graduating to two words. H.O.R.S.E. whinnied assent, and I yanked the steering wheel, whipping her giant sleigh around at the same time as the reindeer curved against the corner, scraping the side of her sleigh against the ice. Something cracked.

"Don't worry, I can fix that!" Celia said over the headset, and I could hear the smile in her voice. She was right. I could do this.

"CRASHER, WATCH OUT!" I yelled, pushing *three whole words* out over the lump in my throat. "STEERING TO MY SLEIGH," I called to horse, beating my personal record and getting to *four*. I helped Crasher slide us around the corner.

Both sleighs broke around the turn into a huge chasm of nothingness. In the distance, I saw two blinking red and green lights. I checked Celia's screen and saw the same thing, in a slightly different place.

I gave instruction to both teams. "We have to fly. Aim for the lights."

Rocker and Crasher both snorted at me. I blushed red, because they were already flying. H.O.R.S.E. had even automatically kicked us both into flight mode.

I heard several loud clangs from Celia's microphone. "I dropped my wrench – don't worry, I brought an extra, and it's even better," she said. "I started with the worse wrench just in case this exact thing happened."

I wasn't sure what made a wrench better or worse, but I figured this wasn't the time. As we flew through the dark space, I looked to my left and right and saw lots of sleighs all flying through the same expanse, lights blinking all the way down. Several blinked out, crossing through the opening on the other side. Some had probably already made it through. Celia and I were behind almost all of them.

No regrets, I thought. *You put safety first.*

As we approached the blinking lights, our sleighs illuminated a big hole in between them. We landed hard on the ground inside, and for a brief moment, I was suspended in the air above my seat before crashing down and probably getting a bruise on my butt.

"I can see a light," I said, squinting at the end of the tunnel. I had to adjust our steering to keep us from hitting the walls and realized why the hole seemed so small. "The walls are closing in! Be careful!"

The reindeer all grunted and tightened their formations. The walls were rapidly closing in, and I asked H.O.R.S.E. to change the volume buttons on the radio to let me switch between sleigh controls, making it easier for me to adjust both.

"Your sleigh is so much bigger than mine," I said to Celia. "How are you not already stuck?" A rock fell from the ceiling, and I slowed us down just enough that it would hit the ground before we got there.

"Maybe these holes were made for us. They could be different sizes." There were several loud pops and scrapes, and Celia yelped into the microphone. "I caught something that fell off, but it is *hot hot so hot ouch oh geez* – OK. Got it. Ollie, I don't think my sleigh is stable enough to get out of here. The engine keeps jumping all over the place. These walls are already breaking apart around us." Several rocks fell past the camera.

"I have an idea!" I said. "Celia, when I ask you to, can you cut the engine totally off? Would that stop the jumping?"

"I see what you're saying, but for that to work we'd have to be aligned perfectly before I did. And I'd have to rip something out to stop it that fast."

"We'll have to risk it. You heard that, Rocker?"

"Aye."

"What?"

"Yes. It means yes."

"Oh. Perfect! Get ready. I don't think there's a lot of room for error." I worked together with Rocker to tilt the sleigh as best we could toward the door. The clanging coming through their head-sets was getting deafening.

"ALIGNMENT AT NINETY-SIX HORSENT ACCURACY," H.O.R.S.E. neighed.

"Not good enough," Celia's voice vibrated. They were bounc-ing a lot.

"NINETY-SEVEN HORSENT."

I shifted the steering ever so slightly, and the reindeer lifted off the ground to pull in the direct centre.

"NINETY-EIGHT HORSENT."

My ears were hurting at the noise. Crasher seemed to have my sleigh under control.

"Thi-i-i-i-s sl-e-e-e-i-i-i-gh i-i-i-i-s cr-a-a-a-a-z-y-y-y!" Celia was barely understandable. That thing wouldn't survive much longer.

"NINETY-NINE HORSENT."

"That'll have to do. Celia, go!"

I heard her growl as she tugged something out of place, and suddenly the noise stopped. There was a steady *screeeeeeech* as some part of the sleigh slid along rock. I crossed my fingers and toes and tongue.

My sleigh slipped smoothly out of the cliff face with no

fanfare, into a blinding white world of snow. Celia's broke through, but it tore a chunk of the cliff off with it.

And then it was falling.

H.O.R.S.E. automatically switched my sleigh into flight mode, and Crasher started pulling us along the line made by lights suspended on little silver balloons. She couldn't access Celia's sleigh, though.

"Uh, Celia, I don't know if you can see this, but you're falling—"

"OLLIE, I KNOW I AM FALLING, I CAN DEFINITELY FEEL IT AND I AM TRYING TO FIX IT!"

"OK. I know you're probably scared, but you really don't have to scream at m—"

"I DIDN'T EVEN WANT TO DO THIS." It was Rocker this time, who was being pulled down by the sleigh. She pushed down and put a hoof on either side of the camera to look me directly in the eye. "AND IF WE DIE RIGHT NOW FOR SOME REASON, I WILL HAUNT YOU SO HARD YOU WILL NOT EVEN BELIEVE IT, MATE."

"Mate?" I giggled a little. What a weird word.

"OLLIE." It was Celia again. "I APPRECIATE THAT YOU HAVE LEARNED TO RELAX IN STRESSFUL MOMENTS, BUT IT SEEMS LIKE MAYBE, CURRENTLY, YOU ARE TOO RELAXED, IF THAT MAKES SENSE, FOR THIS STRESSFUL MOMENT."

"How can I help?"

"YOU CAN'T, I AM FIXING IT, BUT IT WOULD BE NICE IF YOU WOULD ALSO YELL, OR PANIC, OR SOMETHING, SO THAT I DON'T HAVE TO."

I nodded even though she couldn't see me, and cleared my throat.

"Aaaah," I said. "Um, I am scared. Please help, Celia, I am very . . . uh, scared!"

"I HAVE A FEELING THAT YOU CAN DO BETTER THAN THAT."

She was right. I needed to get into the mood. I imagined myself, stuck inside that engine, surrounded by wires and metal and grease and trying to put something back after having totally pulled it out. I imagined plummeting toward the ground. *I imagined reindeer around me, yelling for help. I IMAGINED THAT I WAS MAYBE GOING TO HIT THE GROUND, VERY, VERY HARD, IF WE DIDN'T DO SOMETHING RIGHT THEN, OH GEEZ, CELIA, WE HAVE TO DO SOMETHING, WHAT IF WE ALL GET HURT?! WHAT IF WE DON'T MAKE IT?!?!?!*

There was a click, and a bang, and then a whurrrrrr as Celia's engine kicked back on. I realized I had been screaming for several seconds.

"Oh, wow." Celia let out a deep breath, and then started laughing. "That was pretty nuts, huh?"

"Yeah. Pretty mixed nuts." I grinned, and wiped some sweat off my face.

"Nah, I don't think it was that bad. Probably just cashews."

"OK, well, I don't understand what any of that meant," Rocker said as she tilted the sleigh to follow the downward slope of the lights, "but I've decided I'm going to haunt the both of you no matter how I die, now."

Celia and I laughed. I looked up at Crasher, who was focused really hard on guiding the sleigh.

"Thank you so much, Crasher. I thought, you know, with your name . . . Well, I thought this would be a lot harder."

Crasher glanced back at me. "Well, that's nice of you to say, Captain, but I was named for my landin's, and speaking of which—"

We were coming up on the ground, at a much steeper angle than I thought we would be. Ahead of us was a vast, wide track that all of the paths were routed to. The *real* race. I looked behind us and saw a few sleighs stuck at their holes, but ahead were several sleighs, some already so far ahead I could barely see them.

"Right." I took over steering so Crasher didn't have to handle it. "Let's slow down and link up with Celia. You can take your time and be careful. Whatever you do, don't . . . uh, crash."

"Yeah, right." Rocker snorted over the headset. "That's like asking Jammer not to be *so sick* on the drums. Ain't happenin'."

"I'll show you!" Crasher yelled. "I'm gonna be so careful you won't even know what to do about it!"

We all jostle-and-bumped our way on to the ground. Crasher tripped over her own feet when we landed, but the other two reindeer squeezed in on either side to lift her back up. I guided both of our sleighs gently toward the centre, and H.O.R.S.E. did the rest of the work – Celia's sleigh extended two metal rods that hooked into the side of mine, and drew them close together so they were tightly attached. The two cockpits even lined up perfectly, with our doors sliding out of the way and connecting into one command centre.

Celia poked her head out from inside the giant. She grinned.

"Easy part's over. Now we just have to win."

"Win? We're really far behind!"

"This engine hasn't even got *started*."

H.O.R.S.E. chimed, and whinnied. "COMING UP ON A SLEIGH IN TWO HUNDRED HORSES."

I glanced up and saw she was right – up ahead was a shiny chrome sleigh, sleek and designed like it was from a movie about the future. Bertrand's sleigh.

As we got closer, H.O.R.S.E. connected my headset to Bertrand's using SweetTooth technology.

Bertrand was out of breath, and his voice sounded tired. " – for a giant rhinoceros with a second face on its nose. I wish for a dragon, except it's nice, not one of the mean ones. I wish for—"

"Hey, Bertrand."

"I wish I could talk, Ollie, but if I don't stop wishing, then the sleigh will stop. I wish the sleigh wouldn't stop!" In between every wish, the sleigh would slow down until he finished saying the next one. It looked like hard work.

"I wish you didn't have to wish so much," I said. His sleigh put on a big burst of speed, jumped ahead of us, and then slowly fell back.

"Thanks, Ollie." Bertrand sounded defeated as we swerved around him and started moving away. "I wish you the best."

"Did you hear that, Celia?" I asked when we disconnected from him.

"The Wish Generator is powered by wishes from all over. It makes sense that he, by himself, wouldn't be able to keep it up for ever. Especially since wishes are stronger when you really mean it."

H.O.R.S.E. whinnied. "HORSED TWELFTH PLACE." The map lit up, showing eleven dots ahead of me with labels next to them with names. The next one ahead of us was *SALLY*, and I saw a brightly coloured splotch in the distance kicking up a cloud of snow.

"She's kind of far ahead!" A piece of the engine popped off and hit me in the head. I caught it and tossed it to Celia, who stuck her hand out to grab it. "Don't you need to put that back where it fell?"

Celia made a *mnyeuh* noise, which is the noise she makes when she shrugs. "We do the best we can with the science we have."

"Do you have any . . . uh, 'nitro,' or anything?"

"*Nitro?* No, Ollie, don't be silly, this isn't a movie. We have auxiliary gravity-dampening ionic hyperspace vacuum thrusters."

"Right, of course."

Celia kicked the AG-DIHVTs into gear, and we were all slammed forward by the force of four big green jets of flame shooting out of the back. If the reins didn't tightly (and comfortably) hold the reindeer up ahead of the sleigh, we would have slammed right into them. We came up on Sally at a ridiculous speed, made record time, and then right as we were about to pass her, the jets popped off the back. Fire shot out and melted the snow, leaving a big, warm hole behind us. Celia poked her head out through an opening where one of the jets was, and we watched it die down together.

Then I turned around and looked at Sally's sleigh. The outside was painted in bright colours, like blocks, and had a covering shaped like a train with square wheels. The wheels were rotating a few inches above the treads, creating a cute ornamental effect. Sally had her feet up on the dashboard, and was flipping through a book.

Just as our sleigh was about to creep past Sally's, steam chugged out of the top of the train and a loud horn blew. It put on a burst of speed and stayed just ahead. She flipped another page in the book, and her feet never left the dashboard.

"How are you doing that?" I asked after H.O.R.S.E. connected my headset to hers. Our sleigh caught up again, and her train did the same thing. The reindeer up front looked bored.

"I've got it set to keep me in eleventh place," Sally replied.

"Eleventh place?" Celia wiped some grease off of her hands but on to her face. "Why?"

"She doesn't want to win," I explained.

"I just want to make toys, and cute things, and fun stuff." Sally closed the book and put her hair up in a ponytail with a hair tie she had around her wrist. "This way, it looks like I tried but *just* didn't make it to the next round. Dad will be disappointed, but he'll still have Kurt and Klaus competing."

"OK, well, we want to win." Celia punched some buttons on the sleigh, cutting off some of my screens and adding more speed. "You'll have to let us past you."

The train kept pace perfectly without Sally ever having to touch anything.

"Then you're going to have to help me get past two more people."

I glanced at the map, and saw three dots in a tight triangle ahead of us. *GOLDIE*, *FRANK* and *MYRLE*.

"The triplets are next," I said. "If we pass all three—"

"Then I'll be in the top ten. Which can't happen." Sally patted a harpoon gun attached to the side of the train. "I don't want to ruin your chances, but I need to be in eleventh place. If you push ahead past all three of them, I'll have to pull you back. If you can figure out a way to separate two, I'm happy to let you go."

The three of us stuck together and powered forward, where the triplets were in three sleighs with . . . legs? Thin metal legs. And their sleighs were gold, red and brown pods. Each triplet had a reindeer sitting inside with them.

The legs moved all three forward in unison with a repetitive leap that we slowly caught up to. The speed of Celia's sleigh was really amazing, especially when stabilized by mine. As long as we didn't get physically knocked out, it seemed likely we could catch up to the front of the pack.

H.O.R.S.E. tried to connect the triplets to my headset, but they denied us. Immediately, the three pods moved closer together and sealed over into perfect glass spheres. The two on either side connected on to the middle one and rolled up to click together, creating an upside-down triangle. The orbs rotated individually so the top two triplets were facing us, and their leg pairs slid together to form two big robot arms. The hands clanged loudly as they snapped open and closed.

"I don't like the look of this, Captain," Crasher said.

"That makes—" I paused for a second to count how many reindeer Sally had. "Fourteen of us."

"I think it's pretty cool," Celia said.

"OK, so thirteen."

"Yeah. I mean, it's scary, but I definitely would say that I like it," said Sally.

"Twelve, then."

Slammer and Jammer said, at the same time, "Where can we get one of those?"

"OK you know what it doesn't really matter how many of us don't like the look of this."

A tiny sleigh sped through from behind and tried to slip around us. Sally's train started to react, but before it could, the triplets plucked the sleigh off the ground and whirled it around like a baseball, launching it back down the track where we came from. A little elf I didn't recognize yelled and pushed a button to inflate a protective rubber bubble around the sleigh and its one little reindeer as they blasted off into the distance.

We all stared at the triplets' machine.

"You can add me back into the list," Celia said.

We slowed down enough to maintain a solid distance between us and the robot, which kept opening and closing its hands hungrily. Sally had picked her book back up like it was the most boring thing in the world.

"What if we used your harpoon to pull one of them away from the others?" I asked.

Sally shook her head. "I can only use it once, and I need it for emergencies."

"Emergencies like keeping us from getting ahead of you."

"Yeah, just like those. How'd you know?" She flipped another page.

I covered my eyes with my hands so I could focus, and also so that maybe Sally would feel bad for me since I looked sad. She didn't say anything, and probably wasn't looking, but I *did* come up with a plan.

"Rocker, is it OK if I ride on your back?" I asked. Celia looked at me like I was crazy . . . because I was. "Celia, you and Crasher will have to keep us moving. Sally, you go right; we'll go left. We might get ahead of them for a second – go easy on the harpoon, OK?"

Rocker said, "Aye," and I had H.O.R.S.E. disconnect her from the sleigh. She flew around to the side, and I climbed on to her back awkwardly.

"What's the plan, boss?" Rocker asked.

Celia steered our sleighs to the left, and Sally's train veered off to the right. The triplets' orbs circled to look at them, and the arms reached out to grab them. Pulling against each other, though, they couldn't quite reach either side.

I took a deep breath. "Head straight for the middle. Go between the legs."

"You sure?"

"I'm sure."

Rocker leaned her head forward and kicked off in the air, propelling herself toward the triplets' machine, lightning bolts first. I manoeuvred my feet under me, so I was crouching on her back and clinging for dear life to her neck. The two triplets that had been facing us were distracted by Celia and Sally, so no one noticed us when we slipped between the robot legs.

As soon as Rocker got in front of the machine, I jumped up and grabbed hold of the middle orb, scrambling to find something to hold on to.

"Crikey!" Rocker yelled.

There wasn't really anything to grab, but the forward momentum and my constant wiggling kept me attached enough.

Myrle was inside, in overalls. He looked at my smushed-up face and frowned. His reindeer, who was wearing a nose ring, stuck his tongue out at me. I saw Myrle push a lever back and forth, and the orb twisted left and right quickly. I held on tight, making sure I totally blocked Myrle's view. He spun all the way around, twice, which made me feel sick but didn't throw me off.

"I've hacked into his map," Celia said into my earpiece. Inside, Myrle's screen had several question marks all around it with a message that said, *MAYBE NEXT TIME YOU'LL INSTALL A BETTER FIREWALL FOR ME, HUH?*

Perfect. Now he'll have no idea which way he's facing. I could feel the robot wobbling around, trying to figure out which direction to go.

The glass covering on the orb cracked open just a little, so I could hear Myrle yell, "GET OFFA ME, TWERP!"

"I'M SORRY!" I yelled back. "BUT WE ARE TRYING TO WIN."

I felt something grab my foot, hard, and start peeling me away from the machine.

"Rocker, hurry! Hit the legs!" My hands made a loud squeaking noise as they slid down the glass. I was lifted into the air by my foot, my shirt falling over and the smiley-face button Andrea gave me hitting me in the face. I pushed at the shirt, trying to see, and as soon as I got it out of the way of my eyes, I saw Rocker head-butt one of the knees, then whirl her back legs around and kick the other knee sideways. I guess the legs were flimsier than they looked or Rocker was *very strong*, because they buckled in two totally different directions and Myrle's orb came plummeting down.

The top two triplets disconnected and rolled their legs on to the ground, running like they had before we arrived. Myrle's orb was left behind, cracked and broken in the middle of the track.

The hand that was holding me started to let me go so it could move into being a leg, and I took the opportunity to grab on to it and start climbing toward the knee. I closed my eyes and held my breath while it rotated all the way around so I wouldn't throw up, then figured out which direction I was facing and climbed up to the knee. I looked for a screw or something to pull out, but couldn't find anything that wasn't welded together.

I pulled myself up higher, very proud of my climbing skills, and got to where it attached to the orb. There was a little crack in the orb where the legs connected so they'd be able to move back and forth, which would be *perfect* to jam something into. I patted my left pocket – nothing. I patted my right pocket – nothing. I looked down at my clothes and saw the button.

Pulling a button off without ripping the shirt is already hard on its own, much less while clinging to a swinging metal rod thirty feet in the air. I eventually got it unclipped, though, and waited until the leg was stretched all the way forward. I jammed the button into the gap behind the leg, then yanked my fingers away as fast as possible. The leg swung back around, crushing the button.

The button was just supposed to jam the leg, but when it was crushed, it released an electric energy that shone bright blue. I felt a tingle running through my body, and the legs both shook and stopped moving altogether. The orb tipped forward, and I pushed off of the leg into the air.

"HELP HELP HELP HELP HELP HELP!" I yelled. "HELP HELP HELP HE—" The wind was knocked out of me when I landed, stomach first, across Rocker's back. I heard a crash as the second triplet fell.

"That was brutal," Rocker said. I tried not to worry about it, because if I thought too much, I would feel bad. Also I would feel *bonkers* for ever trying that. "What did you do to the second one?"

"I don't know," I said. "I think that was my button?"

"See you later, Celia, Ollie. Catch!" Sally yelled, and threw something hard up into the air. Rocker swooped over so I could catch it. It was a felt bag, filled with beads. "They're marbles, and there are a *lot* of them. They don't do much at that size but get really big when you sing 'Jingle Bells.'"

"Thanks, Sally," Celia said. Rocker dropped me off at our sleigh and connected back into formation.

"Good luck. Go easy on my brothers."

Celia grinned. "No promises!"

I heard Sally laugh. "Fair."

Without arms to grab us, the other triplet was pretty easy to dodge around and push past. The lights along the side of the track started lifting off the ground, and we kicked into flight mode before the ground dropped out.

"HORSED EIGHTH PLACE."

Celia gasped. "Whoa, Ollie, look down."

I looked down and reeled back, scooting as far away from the edge as possible.

"That is a huge chasm *and* it is thousands of feet deep *and* we could fall and die and *why* did you tell me to look down?"

"People always say 'don't look down.' I wanted to be more interesting."

When I stopped feeling my heartbeat trying to pop my eyes out, I stood up and looked behind us. Frank, the remaining triplet, had moved the legs up above them, where they were rotating like helicopter propellers and bobbing her along in the air.

"HORSED SEVENTH PLACE," H.O.R.S.E. whinnied. Celia and I looked at each other, confused.

"How did we do that?" I asked.

"I don't know. I didn't see anyone." Celia was already climbing back into the engine to fix something else.

Ramp's sleigh was next up, and we were going to fly past him pretty easily, but H.O.R.S.E. automatically connected to his sleigh and he yelled out:

"Now, you wait! You wait for your best friend Ramp!"

I sighed and slowed the sleigh down so we were flying right next to him. He was holding on to his toupee with one hand and steering with the other.

"Uh, hi, Ramp."

"I'm hungry."

"I didn't, uh – I don't think that I brought any—"

"You built this sleigh! Where are the snacks?"

"Well, I actually didn't—"

"Fine. I guess you don't have to help out your poor, hungry best friend Ramp."

I sighed. "Do we have any snacks?"

H.O.R.S.E. whinnied, and a compartment popped open. Powerful, happy organ chords came out of a speaker as two big, delicious, caramel-covered popcorn balls were revealed.

"I was saving those for when we won," Celia said. "But I guess you can give him one if we have to."

I took one out even though I super didn't want to and threw one to Ramp, who caught it and immediately started tearing into it, sticky crumbs falling all over his beard.

"OK, we're . . . uh, gonna go, Ramp."

"Mmnff. Nggmmnnfff!" He didn't stop eating long enough to make sense, so I turned up the speed and we pushed away from that mess.

"HORSED SIXTH PLACE."

The next sleigh was more of an upside-down top hat held aloft by a small army of birds tied to the brim – two big ones, albatrosses, and then a wide variety of colours and shapes in between them. The three reindeer at the front had huge animatronic wings attached to their backs that were flapping as well.

The elf inside, who (from what I could tell) was wearing a snazzy suit, tipped the top hat on her head at me. "Ollie! What a delight. I hope your day has been as marvellous as mine."

"Gadzooks! Is that you? I didn't see you in the first challenge."

"That's me: Gadzooks Gremlin! At your service." She bowed as far as she could, which wasn't very far since the giant hat went up to her shoulders.

Gadzooks wasn't her real name, but that's what she'd started calling herself when she decided she wanted to be a magician. Her father, Richard Gremlin, was in charge of the aviary. There are *lots* of Christmas birds, but everyone knows that – partridges, turtledoves, French hens, you name it. Gadzooks learned how to make birds disappear, and then one thing led to another, and now she talks like a character from a fancy old movie even though she's my age.

I slowed down as we approached her hat. "Do you have any scary tricks to keep us away?" I asked. "Like, are your birds going to peck out our eyes?" Gadzooks and I were friends, but it wouldn't hurt to check just in case. It *was* a competition.

"Why, no! I couldn't possibly imagine causing any hijinks. Here, have a candy bar!" She tossed a candy bar over from her sleigh, which I caught. "Go on, take a bite."

I knew exactly where this was going.

"There's a bird in this, isn't there?"

"A *bird*?! How could you accuse me of such tomfoolery? I would never."

"OK, but, basically every time you hand me anything, there's a bird in it."

"Look at the candy bar. Look at the front, the back, the sides. Could that possibly fit a bird?"

I spun it around in my hands. It looked like a perfectly normal candy bar, except that the label on the front said it was from *Not a Bird! Inc.* and the slogan under that said *This is for sure Not a Bird!*

I opened the wrapper, and it was a real chocolate bar.

Well, this is refreshing.

I took a bite, and it was delicious.

Gadzooks started cackling. "You fool! You've fallen for my trap once again, Sir Gnome. Bested once more by your friend and compatriot, good ol' Gadzooks."

"Huh?" I took another bite of the chocolate. "How did you best me?"

"You thought it was a bird, didn't you? And it wasn't! Not a single bird to be found!"

"I don't feel bested, though. Now I've got chocolate."

"Tell me how you feel after you *look under your hat*."

"You mean my helmet?" I reached my hand up and patted the top of my helmet, where a top hat rested that wasn't there before. "Oh."

I lifted up the hat, and there was a dove underneath it. It

flew around in a circle, then flew back to me and snuggled up in my shirt.

"You've been bamboozled!" Gadzooks cackled again.

The dove cooed and nestled in to get warm. I looked back at my hand, and the hat had disappeared.

"If that's all, I think we're going to move on ahead."

"Absolutely! Keep your wits about you. The birds and I have stayed here because the vehicle up ahead is simply *frightful*. We'd come out nothing but feathers." She shook her head, looking very dramatic and sad.

"See you soon, Gadzooks. I bet your Santa suit will be amazing."

"Same to you, Ollie. Oh, and one last thing." She leaned over and whispered into my ear so it wouldn't go over the radio. "When you get the chance, tell Celia to look behind her ear." Gadzooks winked at me and patted my sleigh as permission for us to go ahead. I cranked up our speed to push across the chasm.

"HORSED FIFTH PLACE," H.O.R.S.E. announced.

At the same time, Celia yelled, "A wild turkey?! How did a wild turkey get behind my ear?!" The wild turkey attempted to explain with a series of loud gobbles as it glided away from the sleigh.

I was starting to get exhausted, and my arms hurt from climbing the triplets' robot, but I knew I couldn't slow down yet.

We had to win.

Or at least beat Buzz.

Chapter 9

The path had been curving back toward town ever since we started flying over the chasm, and it looked like we were going to be landing back on the ground soon. Up ahead was the biggest sleigh I'd ever seen – maybe even bigger than Buzz's. It was painted a dark green and had big rotating cylinders attached to the front and back that were covered in spikes. As we got closer, I saw the words *THE HARVESTER* spray-painted in big, angry letters. On my map screen the sleigh was labelled *ANDREA*.

Up front were *eleven* reindeer, all focused forward with serious expressions on their faces . . . but that might have been because they were scared of getting chomped up in the Harvester's spikes. The width of the sleigh *alone* blocked off the track, and the squad of reindeer made it look even more difficult to get past her.

She's nice though, right? I thought. *She won't crush us to little bitty pieces.*

"WHRRRRRRRRRRRRGHHHH!!!" the Harvester said. It touched down on the snowy ground and churned up a huge cloud of snow, completely obscuring itself and spraying a cold onslaught all over us.

I kicked the sleigh into flight mode. Crasher flew us up pretty high and pushed into the cloud of snow. I couldn't even see the steering wheel in front of me. The Harvester's noise was deafening. Crasher jerked the sleigh to the left, hard, and I grabbed on to a screen to keep from falling. (It wasn't the smartest idea, but it worked.)

"One of those crunchy, spiky things is waving around up here, Captain." Crasher swerved right, and the spinning spike cut through the cloud of smoke just in front of my nose.

Crasher pulled us into a barrel-roll manoeuvre, which almost tossed me totally out of the sleigh.

"What's going on, Ollie?" Celia yelled from inside the engine. "This sleigh isn't supposed to go upside down!"

Andrea's voice came over my headset. "I can't even tell you how sorry I am, Oilie," she said, sounding like she was talking about spilling something on the couch and not *almost killing us*. "I just need to find the button . . ." Crasher pulled up to avoid the snarling spikes rolling by.

"Oh, wait! Here! I found it." Andrea must have pushed some kind of button, because the noise got quieter and farther away. Crasher powered us forward, and I cranked the engine up as high as it could go. As soon as we broke through the snow cloud, we landed back down on the ground.

"Thanks, Andrea," I said. "Good luck on the rest of the race!"

There was another brief second of silence.

Then she said: "Hey, Crowley?"

There is no way she is not doing this on purpose, right?

"My name is, to be honest—"

"I'm sorry about this." A click and a beep from the other side of the mic . . . but nothing happened. "What?" A click again, and then the beep again. And then another click and a beep. *Clickbeepclickbeepclickbeep* – "Why isn't it working?" Her voice sounded a lot harsher than it usually did. Meaner.

"What do you mean?" I asked.

"Are you not wearing the button?"

And suddenly everything made sense. The jokes were a lie. The apology was a lie. The thing the button did to Goldie was supposed to happen to *me*.

I was too mad to think very hard about what I did next. I slowed down our sleigh to let her get right up on our tail so I could see the first of her reindeer. I pulled out Sally's bag of marbles and flung them all out at once – hundreds of marbles slipping under the reindeer's feet and, past them, into where the spinning spikes met the ground.

And then I sang, *"JINGLE BELLS."*

The marbles, which were basically invisible before, all jumped up to the size of regular marbles.

"JINGLE BELLS."

"What are you doing?" Andrea sounded suspicious. I ignored her.

The marbles grew even bigger, like tennis balls. I saw a couple of reindeer stumble over them.

"JINGLE ALL THE WAY."

Beach balls now. I saw the first of them meet the spikes of the sleigh and could hear the *WHHHRRRGGG* get louder as it tried to push over them. Celia, who must have looked out to see what was going on, started singing with me. Slammer and Jammer made instrument sounds with their voice boxes and Rocker started improvising vocals over the top.

"OH, WHAT FUN IT IS TO RIDE IN A ONE—"

"HORSE!"

"OPEN!"

"SLEIGH!" It took Rocker an extra few seconds to finish because she added a riff at the end. By then, Andrea's sleigh had been totally gummed up by marbles of different sizes, since I guess some of them didn't hear us as well. The biggest were two or three times my size, and they were *heavy*. They blocked the track, they broke her spikes, and they tripped her reindeer. Nobody was hurt, but she was totally stuck. We sped away.

"My name is *Ollie!*" I yelled. But we were already too far for her to hear.

"HORSED FOURTH PLACE!"

"Nice!" Celia cheered.

"SHOOT FOR THE HORSE," H.O.R.S.E. whinnied helpfully. "EVEN IF YOU MISS, YOU'LL LAND AMONG THE HORSE!"

I looked at the map: Up next it said *KURT* was very close behind *BUZZ* and *KLAUS*, tied for first.

Before I could ask Celia about strategy, we were coming up on a mostly normal sleigh led by five reindeer with interesting haircuts and faux-leather jackets. The back of their jackets, and Kurt's, said *TREASON 4 THE SEASON* with a picture of a reindeer in heavy make-up sticking out its tongue.

"Blimey!" Rocker exclaimed over the chime of H.O.R.S.E. connecting us to Kurt. "Don't tell me he joined that terrible band."

"Just a big fan," Kurt said over the headset. Rocker looked

down at the ground, embarrassed. "Especially their first album. Obviously."

The reindeer didn't say anything. One of them flipped hair out of his eyes.

Kurt took a candy stick out of his dashboard and stuck it in his mouth. Now that we were riding alongside him, I saw that his sleigh was totally covered in stickers. A big one close to me said *Honk If You're Jolly!*

"Honk!" I said cheerfully.

Kurt looked at me blankly. "You some kind of goose?"

I was immediately very embarrassed. "You know, the sticker? I don't think we have an actual horn."

He snorted, smirked. "Oh, right. I forgot. There are a lot of stickers."

There were. While trying to look everywhere but at him I noticed a big yellow triangle that said *Baby New Year on Board!*

He wasn't going very fast, and we could easily outpace him. Why wasn't he trying to catch up to Buzz and Klaus?

"You see that?" He must have figured out that I was wondering. He pointed at Buzz's sleigh (*car*) and Klaus's sleigh, which looked straight out of a Kris Kringle storybook. They were neck and neck and kept bumping into each other. "They're gonna tear themselves apart. And we're all hitting top ten at this point. Why get in the middle of it?"

"Because you're so close to winning!" I said. "Don't you want to beat them?"

Kurt shrugged. "Nah. This is good enough." He reached over and patted down a sticker that was starting to peel off. *My Other Car Is a Sleigh.*

"Let's go, Ollie." Celia sounded exasperated. "The finish line is coming up any second."

"Have fun." Kurt chomped down on his candy stick as I started speeding up our sleigh.

"See you after the race, Kurt!" I said, still hoping that one day we'd be friends. He did a little two-finger wave as our radios disconnected.

"HORSED THIRD PLACE."

Klaus and Buzz were already too close for comfort, and in the not-so-distant distance was a chequered finish banner stretched across the whole track.

Seeing this, Celia pushed the speed lever all the way to the front, launching us like a rocket at the two big sleighs.

"Celia, they're still slamming into each other!" I shouted. "I don't think they realize we're coming!"

"They'll have to." The engine popped and banged. "Or we'll all blow up, I guess."

I stared at her, alarmed. "I think I am going to warn them we are coming."

"Don't! If you do that, they'll have time to—"

H.O.R.S.E. connected me to their sleighs.

"Buzz, Klaus, we're coming straight for you *very, very fast*. Please get out of our way or Celia says we'll all explode into a million tiny pieces and then *nobody* will be Santa."

Celia put her head in her hands. "Now we don't have the element of surprise, and they're going to—"

The big sleighs split apart, away from the centre, giving us lots of room to power through. We kept up our speed and barrelled in between them. Nothing was between us and the finish line now. I took a deep breath, Celia stuck something back on to the engine—

Klaus slammed into our left side, and Buzz slammed into our right. I was knocked to the floor of the sleigh, then grabbed on to one of the screens and pulled myself up. Buzz looked out his open window and grinned down at me.

"Nice move, Dollie! We're gonna tear your sleigh apart."

Celia frantically tried to catch pieces as they flew off of the giant engine. Klaus, meanwhile, didn't say anything to us. His eyes focused forward, and his foot tapped on the floor of his sleigh like the world was moving too slowly for him. He pressed into Celia's side of the sleigh, and more pieces flew off of the engine that she couldn't catch.

"Faster!" he yelled at his reindeer. "My father didn't hand-select you for me to *lose*. Can't you go any faster?!"

"Yikes," Crasher said. "Double yikes."

What are we going to do?

I turned to the side, reached my arms up to the edge of Buzz's window, and pulled myself inside head first. He didn't push me out immediately – I think he was confused about what was going on – and I flipped around to sit in the seat. Buzz is big, but I'm pretty tiny; it was easy to sit down next to him inside the car. I leaned my head against his arm, closed my eyes, and hummed.

"Wh – what are you doing, Dollie?"

I took a deep breath, enjoying his windshield blocking the wind from blasting in my face for a minute. "I just figured I should get out of my sleigh if you're going to tear it to pieces," I said. "And I also wanted to ask why you're so mean."

Celia's voice came on to my headset. "I hope you know what you're doing, Ollie, because I sort of have my hands full down here?"

I took my earpiece out and moved my head from Buzz and rested it on the dashboard.

"Mean?" he asked. "What do you . . . uh, mean?"

"I tried to be friends with you, but you're always ignoring the rules at the shop. And bullying me and Celia, and everybody, with your mean crew. And you cheated in the first challenge. If I win this challenge, I get to do the next challenge with my *actual, for-real mum*. But if you win the challenge, and then win the Trials, I'm going to have to move to *Florida*."

After a second, he said, "Why?"

"Because you'll make the whole North Pole a mean place, and I don't want to live in a mean place. Even a mean place where I was born, and my family lives, and my best friends live. The North Pole should be for *everybody*, not just you and your squad of rude jerks."

Buzz opened his glove box and handed me tissues wrapped up in plastic. I used one to wipe off my eyes, and another to blow my nose.

"Get out," he said, and reached over me to push open his door. I looked down with my puffy eyes and saw Celia working extra hard to keep the engine going. "Klaus is still gonna tear you to pieces," he added, looking away from me and fidgeting uncomfortably. "So it doesn't really matter. Besides, if I won, I'd have to work with your *mum*. That's super lame, and also she'd probably make my suit blow up or whatever."

I laughed. "She's too proud of her work to do that. But she might use a really itchy fabric."

"Yeah, see? And I've got . . . sensitive skin, so . . ." He looked up at the ceiling, and then at the chair next to him, and then out the window. Everywhere but at me. He tapped his fingers on the steering wheel. "Get out, please?"

I put my headset back in.

" – would really like an update on what's going on, best friend, best buddy, best pal!!!"

"Thanks, Buzz."

"This isn't over, Dollie."

"Maybe you *can* be nice."

"OK, I didn't mean – *this* part, right now, *is* over. So if you could—"

I swung out of the car and landed on the floor of my sleigh with a thud. Buzz moved out of the way and fell back a little to give us some breathing room. I steered us away from Klaus to stop the scraping sound, but he kept pushing. It wouldn't work for long; eventually we'd be run off the track.

The finish line was close, though.

"HORSED SECOND PLACE."

"Can we make it, H.O.R.S.E.?"

"CALCULATING . . . CALCULATED ZERO PERCENT HORSE OF SUCCESS." She whinnied, then pulled up a helpful little animation of what would happen if we kept pushing forward; either our engine would blow up completely or we'd be run off the track.

"Come *ON*!" Klaus yelled at his reindeer again. "We should have won by now. This is ridiculous."

I had an idea. "H.O.R.S.E., do Klaus's reindeer have headsets?"

H.O.R.S.E. neighed affirmatively.

"Can you connect me to their leader but *not* Klaus?"

Instead of answering, she did it. I heard a chime as we were connected, and then heavy reindeer breathing.

"Uh, hi. This is Ollie, your race neighbour. What's your name?"

"Prancer XII." The answer came quick, no-nonsense. "What do you want?"

Oh, wow. A direct descendant of the original reindeer. They were usually reserved for Santa sleighs.

"I just wanted to see how you were doing," I said. "It seems like he's working you pretty hard."

"It's our job," Prancer XII said.

"OK, but, did you know that he's already qualified to make it to the next round?" I asked. "Right now he's basically only pushing you this hard for bragging rights."

Klaus pulled the sleigh away briefly, then slammed it back into ours, jostling us and knocking a huge chunk off the engine.

"He's our commander. It's up to him."

"Yeah, sure, but if you were to keep him from blowing us up, and he got second place, it wouldn't be a big deal."

"Santa is his father. I want to be on *the* sleigh team someday. I can't disobey a direct order."

"FASTER!" Klaus yelled. I winced.

"OK, then how about this? Celia and I are trying to be Santa, too. If you don't disobey orders, but maybe act a little more tired than you are, we'll promise to put you on our sleigh team one day, too. You can make it look like you're doing your best, and then you'll have *tripled* your chance to be on '*the* sleigh team.' " I held my breath. *Let this work, let this work, please let this work.*

A moment later, Klaus's sleigh started lagging behind us just a little. I took the opportunity to swerve us away from him. As we pulled ahead, I got a look at all the reindeer – they were gorgeous, tall, long-antlered and strong. A traditional nine-reindeer team with Prancer XII at the front. They even had bells attached to their reins, jingling and jangling.

"*What?!*" Klaus yelled.

I heard Prancer respond to him: "We're trying, Commander, but we're exhausted. We're doing our best, but you've had us flying full speed since the beginning."

"Thank you," I said, and disconnected us. Our engine was crumbling to nothing, so Celia jumped on to my sleigh and slammed down on some buttons to shift all six reindeer to my sleigh. She disconnected hers, letting it tumble off behind us. It burst into flames, and we both winced and looked away.

"What did you do?" she asked.

"Talked."

Our existing momentum kept us going, and the engine of my sleigh alone kept us from falling behind. Crasher pushed through the yellow tape of the finish line, and suddenly we were in the centre of an enormous, cheering crowd.

We won.

Chapter 10

There was another month before the next challenge. We got another email explaining that we needed our suits to be "prepared for anything," so we had until the beginning of November. We went to work.

Part of work was being on TV. Celia still didn't enjoy it, so most of the time I did interviews and events for both of us. We weren't the only ones, either; everybody was trying to convince the North Pole they should be Santa. Klaus even hired a whole campaign team.

I never thought I'd get tired of seeing my own face on TV. Before this, the only time my face had been anywhere on a screen was when the camera crews around big Christmas events would pan over the crowds. Actually, that's not totally true; I was also on the Jumbotron once during the Reindeer Games because I had painted my face with the colours of my favourite team, the Abominable Throwmen, when they were competing in the Big Game against the Grim Wreathers.

Now Maria Duende had my face on the news every hour, when she did her "Contestant Countdown." She made all of us film "catchphrases" while a big computer-animated banner with our name and rank flew by in the background.

> **Ollie Gnome: #1.** "I'm here to make friends!" (I couldn't think of anything else in the moment.)
>
> **Celia Pixie: #1.** Hers is actually just fifteen seconds of uninterrupted glaring at the camera.
>
> **Klaus Claus: #2.** "Wait, you're just going to let Kurt plug his merchandise on the air? He's not even taking this seriously. I refuse to participate in something so ridiculous, and furthermore—"
>
> **Buzz Brownie: #3.** "I'm gonna win this competition, and none of those dorks are gonna stand in my way." (His heart didn't sound like it was in it any more, though.)
>
> **Kurt Claus: #4.** "Buy my T-shirt, if you feel like it." (They said *I Don't Care Who Wins* on the front, and *Kurt for Santa* on the back.)
>
> **Frank Fae: #6.** "My brothers will be avenged." (They didn't die or anything. She was just being dramatic.)
>
> **Gadzooks Gremlin: #7.** "I'll make your chances … disappear!"
>
> **Ramp Claus: #8.** "Is the light on? Am I supposed to talk now?"
>
> **Andrea Claus: #9.** "I came all the way to the big city to win, and I'm gonna do anything it takes!" *Tell me about it.*
>
> And the big surprise: **Sally Claus: #10.** "I'm glad I still have a chance. I guess."

I never caught #5 when it came on. I wasn't even sure who it was.

Celia and I tied for first, which was awesome, but because we worked together they punished us by giving the both of us only one tailor: my mum. That freed up the number-ten spot, which pushed Sally (who had successfully stayed at number eleven) into the running again. She was definitely not happy about it.

The worst thing, though, was that Celia's feud with Maria apparently extended into the reporter's professional decisions; there was an entire segment analyzing whether or not we cheated in the race and lots of live interviews with the Klaus Claus Fan Club. Somehow Maria had recorded a clip of Celia talking to Bertrand before the race, and instead of drawing attention to his invention, which would have been the nice thing to do, she took the opportunity to play Celia yelling "Who cares about *winning*?" over and over, without context.

"Why do you think Celia Pixie would say such a thing, and then go on to win the Trial?" Maria asked a man on the street with very shiny teeth and no eyebrows.

"I think, and this is just my opinion," the man said, his teeth so bright they caused a lens flare, "that she acted like she didn't care so everybody else wouldn't try as hard."

"That's not true!" I yelled at the TV, but Maria Duende was nodding seriously.

She said, "I think you speak for most of us with that one, sir."

"Uh, well, it's just my opinion, but—"

"You heard it here first," Maria interrupted. "Did Celia Pixie knowingly trick the competition, including our Santa's own son, Bertrand? Use the hashtag below to cast your vote!" At the bottom of the screen #trickypixie flashed on and off in bright letters.

Celia clicked off the TV from behind me. "I'm tired of hearing her voice."

My mum called from the other side of our office through teeth clamped around bobby pins. "We need to focus, anyway. Bring your sister over here so we can use her head."

I picked up Polly, who had been watching the TV with me, and walked her over to my mum.

"Why do I always have to be the model?" she whined.

"'Cause you've got a big head," I teased. She stuck her tongue out at me.

"Let's talk about *clothes*." My mum spread out some sketches and designs on a table in front of us, along with a pile of blank sheets of grid paper. "Ollie already knows a lot of this; design is one of his *strong suits*."

Celia groaned at the pun. I giggled.

"As you know, there are two major parts of fashion: *form*, which is basically looks, and *function*, which is what the outfit can do." My mum gestured to Celia's clothes: a lab coat and goggles over a green shirt tucked into cargo trousers that were a slightly different green. "Celia needs help with form, while Ollie . . ." She turned to me. I was wearing striped tights and shiny wooden shoes under a long blue tunic. It was *very* adorable.

"Ollie doesn't even have any pockets." I blushed. "Plus, those shoes will hurt his feet if he's not careful."

"He got a blister," Polly added. "He told me!" I put my hand over her mouth until she licked it to make me let go.

"Why does it matter how our suits look?" Celia asked. "It's just like all this wasted time on TV. We just need to win the challenges. Why should we care what anyone thinks of us?"

Mum explained, "People want to feel included. Nobody is forced to listen to Santa; they do their jobs because they believe. Talking to them, showing them who you are, helps them believe in *you*."

Celia gestured to her outfit. "This *is* who I am. Dressing like Ollie would be lying."

Mum shook her head. "You won't be dressing like Ollie. I'm not trying to change you, just bring out the best version of you."

Celia frowned but didn't have an immediate comeback. I was already distracted looking through the sketches Mum had drawn up.

"I'm thinking something with gold leaf," I began. "I'd have to be gentle with it so it didn't crack, obviously, but – or, ooh, what about a suit that changes colours based on my mood? Teaching it to recognize emotions would take a lot of time, but it would be so *dramatic*! Or what if it had huge feathered wings on the back, like, twice my size? That would be impressive—"

"This is why it's lucky you're working together." My mum handed each of us pencils and blank sheets of gridded paper. "I'm going to help you design *each other's* suits."

Celia and I looked at each other and thought about this.

I had to admit, "This is a good idea."

Celia frowned. "It's a very good idea."

"That's why I'm the best." Mum tapped her fingernails on the paper. "Get to work."

I started scribbling furiously. Making something for my friend was a lot more exciting than making something for myself, but it was a much more difficult challenge. I had to consider what Celia would like, but also something that showed my strengths, too.

"But, Mum, Celia is a scientist. A genius scientist." I was having lots of ideas, but none of them seemed good enough. "How am I going to make something for her that's any better than what she can make for herself?"

She ruffled my hair and pulled up on a chair next to me. She shuffled some of my papers around and pointed at one of my doodles: basically a suit of armour with a Santa hat on top.

"That idea was stupid. It's too bulky."

"No idea is stupid." She ripped the picture out of the paper and set it next to another one of my doodles I had drawn in a moment of frustration: just a laptop strapped to Celia's head like a hat.

"That one's even worse. I drew it as a joke!"

Mum ripped that one out, too, and set both of the designs next to a third design. I had covered an entire Santa suit in pockets, like Celia's cargo shorts. It would probably just make her look like a toad, though.

"That one's ugly. And *just* having pockets isn't very useful."

She set all three of my designs beside each other, and pointed. "Why did you make each of these?"

"Uh, I made the armour because I know Celia would want something to be protective. And the reason she likes cargo shorts is so she can put her gadgets in all the pockets. One time she told me, 'I like to have the best tool for the job, so I make sure I always have *every* tool.' That's why I made the pocket design. The computer one was really just a joke because—

"Wait a second!" I cut myself off and pulled a new sheet of paper over next to those three designs. "So it needs to be tough, of course, and it needs to have places for all of Celia's things. But that doesn't necessarily have to be pockets, right?"

My mum's smile grew big. "What are you thinking?"

"Armour. But not like a full suit of armour, more like body-sized, with gadgets built in. And maybe a computer that lets her use all the different tricks – like a superhero suit!" I started sketching out ideas. "If the gadgets are *part* of the armour, then it doesn't need pockets, and I can still make it look one hundred percent so very amazing."

Mum clapped me on the shoulders and kissed the top of my head. "You got it. Get some designs together, and let's get started."

Even with almost a whole month I felt rushed. Celia and I had to balance making these suits, doing public appearances, *and* working at the Games & Puzzles department. Our workload was a little smaller than normal because everyone knew we were competing, but Christmas couldn't be put on hold! By the last week, everything was running together: I accidentally made a Big Red Suit for a superhero action figure, showed up for an interview on NPNN half-dressed, and kept checking to make sure my mic was on when my dad asked me what I wanted for breakfast.

We had to keep our designs secret from each other, which was half the fun. Celia, in particular, was very nervous about what I was making, and kept trying to find excuses to sneak into my room, like:

"I just need to borrow one of your stuffed animals."

I peeked through a very slim crack in the door. "Oh, really? No other reason?"

She shrugged. "I'm kind of bored sleeping with mine, and you have so *many*."

"Which one do you want?"

She paused. "Uh, my favourite is the leopard. Or if not the leopard, then maybe the snow leopard."

"Great! Then I'll just get it for you." I tossed the snow leopard out (it landed with a squeak) and shut the door.

I was nervous, too, but if Mum was coaching Celia as much as she was coaching me, then everything would be fine. She kept crossing out my sketches in red pen and writing things like *Unnecessary* or *Cute, but you can do better.* Seeing all those red lines could be tough, but I knew she was trying to help me, so I listened.

When we had finally finished, Celia and I presented in the living room with my mum, my dad, and Polly as our audience. I went first.

"For Celia's Big Red Suit, I've gone pretty nontraditional. Other than the hat, the only thing I've kept from the original Santa design is the colour scheme." I ripped a sheet off the mannequin with a flourish, presenting the red-and-white suit I built. "The base is a very tough fabric – the same kind of thing in our suits from the first challenge – but it's bulkier because I've modified it a lot. There's a lot of stuff going on in it, but I'll focus on the major points."

I took the gloves off the mannequin and put them on my hands. "Everything the suit does is activated by specific hand gestures I can show you." I waved my hands like I was fanning myself and a soft whirring noise came from the suit, like a fan. I put my hands to my shoulders like I was shivering, and the whirring noise shifted to a low vibrating sound. "It's got air-conditioning, so you'll never be too hot or too cold."

I pushed my palms down toward the ground like I was imitating a penguin. Super-concentrated air shot out of the armholes and legholes of the suit and lifted the mannequin off the ground. I tilted my hands, and the mannequin shifted forward and back, then I gently lowered my hands flat against my legs, and it gently settled on the ground. Everybody clapped.

"And now . . . Polly, could you get the lights?"

She crossed her arms. "I don't wanna."

"Polly, why do you have to be so *three* all the time?"

My dad shook his head. "You can get the light yourself, Ollie. You're already standing up."

"But it'll ruin the moment!"

"I can get the light!" Celia offered.

"No, Celia, let Ollie do it. He shouldn't order his sister around like that."

I groaned and trudged *all the way across the living room* to flip the light switch. Then I twisted my left hand like I was screwing in a lightbulb, and the whole room lit up with bright white light. The lining of the suit – all the white parts, including the gloves and the ball at the end of the hat – were lit up. I twisted my hand back and forth to show that I could dim and brighten the light however I wanted.

I flicked the light switch back on. "The hat can be pulled over your head and tightened to be used as an air filter, in case you get somewhere with dangerous air, and it's got its own oxygen, in case you end up underwater. You can tighten it to seal around your neck. That's all the big stuff."

Celia was already up and inspecting it. "There isn't any room for carrying extra stuff, though."

"This small pack attached to the back can build small tools for you on the fly! For example, if you need a hammer . . ." I made a hammering motion with my left hand, then reached around the back of the suit to where a hammer was moving out of a hole in the top. I pushed it back in through the side, then did the same with a screwdriver twist.

"It only has enough material to make one or maybe two at a time, but it can handle most of the small stuff you need. That way you won't have to keep track of where everything is!"

Celia nodded. "Awesome. My turn!" She tossed the sheet off of her mannequin as well, revealing a skintight black bodysuit, like a diver's suit, with a red belt around the middle and a hat on top. That was it.

"Honestly, this one might be best if I just show you how it works." She unclipped the belt and wrapped it around her waist. "The bodysuit is there for protection, but *this* is the real suit." She pressed the buckle and struck a pose like she was ballroom dancing. The red fabric of the belt billowed out and stretched, wrapping around her other clothes into a red gown. She shifted like she was punching, and the red shifted and shrunk into a tighter-fitting tank top and shorts, like for exercising.

"The poses help, but they aren't technically necessary. The suit picks up on what you're visualizing and changes to look like whatever you want. It can be almost anything you can imagine, as long as that thing is connected to your body." She shifted it through a few more forms; the suit could even change your shoes! "It can expand to way bigger than it looks, but there is a limit, so don't go too crazy."

"Does everything always have to be this one shade of red?" I asked, poking at the stretchy fabric.

Celia grinned. "I knew you would ask." She furrowed her brow with intense focus, and a ripple of blue spread through the suit from her neck until the whole outfit had changed colour. She shifted it to green, then to yellow, then a cheetah print.

"It has a light-up setting, too!" I saw her shift her focus again, and the suit glowed with a dim light.

My mouth fell open. "How does it do that?"

"Nanobots, a little receiver that interprets your thoughts. Basic fashion stuff."

"Oh, so now you're a big-time fashion expert, huh?"

She shrugged. "It turns out fashion is basically science."

My parents both clapped, but quietly, because Polly had fallen asleep in my dad's lap.

"You've done an amazing job. These suits are some of the best things I've ever seen, and I've been in this business for a long time. Your transforming outfit might put me out of a job!" She winked at Celia. "For now, though, it's late, and you need to rest."

My dad picked Polly up and gave me and Celia a hug. "Good luck, kiddos."

Celia unclipped her belt and put it back on the mannequin. I took off my gloves and did the same. We stared at our suits while our parents went to bed.

"I can't believe the trial is tomorrow," Celia said finally. "What do you think it is?"

"I don't know. But I don't need to." I wiggled the mannequin's fingers and made the suit light up again. "I just know we're gonna win."

Chapter 11

The next trial wasn't actually just one trial: It was *seven*. One for every day of the week. On the first day, the eleven remaining contestants all crammed into one of The Workshop's conference rooms. An elf passed out a paper with all the challenges we'd have to endure using our Big Red Suits.

THE SANTA TRIALS CHRISTMAS MERRY-THON SPECTACULAR

DAY ONE: *The Amazing Chimney Race!*

DAY TWO: *This Old Gingerbread House!*

DAY THREE: *Cookies and Milk and Cookies and Milk and Cookies and Milk and Cookies!*

DAY FOUR: *North Pole Idol!*

DAY FIVE: *Reindeer Rodeo!*

DAY SIX: *Next Top Nutcracker!*

DAY SEVEN: *Heatmiser and Snowmiser's Around the World in Eighty Minutes!*

This was an overwhelming amount of information. Was the cookies one an eating challenge? What would we do in the rodeo? *North Pole Idol* sounded fun, though, and so did the one about gingerbread houses. And the last one – what did that even mean?

"This is ridiculous." Klaus had his feet propped up on the conference table. His suit looked the most like a traditional Kris Kringle outfit – except for the shoes, which had little heels to make him seem taller than he actually was. "Singing? Dancing? What does this have to do with being Santa?"

"What's the problem, bro?" Kurt was leaning against a wall in his normal clothes, all black with one of his *I Don't Care Who Wins* shirts. The back of his leather jacket said *THIS IS MY BIG RED SUIT.* He did a few body rolls in Klaus's direction. "Don't got the moves?"

"This is not about my '*moves.*' It's about how this whole circus is ridiculous."

"*Ridiculous, ridiculous, ridiculous.*" Sally crossed her arms and kicked Klaus's chair so he had to quickly adjust to keep from falling on the ground. "Do you hear yourself?" Her Big Red Suit looked like it was nothing more than dirty red cloth lazily stitched together. She was still trying to lose.

"I just don't think my moves have anything to do with my ability to lead a city."

"Well, I'm all for it!" Ramp's grumbly voice came from across the table. He looked like an old-timey prospector with suspenders hiking his trousers up to his chest and a wide-brimmed hat. A small fan dangled off the brim and blew on his face. "I know all the hip dances, like the 'fox-trot,' or the 'Charleston,' or the 'electric slide.' And I've got my eye on those cookies."

A kid about my age wearing a beige sweater over his Big Red Suit nudged me. He looked kind of familiar, but I couldn't place from where. *How have I never seen him before?*

"Ramp is really old, right, Ollie?" the kid whispered to me. "It seems like he's definitely really old."

How does he know my name? Oh gosh, uh, I don't have any idea who he is. But I guess he's a competitor? Gotta play it cool.

"Uh, yeah, my pal," I whispered back. *So far so good.* "I think that's probably true, and also I totally know your name." *Mayday! Mayday!*

"That's a relief." The kid smiled and patted my shoulder. "Nobody else seems to even remember me. Maria said I wasn't a 'good enough character,' whatever that means, so she didn't put me on TV at all."

When he shifted away in his chair, Celia leaned over to my ear on the other side. "Who was that?"

I shrugged. "I guess we can't keep track of everybody."

The elf cleared his throat. "Now, if you'll please wait here, there is someone who wishes to speak to you. He'll be here shortly."

The elf left, and the eleven of us sat in silence, looking around at each other awkwardly. Kurt broke the silence by saying something to Sally, Andrea said something to Klaus, and then

Celia started talking to Buzz. Gadzooks walked over and pointed at my shirt.

"How gracious of you to keep track of my little friend." Gadzooks bowed her head. A dove wriggled out of my collar and flapped on to Gadzooks's finger.

"That . . . that's the bird from the race." I blinked at it. "That's the one that was in my shirt that whole time."

"Quite a long time, in fact." Gadzooks grinned at me with all her teeth. She lifted her top hat – which was covered in puff balls to match the rest of her Big Red Suit – and the dove flew into it, disappearing completely.

"But it couldn't have still been there. I haven't seen it in weeks!"

Gadzooks lifted both palms up and shook her head. "I don't know what to tell you, my friend. He's been there since the race."

"This isn't even the same shirt!"

But she was already walking away. Behind her, I noticed Frank Fae in the corner with no one to talk to. *It must be hard to lose both of your brothers.*

"Hey, Frank!" I started to lift out of the chair, but I pushed my feet off wrong and just ended up spinning it around in a circle. My feet were too short to reach the floor, so I couldn't stop it and just pushed myself out on to the floor. I felt too embarrassed to stand up, so I rolled the rest of the way to the corner. I stared up at Frank. "I wanted to apologize. For knocking your brothers out of the race."

"Don'tevenworryaboutit," she said, like it was all one word. "Ya did us a favour."

I pushed up on to my arms and tilted my head. "What do you mean?"

"We woulda had to fight each other at this point, ya know? Ya saved me from havin' to punch 'em in the butt."

"In the butt?"

"Right in the butt." She punched the air to demonstrate. "Just like that."

"Oh."

She scratched at a bright red rash on her neck. "This suit's itched me all over. You got any lotion or anythin'?" Her suit was shiny – like it was made of plastic – but then there were also patches that looked scratchy, like wool. Not a comfortable combination.

I shook my head. "Sorry."

"Don'tevenworryaboutit."

The door to the conference room opened and Santa walked in.

For the first time ever, a room with Santa in it got *quieter*. Usually people cheer, or he's having to walk-and-talk for Christmas, or he's doing inspections of The Workshop, or *something, anything*, but instead he stood in silence while everyone shifted uncomfortably and stared at him.

This was the first time I'd seen him since the competition had started, and it was with all ten other competitors. Everything felt really real, really fast. We were even *dressed* like him.

This was very weird.

Klaus broke the silence first. "This is ridiculous. You know that, right? You know this is ridiculous."

Santa looked very tired. He smiled at Klaus anyway. "Trust me, son. There's a reason for everything."

"Really? Please tell me the *reason* you had us work for weeks on suits just to make us dance like windup toys for the public."

Sally put a hand on his shoulder. "Klaus, this isn't the time—"

He swatted her hand away and stared straight at his father. "No, I mean it. Is this some kind of game to you? Do you really hate me *this much?*"

Santa winced. Sally stepped in front of Klaus. I saw most of the other competitors pretend the floor was suddenly really interesting, but I couldn't look away.

"Klaus, I'm serious," Sally said. "This is a conversation for the family."

"Yeah, fine. You're right. I shouldn't have left you out." He stepped around her and got up in Santa's face. I had never seen *anyone* angry with Santa. Not like this. "Sally doesn't even want to *be here,* Dad. She feels forced to do this because she doesn't want to hurt your feelings."

Santa scratched his beard and looked at Sally, who was staring at the ceiling.

"Is this true?" he asked.

"No, it's—"

Klaus interrupted her again. "It's true."

"You don't get to say how I *feel,* Klaus!"

Kurt finally stepped up. "Bro, chill." He pulled a candy stick out of the pack in his sleeve and offered it to Klaus. "Here."

Klaus took it and crunched on it loudly and angrily. It didn't seem to help his mood, but at least he stopped interrupting Sally.

She said, "I just want to make things, Dad. I like toys. I like The Workshop, and the elves."

Santa stepped closer to her. "But you'd be so good at it."

Sally's eyes flipped to the ground, and she sighed like she'd heard that a million times. "Yeah, maybe. But so what?" She finally worked up the courage to look at Santa in the eyes. "I don't want to do it. Can that be enough?"

Santa tugged at his beard and looked at her with stern eyes. Everybody held their breath. He stepped forward, held his arms out, and pulled her into a huge hug.

Something in his suit beeped, and he pushed her away very quickly and reached inside.

"One second." His hand rummaged around until something beeped again. "Smoke bombs. Would have ruined the moment."

Sally laughed and pulled her dad in for another hug. "You already ruined the moment, Dad."

Celia leaned over to me and whispered, "Should we have put smoke bombs in our suits?"

I whispered, "Shh, shh, I'm watching them hug!!"

She swatted my hands. "Stop biting your fingernails."

I put my hands in my pockets and tried not to get all teary again.

"Well, what about Kurt?" Klaus had finished his candy stick. "He doesn't care, either. He's just doing this to bother me. Literally everything in his suit was built to counteract mine." I looked at Kurt again. It didn't even look like he was *wearing* a suit. Kurt must have been a better designer then I realized.

"Is that true?" Santa asked.

Kurt shrugged. "Yeah."

"Well, that's very funny, and I completely support it."

"WHAT?!" Klaus yelled.

Santa sighed. "I'm kidding, son. I—" He looked around at all of us, then opened his mouth to continue.

Klaus didn't let him. "Again: Do you hate me? Do you really think I can't do this?"

Santa's eyes cut down and to the side, like he was thinking, but also a little sad. "This is as good a time as any, I guess."

Celia and I looked at each other. *Time for what? Does he really not think Klaus can do it?*

"Every single one of you would be a great Santa. Even you, Klaus. I think you're a natural leader, and you work harder than I ever have."

Klaus threw up his hands. "Then why—"

Santa looked at him like a dad does, and Klaus got quiet.

"I didn't decide on the Trials because I don't think you could be Santa, Klaus. I did it because *I* shouldn't have been."

That got everyone's attention. *What?*

"I'm not a good Santa. I don't even *like* the job. I wish you had felt comfortable telling me sooner, Sally – I would never force this on you. Being Santa is *tough work*. You know what I love? Sleighs. I love flying, and racing, and working with the reindeer. The night before Christmas is *amazing*. But the rest of it? The planning, and the meetings, and all the paperwork! So much paperwork!" He took his hat off and wiped some sweat off of his brow. "Mrs Claus has been doing most of that, honestly. She has a knack for it I've never had. And it's not fair to her, because she has her own things to do." He stared at the floor for a second, then looked at Klaus right in the eyes. "My name isn't Santa. It's just Matt. And it should have stayed Matt."

Everyone was dead silent. There was nothing to say. Santa took off his little round spectacles for a moment to wipe his eyes.

"So that's a warning for all of you. Being Santa is tough. There's a lot more to it than you think. It's a heavy stocking cap for one head." He laughed, just a little. "It needs to go to the person most qualified. Maybe that's you, Klaus, but if it isn't, and someone else in this room is better for the job, isn't it best for the North Pole, for Christmas, that *they* become Santa?"

Klaus didn't answer. He stared at Santa's – *Matt's?* – feet. Santa walked over and hugged him around his shoulders, but Klaus didn't move.

Santa cleared his throat and looked at each of us in the eyes one at a time. "Anyway. I came here to tell all of you that every challenge this week is going to push you to your limits. Like my letter said, be prepared for *anything*. Let's go, Sally." He fist-bumped with Kurt, then walked to the door held open for him by the serious-looking elf man. "I'm excited to see what happens. And I'm excited to meet the next Santa, whether they're Santa Claus, or Santa Gremlin, or Pixie, or Brownie, or Fae, or Gnome."

I got chills when he said my last name. Celia reached over and squeezed my hand. Sally waved as the door shut behind Santa. The whole room felt like it was full of Jell-O that nobody wanted to move through.

The boy in the beige sweater, whose name I didn't remember, and who I didn't know was standing right next to me, said, "I guess even Santa forgot my name, huh? At least we're friends, Ollie."

This is a horrible nightmare situation that I will never be able to fix. "Yeah, totally."

Klaus looked around at all of us. "This doesn't change anything. I'm still going to win."

Buzz snorted. "I'll believe it when I see it, Claus."

Looking around at the room made me nervous. Everyone was so smart, and tough, and talented. Santa's voice kept ringing in my ears.

My name is Ollie, I thought. *Is it going to stay that way?*

Chapter 12

DAY ONE: THE AMAZING CHIMNEY RACE

The challenges were all held in the Reindeer Games Stadium and Spa Resort. All in our Big Red Suits, the ten of us gathered on the field. Ahead of us were two straight lines of big, featureless grey boxes with chimneys of different sizes and shapes poking out of the tops.

Rudolph was waiting for us when we arrived. Since Celia and I had been first in the sleigh race, he made us team captains.

"I'll take Buzz," Celia started.

"Uh, Kurt," I said.

"Gadzooks."

"Ramp."

"Frank."

"Klaus."

"Andrea."

"That leaves me!" The boy in the beige sweater walked cheerfully over to my team. "What a good group."

Klaus rolled his eyes. Kurt rolled his eyes and made a goofy face to make fun of him. Klaus started rolling his eyes again, and Kurt mimicked him again, this time rolling his whole body at the same time as his eyes. Klaus almost rolled his eyes at *that,* but caught himself and just grumbled.

Rudolph shone his nose as bright as it would go, getting our attention.

"Each of you wannabes will pick one of the chimneys," Rudolph explained in his robotic drone. "Each chimney has a different challenge, and at the end of the chimney is a room with a tree. Press the button under the tree, and a buzzer will sound, signalling your next teammate to drop down theirs. One of the members of the losing team will be randomly chosen and eliminated from the competition. Understood?"

"Randomly?" Celia scrunched up her face at Rudolph, which was very brave because he was terrifying. "Are you serious? That's not fair!"

He swivelled his dark eyes at her. "Are you questioning my challenge, Pixie?"

Celia huffed but didn't say anything else. We all split up and picked our chimneys. Celia and I both chose the last box in our line, with a simple redbrick chimney on the top. The rest of our teammates took their places along the line.

The start buzzer sounded. Buzz and Kurt jumped down their black metal cylinders. There was a loud clanging as they went down, and a huge cloud of soot flew out. A few more seconds of clanging, and then a steady stream of smoke started coming out of the top.

Fire??? I thought. *Are they being set on fire?!*

Buzz's box lit up, and the buzzer sounded, sending Gadzooks down her chimney. Ramp was still waiting on Kurt, and I started to get worried as the smoke churned out of the top. Buzz shimmied out of his chimney and fell on top of the grey box, gasping for breath and covered in soot.

Kurt's buzzer sounded. *Phew.* Ramp jumped down into his chimney: a wide, clear one. There was a loud splash, and his chimney sealed closed at the top. The entire grey box turned over sideways – like I saw had already happened on Celia's side – and the clear chimney filled up with water.

Can Ramp even swim? I thought. Apparently, he could swim even better than Gadzooks; their two boxes lit up and buzzed within seconds of each other. Frank and the boy with the beige sweater were next. Each of their boxes had two very long chimneys they had already climbed to the top of.

They both jumped in, and a moment later, the boxes shook, rolled over, and stood up on their chimneys. Using the chimneys as legs, the boxes ran around the field in a way that didn't seem to follow any particular pattern. They even crashed into each other a few times, fell on their backs like toddlers, then wobbled back up and started running again.

I looked over to Ramp and Gadzooks, who were sliding out of their clear chimneys, followed by a rush of water. They were both soaking wet, and Ramp had a little crab wearing a sea captain's hat clamped on to his nose.

"Off! *Off!* Get off, you!" Ramp jumped around and finally knocked the crab off. The crab picked its hat off the ground and scurried back up the cube and into the chimney.

Frank's cube buzzed and lit up. It flopped over on to the ground and wiggled its chimney legs in a little dance. The other cube ran around it in circles for a few more laps and then buzzed and lit up. It flopped over on the ground and danced, too.

Klaus dropped down into his yellow chimney a few seconds after Andrea. I waited for a few seconds, but there was no sound. There was no movement. Nothing happened for the next five minutes.

Or the next ten minutes.

Or the next *two hours*. Finally, Andrea's box buzzed, and she climbed out, quietly. She sat down on the top of the grey box and leaned against the chimney. She closed her eyes and took a deep breath.

Klaus still wasn't finished, but Celia didn't go down her chimney yet.

"What are you doing?" Frank yelled at her. "Get in there!"

Celia acted like she didn't hear him. She winked at me. We stood there for another ten minutes while Celia's team yelled for her to hurry up. She just yawned.

Finally, Klaus's buzzer sounded, and he climbed out of the chimney quietly, just like Andrea had. He looked very, very tired. I looked over at Celia, and she held up three fingers. *Three . . . two . . . one!*

We jumped into the chimney.

And didn't fall. My eyes were still peeking out over the top. Celia shrugged with her eyebrows, and then I saw her head disappear, so I looked down and crouched, too. The chimney became a small tunnel I had to climb through, just barely big enough for my body. I tapped my belt and shrunk my suit so it was more form-fitting and pushed myself forward.

Shuffling on my hands and knees was slow but steady. I thought I heard something like chittering in the darkness, but I ignored it and kept moving forward. My hand felt a drop-off in front of me, so I twisted around awkwardly and lowered my feet down. Even with my fingertips just barely gripping the edge, I couldn't feel the bottom, so I took a deep breath and let go.

I expected to hit the ground right away, but the fall was way farther than I could have planned for. I pressed my belt and focused on an image: cushy shoes and a big cape. I grabbed the corners of the cape and tossed it over my head so it would catch some of the air as I fell and slow me down. My shoes ballooned into big shoes with huge soles full of air, and when I finally hit the ground they took most of the force and deflated.

The chimney took a hard turn sideways again, so I crouched down and crawled some more. I heard the echo of quiet chittering come down the chute. The metal down here felt warmer somehow, so I formed gloves over my hands to protect myself. A few more feet forward, and it felt even hotter – I thickened the gloves into oven mitts and formed knee pads over my legs. Another few shuffles and the heat was unbearable! I *had* to get off the floor.

I lifted up one hand and focused. The palm of the glove reshaped into a big suction cup, which I tried against the roof. It held! I did the same with my other hand and then my knees. I crawled along the ceiling, holding myself tight to the top so I wouldn't touch the bottom of the chimney, which was glowing with the heat and making me sweat.

The chimney sharply turned straight back up, which I expected at this point. I pushed all the fabric straight down to my feet, forming longer and longer stilts that raised me up the long chimney chute. I felt the corner at the top, pulled myself over . . .

And was face-to-face with a squirrel. A very cute, very small squirrel with wide eyes and a bushy tail that was twice as big as its body. It held both little paws out to me and chittered.

"Aw, hey, little friend." I tried not to make any sudden movements. "I kinda need to keep moving past you."

The squirrel chittered and pushed its paws out closer to me.

"I don't have any nuts or anything."

It cocked its head to one side, then darted forward to sniff at my fingers. I lifted my palms up to show I didn't have anything. "No. Nuts," I explained it slower this time. "I'm. Sorry."

It flipped my left hand over and back, then went to my other hand and flipped it, too. It looked up at my face and I swear I saw its big eyes narrow.

"I'm gonna . . . go . . ." I started shuffling past it and tried to lift my arm gently over the squirrel so I could try moving around it. It chittered a little louder and slipped through my arms to get in front of me again. "Excuse me, please!" I started moving again. It crouched low to the ground and flicked its huge tail back and forth. It growled. "Oh geez. Please calm down! I'm sorry!"

I tried to pull myself backwards, away from it, but as soon as I moved, it leapt up and latched on to my nose with its teeth.

"Ow!" I reached up to grab it, but it slipped out of my fingers and bit my ear. I tried to swat it away, but it grabbed the back of my hand and bit my fingers, too. I tried to push myself forward to get away from it, but the squirrel kept circling around my body, scratching and biting. I focused and shifted the suit to cover all my exposed skin, but the squirrel moved fast enough to get inside and started going even crazier trapped under my clothes.

I slammed against the walls of the chimney, trying to get out, yelling for the squirrel to leave me alone.

"Stop, please! STOP! *WHY ARE YOU DOING THIS TO ME?!*"

A lit sign swung down from the ceiling and hit me in the face. I rubbed my nose and looked at it. *SHHH! YOU'LL WAKE THE CHILDREN!*

"WHAT?!"

Another sign swung down and hit me on the back of the head. I whirled around to look at it. The squirrel kept struggling inside my suit.

I SAID SHH! SANTA NEEDS TO BE QUIET!

"I'm trying, but there's a – *ouch!* – squirrel in here trying to kill me!"

A third, smaller sign folded out from the first sign and poked me in the nose. *I WARNED YOU!*

A low rumbling came from the end of the chimney. The signs folded up out of the way, but before I could worry about what was coming, I had to deal with the squirrel that was currently rolling around near my armpit.

I focused hard on the fabric around that space, and it separated and reformed behind the squirrel, pushing it out. I imagined a hand, grasping the squirrel, and the fabric in my armpit stretched out into five fingers that gently held on to it around its tummy. The squirrel struggled and bit on the hand, but since it was made of fabric, I couldn't feel it.

OK, I thought. *I'm scratched and beat up, and I've got a hand coming out of my armpit, but at least I've still got my positive attitude.*

The rumbling got louder. A strong gust of wind started blowing, and I came dangerously close to losing my positive attitude. I got knocked back, but before I could fall back down the chute, I panicked and expanded my suit, cramming fabric into all four corners of the chimney with me in the middle. I braced my feet on the floor and pushed forward, fighting against the strong wind. I looked like a big red cube sliding down the hallway (a cube with three hands and an angry squirrel attached to the front).

Moving through the tunnel with the wind blowing straight on me took twice as long. I couldn't see when the tunnel ended, either, so I tipped over and started sliding straight down before I realized what was going on. At the bottom of *this* chute was a fire, and I accidentally breathed in some smoke and started coughing.

I shifted away from the cube into my outfit from before but covered up my face and the squirrel's face so we wouldn't choke on the smoke. I held out my arms and legs and dragged against the wall until I was wedged tight enough that we stopped, my feet just barely above the fire.

If there are any real chimneys like this, I don't think I want to be Santa.

There was no way I could put out the fire with my shape-shifting suit. The fabric was heat-resistant but not fireproof. My bodysuit underneath was fireproof, but that didn't protect my face and hands. The fire was too high for me to swing around it.

You're stuck, Ollie. What are you supposed to do?

I was positive Celia already had a solution. I looked at the squirrel, who had stopped fighting my armpit hand out of fear for the fire, and decided I could at least save *it*. I extended my third hand down and around the edge of the flame, then let go. The squirrel ran away from the spitting logs, out of sight, and I closed my eyes. *Maybe if I just hold myself here long enough, the fire will go away.*

I heard a loud clang, along with several smaller clangs. Something had been knocked over in front of the fire – one of those things that holds the fire irons. The pokers. I focused really hard on stretching out a third hand again and reached down to grab the poker. The metal was heavy, and the suit couldn't pull it up by itself, so I focused on wrapping around it and used my real hands to pull it up to me, like a rope. Without my hands holding me up, though, my legs started slipping a little.

I was running out of time, but I grabbed the poker with both hands and started pushing the logs out of the fireplace, taking the fire with them. *I hope there's nothing important in front of the fire.*

Once the logs were out from directly under me, I landed in the warm soot and quickly jumped over the flaming logs. *A living room?*

I had finally reached the end of the chimney, and was in a really nice-looking living room *that was on fire now, oh, yeah!!!* I looked frantically around for something to put out the logs while the squirrel screeched loudly from the mantel. I found a pitcher of milk next to a huge plate of cookies and dumped the milk all over the fire. It didn't work as well as water would have, but I was able to stamp the last few burning bits out with my foot.

I couldn't slow down; Rudolph said I had to find the button under the tree. I glanced around the room and didn't see any trees. There was a painting of a beach scene, a stressed-out squirrel, some chairs, a couch, a coffee table . . . *wait a second.*

The beach painting had a big palm tree on it. *Could that be . . . ?* I looked at the floor below the painting and didn't see anything. I nudged the frame gently to peek behind it – *there!* Built into the wall was a small red button. I pushed it, and immediately a loud buzzer sounded from my box. The wallpaper below the painting split open and revealed a hatch that led directly up to the original chimney entrance. I turned my shoes into stilts again – the squirrel hitched a ride on my shoulder – and rolled myself out of the top.

Celia met me in the middle between our two boxes, and we started yelling over each other about what happened.

"The chimney just kept going around—"

"—and your suit was AMAZING I couldn't even BELIEVE—"

"—I used the toolbox to build a—"

"—I hope squirrels don't have rabies?"

"I'm pretty sure these don't, at least." Her squirrel was meeting my squirrel, and they were jumping around each other to say hello.

"You guys tied!" Buzz ran over to us. He had wiped most of the soot off of his face, but there was still some on his nose, so I reached up and rubbed it off. "Your boxes buzzed at the exact same time."

Rudolph strode over to us, and glared down his nose. "I suppose that means you're all safe. For now."

Celia crossed her arms. "Good. This challenge was unfair anyway."

Rudolph's nose shone red, but I saw a little twinkle in his eye. "You could be right. Good work, wannabes."

Chapter 13

DAY TWO: THIS OLD GINGERBREAD HOUSE

On the second day, the grey boxes were replaced with ten huge piles of gingerbread. Waiting for us that day was none other than *The* Gingerbread Woman. She was known throughout the North Pole for being exactly who you call when your gingerbread house is a fixer-upper. She was a master with the stuff and worked *very fast*. "The competition can't catch me!" her TV promos said. "I'm The Gingerbread Woman!"

"Today you will be using the reclaimed gingerbread we've given you to build a full-scale house. Along with the gingerbread, you may order anything from my specialty catalogue, *Run, Run to the Deals as Fast as You Can*. We'll be touring the houses at the end of the day; the designer of the best house will receive a free shopping spree from my catalogue, and the designer of the worst house will be eliminated from the competition. Judging is tonight. Ready, set, go!"

We all immediately took off running. The good thing about gingerbread was that it was soft and light – it was easy to hammer together and build a frame for the house. The worst thing was that it wasn't super sturdy, and it was easy to snap if you weren't careful with it. I grabbed some blueprint paper and drew out my design, but a lot of the other contestants just jumped right into building, which made me nervous.

This is a challenge I can win, I thought. *I'm good at making things look good.*

Every contestant was good at a lot of things, though. We were the final ten!

❄ ❄ ❄

My idea was maybe a little overboard: I wanted to make a scaled-down replica of Claus Castle. The inside would look like a real house you could live in, but the outside would look *exactly* like the castle, except made of candy.

Ramp wasn't doing so hot. He kept using marshmallow glue to stick gingerbread boards together without any kind of plan or foundation for the house.

"Back in the day, no one built houses," he explained when I asked how it was going. "They sprang up out of the ground like trees! Us kids today, ruining the housing gardens just like we're ruining everything else."

After a few hours of work, The Gingerbread Woman came by to check on my progress.

"How's it coming?" she asked, surprising me as I was adjusting a butterscotch lamp.

"It's going well, you know." I tried to think of some words from her show I could use to sound smart. "I'm thinking kind of an open-concept, ranch-style dream home with nice interiors and, for the final touch, a yard with room to grow, you know, as a family? We're looking for something in our budget that isn't going to break the bank, and I really think my husband is going to love it. Something modern and chic, but also with a traditional, classic feel. And I can't stress this enough: Everything is a deal breaker."

She nodded seriously. "It sounds like you've got this all under control. See you tonight."

Nailed it, I thought.

That night, The Gingerbread Woman led us on a tour of the contestants' houses, carrying a clipboard and making no facial expressions the entire time. She would scribble notes every once in a while or make an *mm* noise that could have been either positive or negative.

Andrea's house was first, and while I hated to admit it, it was *pretty cool*. At first glance, it just looked like a boring barn, but once we were inside, she showed us all these amazing hidden compartments and passageways that made the house feel much bigger and more mysterious than it looked on the outside.

Klaus built a tower with a spiral staircase in the centre and Claus flags all around. He was clearly *very* proud of it. I got some satisfaction watching him sweat when The Gingerbread Woman straightened one of his candyfloss curtains and said, *"Mm."*

Frank made a house that looked like a submarine and was very spacious and comfortable for one person on the inside. The portholes even had screens behind them so it looked like you were really underwater!

"I didn't know you were so into the ocean," I said.

She scratched at the rash glowing red on her neck. "We're not really friends. You don't know a lotta stuff about me."

Burn, I thought. *But I guess that's true.*

Gadzooks built a giant birdcage where the space between the cage bars could open or close however you wanted, giving full control of the sunlight. Inside, she had released a lot of birds that pecked around at the gingerbread but looked cute. One of them pooped on The Gingerbread Woman's clipboard, though, which I was sure would lose her some points.

Kurt just built a totally normal, cookie-cutter two-bedroom house. "It's backwards," he explained. The rest of us looked around, confused.

"It just looks like a house," Celia said.

"Yeah, I mean, it's basically a house, except it's backwards."

Klaus banged his forehead against a wall, dusting the floor with crumbs. "Everything you do is nonsense, Kurt."

Ramp was having such a hard time making his house that I broke down and secretly helped him. I didn't want to spend too much time on it, but I guided him toward a re-creation of the traditional witch's house from "Hansel and Gretel." It was classic: frosting lining the roof and walls, candy accents of a variety of kinds, and I even convinced Ramp to wear a big witch hat when he gave the tour. His grumpy face really sold it.

Why did the witch want to eat those kids? I wondered while I hammered a peppermint wreath above the door. *She had a whole house made out of candy. She had so much food to fatten them up with. Are humans really that tasty?* I watched Ramp pick his wrinkly nose and then eat the bogey. *They don't* look *tasty.*

Buzz built a gingerbread gym ("A gymgerbread!" I said, and Buzz punched me in the arm disapprovingly) with workout equipment and dumbbells of varying weights all built out of candy. I lifted a ten-pound weight, and I felt *very* strong. Buzz lifted a hundred-pound weight, and I felt *very* weak.

Celia made a secret lab. ("It *would* be secret, I mean, in real life. But obviously I have to tell you about it so you can judge for the competition.") It was full of edible replicas of state-of-the-art science equipment. There were marshmallow lab rats, lab coats made out of gummy fruit candy, and even a cloning machine that would make a life-sized replica of you in the candy it decided was most like you. When I got in the machine, it just dropped a huge pile of gross-looking gummy worms.

Celia laughed. "I put that setting in as a joke just for you."

"I hate gummy worms!"

"I know." She scooped up a handful and tossed them at my face. I picked up a whole bunch of them and threw them back at her. A few hit The Gingerbread Woman in her glasses.

"Mm," she said.

I was very, very proud of my house; the outside looked *just* like the castle. I analysed pictures as I built to make sure I got it perfect, down to the last detail. On the inside, it was totally different because otherwise it would make you feel like a giant. I structured each wing of the castle as a big bedroom and turned the grand hall into a living room. For fun, I designed one bedroom to be perfect for me and the other to be perfect for Celia. (I made the third bedroom perfect for H.O.R.S.E. and put the prettiest and most majestic stallion stickers on the walls.)

The best part, though, was watching The Gingerbread Woman walk inside. She admired the replica, of course, made her notes and said her *mm*, but when she opened the door to the living room

I had meticulously filled with the most Christmas spirit–y things I could find, she said her first word of the evening:

"Wow."

My face turned bright red, and I tried really hard not to cheer. Celia grinned, and Buzz punched me in the arm supportively.

"Nice work, Ollie," Kurt whispered to me. "For real."

The Gingerbread Woman turned away from me to inspect one of the tiny portraits I had hastily drawn of an old Santa.

"Oh, and one last thing!" I remembered. I gave a thumbs-up to the squirrel, which had been following me around since the day before. It took a break from nibbling on a candy and pushed a button on the roof.

The chandeliers and overhead lights in the house flickered off, and red and green Christmas lights hidden in the wallpaper and in various places around the living room lit up and blinked on and off in a stunning pattern.

"I've seen all I need to see." The Gingerbread Woman marched out of the house, making marks on her clipboard. It wasn't another *wow*, but it was something.

The Gingerbread Woman brought out a trophy made, appropriately, of gingerbread coated in edible gold leaf. She presented it to me, and I broke off pieces to share with the other contestants (except for Klaus, who was too grumpy about losing to take a piece). It was delicious, because it tasted like *victory*.

The boy in the beige sweater lost, but The Gingerbread Woman didn't say his name, *of course*.

"You lose," she said while pointing at the boy in the beige sweater, "because your house was completely unmemorable."

Come to think of it, I don't remember his house, either.

The boy in the beige sweater nodded. "That's fair." He walked to the front of the group and waved at all of us. "Thanks everybody for this opportunity! I had a really great time with you all. And thanks especially" – *oh no* – "to my good" – *please don't* – "friend" – *this can't be!!* – "Ollie!" *Why am I being punished?*

The boy walked over and gave me a hug. I patted him on the head. He left, and I let out a deep sigh of relief.

A few minutes later, Ramp came up to me and asked, "Who was that kid?"

Chapter 14

DAY THREE: COOKIES AND MILK AND COOKIES AND MILK AND COOKIES AND MILK AND COOKIES

The nine remaining contestants sat on a long bench in front of a table piled high with nine cookie platters and nine jugs of milk.

"Alright, kids." Chef's metal hand morphed into a rolling pin, which he rolled along the table while he paced back and forth. "Time fer yer eatin' challenge. Kids these days leave *a lot* of cookies and milk for Santa. A *LOT*." He slammed his rolling pin on the table in front of Frank, who was too busy scratching her rash to pay attention. (I was sitting next to Frank, and it scared me more than her.)

"So yer gonna prove yeh can handle it. These're some of the best dern cookies I ever made – but there's two hundred of 'em fer each of yeh and a gallon of milk to wash 'em down. Yeh don't gotta drink the milk because fer some reason the higher-ups think that's 'too dangerous,' and would 'get vomit everywhere.'" He spat on the ground.

Ramp added, "In my day, we drank a gallon of milk for every lunch, and we *liked it*."

"Hear, hear!" Chef giggled his tinny laugh. "Yeh've got all day,

but the last one to finish gets the boot. First gets free lunch for a year. And be careful, kids . . ." He rapped his rolling pin on the table. "They're *spicy*."

A loud buzzer sounded, and we dived in.

Buzz crunched into his cookie and made a confused face. "This isn't spicy at all."

"That's just a thing he says," I explained through a mouthful of crumbs. The cookies *were* really good.

This is going to be a breeze, I thought after the first two cookies.

This is absolutely not going to be a breeze, I thought after fifty cookies. *This is going to kill me.*

I looked around while I picked at a piece of macadamia nut that got wedged between my teeth. Buzz was doing better than most because he was bigger and stronger than everybody. *Lucky.* Celia was about as miserable as I was. Gadzooks looked like she was having the worst time, though; she was thin and long like a bird, so I wasn't surprised. Frank was—

Hm, I thought. *There's something weird about Frank.*

Frank didn't look like she was uncomfortable at all. She was munching down on probably around her fiftieth cookie, too, but she looked like she was still hungry. She looked totally happy, even comfortable. Plus, her rash was gone.

"Where'd your rash go?" I asked her.

"Huh?" She glanced at me and took a big bite out of a double-chocolate chunk. "Whattayoutalkinabout?"

"Earlier. You had that big red rash, from your suit."

"Oh, uh . . ." She shrugged. "It went away, I guess."

I guess. "Have you always had that mole on your cheek?" I asked.

She poked the mole just to the left of her nose. "Yeah, always. Since I was born."

"I didn't know that."

"We're not really friends," she said. "You don't know a lotta stuff about me."

I frowned. "Have we had this conversation before?"

She shrugged. "I don't think so."

Then things got even weirder when everyone was around one hundred and fifty cookies, a couple hours later. I was talking to Celia about how I never wanted to eat another snickerdoodle again in my life when I looked over and saw Frank coming back from the bathroom.

"Wait, where did your mole go?" I asked.

She caught a colourful candy that fell out of her mouth. "What mole?"

"The one you've had since you were born."

She stared at me blankly and shoved another whole cookie in her mouth.

I struggled to nibble on mine. "And is your rash still gone?"

"I don't know what rash you're talking about." She shoved a few more cookies in her mouth. "I gotta go to the bathroom."

I waited until she was almost to the end of the table before getting up and sneaking after her. She walked down the steps off the eating stage and headed to the edge of where the stadium part met the spa part. (The spa part had the best bathrooms.) She turned to look behind her, and I jumped behind a tall human with a big white bathrobe.

"Oh, good. Are you the towel boy?" The man dropped his bathrobe on top of me and stood in just a swimsuit. "I need a new robe. That one fell in the mud bath."

I felt mud dripping on my face and quickly shook the robe off me and on to the ground. I peered around the man just in time to see Frank *coming out of a hole in the bathroom wall?!* I watched her leave the bathroom and walk back toward the cookie table.

"Sorry, sir! I'm not the towel boy!" I yelled as I ran toward the hole. "I hope you find one, though!"

Attached to the edge of the hole was a rope ladder. I took a deep breath and climbed down into the darkness, moving slowly since I couldn't see the rungs. The hole was only just big enough to fit my body through, so I was squished by gross damp walls on all sides, and everything smelled like a toilet. About ten feet down, I felt the space open up and the floor under my foot, so I stood up and looked around. Even with my eyes adjusted, I couldn't see anything, so I focused and changed my suit's colour to a dim light.

The gentle glow revealed not one but *two* Franks napping in sleeping bags. I moved closer to one of them to light up her face: a *rash*. I moved to the other one and lit up her face: *no mole*. I finally understood. I knew there was only one possibility:

Goldie and Myrle were pretending to be Frank.

That's why she was so calm about her brothers losing the racing challenge; now they could cheat together. And since they all worked in the mailroom, they had access to the underground service tunnels at the North Pole. One of them must have snuck in and set up this little camp for the challenge.

Before I could decide what to do with this information, one of the Franks blinked open their eyes and shouted, "Turn that light off, Frank!"

I quickly turned my suit's light off, so we were in complete darkness.

"That's not Frank, Goldie. I'm Frank. That's Myrle." The other one turned over and faced the wall.

"I thought Frank just left to go eat. Musta slept longer than I realized. And I'm Myrle! Aren't you Goldie?"

"No, I'm Frank." I heard a rustle as she turned back to face me. "Goldie, I don't think that's Myrle."

"I know that's not Myrle. *I'm* Myrle!"

"Nah, I mean, I don't think that's Goldie *or* Myrle."

"So it's Frank?"

"No, *I'm* Frank! That's somebody else altogether!"

"No it isn't!" I said, trying to fake my voice like theirs. "You think I'm . . . some kinda twerp?"

"*I* think you're Myrle."

"He can't be Myrle, you idiot! HowmanytimesIgottatellya: I. Am. Myrle."

"Fine then: Tell me somethin' only *Myrle* would know."

I cleared my throat. "One of us has gotta go eat," I said. "Who cares who it is?"

"Fine, I'll go." Goldie – or Myrle? Or maybe Frank? – got up and pushed past me to the ladder. She climbed up and out, and I waited until she reached the top before I climbed up quickly, too.

The new Frank was still yawning and rubbing her eyes as she

walked over to the benches, so she didn't notice the other Frank already sitting there. I ran up behind them and yelled:

"HEY, EVERYBODY, LOOK! THERE'S TWO FRANKS!"

The contestants gasped. Frank and Frank looked at each other. One of the Franks put her face in her hands.

Chef crossed his arms and frowned.

"You buncha idiots." One Frank advanced on the other. "We had a system!"

"*You're* the idiot. You just came down and told me to leave, Myrle."

"I'm not Myrle. I'm Goldie."

Not this again.

"I don't care who you are! Now none of us are gonna be Santa!" One Frank punched the other Frank in the arm, and then the other Frank pulled the first Frank's hair. They pushed each other on to the table and sent cookies and milk flying everywhere. Chef came up onstage and used his hand, now a spatula, to push them away from each other.

"Yer all disqualified." His hand morphed into tongs, and he grabbed both Franks by their collars. "The rest of yeh, get eatin'! Lunch is at stake!" *At steak*, I thought.

I sat back down and stared at the small pile of cookies I still had left. Ramp was snoring, asleep on a pillow of uneaten cookies. Buzz was a few cookies ahead, but even he slowed down around the hundred and fiftieth. Celia had used her suit to build a little chisel and was breaking the cookies into very, very small pieces before eating them.

I focused and loosened the belt of my suit. I picked up a cookie and stared into its chocolate chips.

Leave me alone! I imagined the chocolate chip begging. *Just put me back down on the plate and let me live!*

Buzz took another big bite and groaned.

"I can't!" I apologized. "I have to keep fighting to the end!"

"Stop talking to the – *urp* – cookies, Ollie." Celia shook her head at me. "It only makes it harder. I figured that out – *blech* – earlier."

"Me and macadamia nuts had a thing going for a while," Kurt interjected, equally loopy. "But in the end, you always have to eat them."

Klaus glared over his substantial plate of cookies. "Are you *crying*?"

"*Everything crumbles.* That's just life, man."

I took another bite and felt like I was going to throw it all back up. "I never guessed the hardest thing about being Santa would be all the *cookies.*"

"Speak for yourself!" Buzz yelled, too loudly. "This is *muscle fuel*!!!" He put three cookies in his mouth at once and chomped down on them. *"THESE COOKIES AREN'T GONNA BRING BUZZ BROWNIE DOWN!"*

He caught all the big crumbs as they fell and put those in his mouth, too. I looked at my plate. *Only ten cookies left.* I grabbed a snickerdoodle and broke it into halves, and then quarters, and then gently placed one of the quarters on my tongue.

"RAAAAUGUUGHHHH!!!" Buzz tilted his plate into the air and poured the final four cookies into his mouth. With a final burst of energy, he crunched like a lawn mower, eating up every bit left on the plate.

Chef, back from kicking out the triplets, lifted Buzz's hand in the air with his tongs. "We've got our champion! Congrats, Brownie! Free lunch fer a whole year!"

I let out a sigh of relief and pushed my plate away. Buzz rolled backwards off the bench and curled up on the ground. "I'm never eating again."

Chapter 15

DAY FOUR: NORTH POLE IDOL

This time, the eating bench was replaced with a huge lit stage, complete with several instruments propped up and waiting in the back. Directly in the centre and all the way at the front was a microphone. A bigger surprise, though, was the crowd; most of the North Pole must have shown up for this challenge.

"What do you think's going on?" I asked.

Buzz raised his eyebrows at me. "You haven't heard?"

Celia frowned. "Heard what?"

"Pa-rumpa-pum-pum, y'all!" came a voice. A platform slowly raised someone up from under the stage. The huge crowd behind us, barely held back by Santa's Secret Helpers, yelled things like *NO WAY!* and *Oh, holy COW!!!*

"It's LDB," I said. "*The* LDB. I can't believe it. Why is he here? What's going on?!"

"Who's LDB?" Celia asked.

"Where have you *been*?!"

The platform finished rising all the way up, and there he was: LDB. He was a tall, bulky human with dangly earrings that looked like miniature drumsticks. Around his neck was a big thick chain necklace with a small drum hanging in the centre of his chest. He already had his arms outstretched like he was receiving the crowd's cheers directly into his body.

I couldn't help it; I screamed a little, too. Celia rolled her eyes at me.

"I don't really listen to Top Forty," she yelled over the noise.

"Your loss!" I yelled back. She laughed.

LDB cleared his throat. "Come *through*, they told me!"

The crowd responded, "PA-RUMPA-PUM-*PUM*!"

LDB was *the* North Pole music-producer-slash-pop-star. He sang in, rapped in, and/or produced every major track of the last year. (He was known best for his beats. They were *very good*.)

"I have the *pleasure*," he paused for a moment, relishing the sudden silence, "of telling y'all about the next trial. Y'all wanna hear it?"

The crowd screamed again, even louder. Someone yelled, "I LOVE YOU LDB!" and LDB yelled back, "COOL, THANKS." He stretched his arms out, palms down, and the crowd quieted down.

"The third official Santa Trial is . . ." He paused for a looooong time again, and you could feel everybody even lean forward a little. "A gruelling test of your abilities. It's . . ." He tapped the drum on his chest with his fingers, and everybody leaned forward even farther. "Gonna drive y'all crazy. In fact, it's . . ." He leaned toward us a little, and the whole crowd leaned forward so far that a lot of them fell over. *"A singing competition!"*

The crowd went nuts. The eight of us, however, got very quiet.

"This is why our suits needed to be 'prepared for anything'?" Buzz mumbled. I didn't even realize he was standing behind me. "I've been prepared for this since I was *born*."

"You perform?" Celia asked.

Buzz blushed. "Sort of. I've taken dance lessons since I was a kid."

A realization hit me. "You were in LDB's music video, 'Santa Claus Is Coming to the Club.' You were wearing a mask, but I always thought—"

"*Shhh.*" Buzz covered my mouth with his hand. "Just . . . don't make a big deal out of it, alright? It's embarrassing."

"Maybe you can help Celia," I said. "She doesn't know how to dance."

"Neither do you!" Celia protested.

"Yeah, but that doesn't stop me!" I waggled my fingers and shook my shoulders. "I've got the *spirit.*"

"This isn't a dance competition anyway," Celia grumbled. "It's a *singing* competition."

LDB continued explaining, "Each contestant will pick a song to perform, and you, the audience, will judge the winner using our patented Cheer-O-Meter judging system! The louder you cheer, the better they'll do! Winner gets featured on my next album, but the loser's out for good. Oh, and I almost forgot . . ." He banged the drum on his chest, and a group of reindeer in faux-leather jackets and crazy haircuts flew down from the sky.

One with a bright red Mohawk sat at the drums and used his antlers to hit them. One with very long blue hair sat in front of a piano. The one who had somehow shaped his antlers into the outline of a mouth with a tongue sticking out went up to the microphone.

Kurt was the first person to start screaming. "That's Treason 4 the Season!!! I can't believe they're breaking their vow of silence!"

His sleigh team? I'd never seen him this genuinely excited. He jumped up and down and pumped his fist.

"Play 'Christmas Chriminal'!" he yelled. I guess because I was closest to him, he grabbed my shoulders and shook me a foot off the ground. "It's from their first album, which is *amazing*. They never play live any more!" He dropped me and I tried to make dizzily teetering look cool and intentional.

Treason 4 the Season starting playing. Kurt immediately started jumping up and down and thrashing his arms around to the music.

"He's never been this sincere about anything," Celia said.

I nodded. "It's very weird."

As Kurt started mouthing the words along to a song about snowboarding, Celia scrunched up one side of her face and shrugged her shoulders. "Turns out he's just been a big fanboy this whole time."

They gave us some time to pick our songs, and then one by one we went up and performed. Most of the contestants (including me) sang Christmas carols, of course. They were easy crowd-pleasers, and you could maybe trick the audience into singing along and contributing to your score. Andrea sang both parts of "Baby, It's Cold Outside," which was even more impressive than it sounds. Even I was moved to tears by her very convincing emotional performance of both roles.

"She *really* can't stay!" I explained to Celia with watery eyes.

She patted me on the back. "I know, Ollie. I know."

"But it's *so cold*."

Next Kurt walked on to the stage, and things got even more interesting.

"I'm going to be singing Treason 4 the Season's song 'I Don't Care If You Care (That I Care).'" He looked terrified, and his hands wouldn't stop moving. He crunched a candy stick down to nothing very quickly while the band got ready.

The reindeer with a Mohawk started hammering a beat out on the drums. The one with blue hair started playing an intro on the piano. The singer said, "ONE TWO THREE FOUR."

"I know—" Kurt's voice faltered, and he cleared his throat. "You think that I—" His voice squeaked away, and he stopped completely. After a second, the band caught on and stopped playing.

"Sorry, guys, I'm just – well, performing with you guys is a dream of mine, and I'm kind of nervous, so if we could . . . can we start over? Is that OK?"

The reindeer with a Mohawk hammered out a beat again. The one with blue hair played the same intro. The singer said, "ONE TWO THREE FOUR."

"I know you think that I don't think—" Kurt's voice hiked up sharply a couple of octaves, and then he kept mouthing words but nothing seemed to be coming out. The band stopped again. Kurt's face was turning bright red, and he was obviously sweating. He combed his hair back with one hand and fidgeted with the other one.

"Sorry, I'm so sorry. Just one more time."

A hammered beat. A played intro. "ONE TWO THREE FOUR."

Nothing came out of the speakers but a garbled noise like a bird trying to scream at you.

"Sorry, Kurt." LDB's voice washed over us. "I can't let you start over any more."

People in the crowd said, *"Aww,"* which added a few points to his score, but he definitely lost.

"Whatever," he said, and put a candy stick in his mouth. "Who even cares, anyway?"

Before he could leave the stage, the lead singer of Treason tapped on the stage twice and a guitar rose out of the ground. The reindeer gestured to it, and Kurt stopped.

"Me?" Kurt asked.

The reindeer nodded.

"Are you sure?"

The reindeer nodded again, but Kurt still hesitated.

The reindeer leaned over to the microphone. "You've got the music in you, bro. Who cares about the competition? Let's rock."

I yelled through the silence, "You can do it!"

Kurt laughed and nodded, surprised out of his nerves. He picked up the guitar and whispered something to the singer. He cleared his throat.

"MY NAME IS KURT CLAUS, AND I WON'T BE SANTA BUT I WILL ROCK YOUR WORLD!" He played a few quick chords to open up the real version of "I Don't Care If You Care (That I Care)." Fireworks flew out of his jacket and in the air spelled out *KLAUS STILL WEARS WHITE SOCKS!* The crowd cheered.

"Was that all that was in his suit?" Celia asked.

"I kind of hope so." I couldn't take my eyes away from his performance.

Kurt was out of the competition, but he didn't seem too sad about it. Andrea won. We spent the next few hours dancing and relaxing, which was nice for a change.

Chapter 16

DAY FIVE: REINDEER RODEO

A tall, hefty reindeer was waiting for us this time. He was the biggest reindeer I'd ever seen, with little stubby horns but huge, marble-slab hooves. I recognized him immediately.

"That's Brutalizer!" I whispered to Celia. "He's the captain of the Abominable Throwmen!"

"I know, Ollie. Everyone watches the Reindeer Games."

"He's the toughest reindeer on the team! And the second-fastest flyer!"

"I know that, too. He was on my draft team last year."

Oh, yeah. Celia always won the draft league. "It's just statistics," she would say. "And statistics is basically science."

"Morning, buds!" The voice coming from Brutalizer's translator was kinder than I expected. He always looked so scary on the field, like he could kill you with one mean look. He wasn't making any mean looks at us, just doing the closest thing to smiling a reindeer can do.

"I'm going to tell all y'all a story." Brutalizer shrugged his shoulders and look at the seven of us remaining. "I've always been pretty big. Being tough and strong came naturally to me, you know? And since I was already good at it, it was fun to get even tougher and bigger. But then when I tried out for the Reindeer Games, I got turned away for being too slow."

I gasped. *Too slow? But he's always so fast!*

"I tried to be a faster flyer, but I convinced myself over and over that it just wasn't going to happen. It didn't come naturally to me, so I gave up." He kicked off the ground and lifted up into the sky. He did a barrel roll in one direction, then the other, then sped around us in a tight circle. "Took me a while to realize that you have to work *twice* as hard at the stuff you're not already good at, but it's worth it. Now I'm the second-fastest flyer in the Games, thanks to serious practice. *Every. Single. Day.* Today I'm going to show you what my practices are like."

Klaus scoffed, "So we're just going to sit here and watch you practise?"

Brutalizer laughed. He stomped on the ground with his hoof twice, and behind him the field came alive. Hoops and steps and targets and balls, some of them on fire, flew up into the sky and formed a course in the air. "You're not going to watch. You're coming with me."

A team of elves rushed in and started putting a saddle, helmet and goggles on Brutalizer. They passed each of us a set of protective gear, too. The reindeer explained while he got suited up.

"I'm going to do my daily flight training, like normal. Your job is to stay on my back no matter what. Anyone falls off – they're out. Anyone gives up and asks me to stop – they're out. Up in the air, Santa has to stay in sync with his reindeer. No one knows what's going to happen once we're flying, and light speed is *very dangerous.* Y'all got it?"

I nodded along with everyone else. I saw one of the spinning hoops light on fire. *We're going to have to go through that?*

"Up first is Ollie Gnome. You ready?"

I gulped. "Yes, sir."

Brutalizer laughed. "Please. Sir's my father. Hop on."

I clambered on to his back and wrapped my hands around the horn of the saddle.

"I would just like to say, Mr Brutalizer, that I'm a *very* big fan. I paint my face and dress up for all your games."

"I know! You gave me that cool helmet after last year's Games."

"You remember that?!" I had hand-bedazzled a special helmet that probably wouldn't have protected him very well, but it looked great.

"Of course I do. I keep it on the wall in my room."

"Wow! Oh, wow. That's so – and now I get to *train* with you, and—"

"Let's get going, huh?"

I nodded . . . and then realized he couldn't tell because I was sitting on his back. "Yeah! Yes. Let's go."

He trotted over to the edge of the stadium, looked up into the sky, and *launched*. We were flying faster than I had ever flown, even during the sleigh race. The first section of the course seemed to be some kind of sprinting challenge – he was bouncing back and forth between two balls floating in the air so quickly I was struggling to not get whiplash.

"The trick when flying," he yelled over the wind, "is to lean into the movements of your reindeer. We've been flying since we were born, basically, so we know what we're doing. Even if you're steering, you have to trust our instincts."

"That won't be a problem!" I yelled back. "I mostly let Crasher do the work!"

"Not a bad choice. Crasher's good. I bet she'll make it in the Games when she gets a little older." He looped through a flaming ring, and I had to push my hat against the saddle to smother a little flame. "Don't tell her I said that, though. She's already pretty cocky."

I took his advice and leaned with his turns. With every bob and weave, I got a little better at predicting where he was going to go.

"You're doing great!" he yelled as he dived toward the ground really fast to tag a checkpoint flag. "Remember: Being in charge isn't just about being in control. You have to know when to just trust your team." He rolled around on to his back and flew straight ahead, but I held on with my legs and didn't fall. "It seems like you've already got that down, though. We'll see how the others do."

The final stretch of the course was a series of spiked balls flying through the air. Brutalizer dived straight into the middle of them without stopping, and I had to duck my head to avoid getting hit by a spike. I started guessing his movements and following his shifts around the spikes before they hit – maybe even helping him dodge better, if I wasn't imagining things. We grabbed a flag at the end of the spikes and then dived back through them, putting the flag in a holster on the other side.

And then the flying course was over. Brutalizer's hooves landed on the ground with a *whumph* and I made a similar *whumph* when I rolled off his back and fell on the ground.

"Thank you," I said, panting. "That was *awesome*."

"Celia Pixie, you're up next."

"How are you not already worn out?" Celia asked, amazed. "That course was *crazy*."

"I do it ten times a day. Since you guys are added weight, though, I'll probably only do the seven."

Celia climbed on his back, and they took off. Watching her was even scarier than actually doing it; when I was up there, I was mostly distracted with trying to hold on. From the ground, you could see how high up they were and how fast they were moving.

After Celia was Buzz, and then Andrea, and then Ramp; I was nervous about him, but his Big Red Suit had some kind of feature where it locked in place and seemed to do most of the holding-on work for him. After Ramp was Klaus, and then finally Gadzooks.

Poor, poor Gadzooks. For someone who spent so much time with birds, you would've thought she'd handle flying better.

Almost immediately after they took off, her coat flapped in a weird way, and a flock of doves flew out.

"Pay them no mind!" she yelled. "Nothing to see here!"

But the birds were spooked, and they whirled around to try to land back on Gadzooks. She tried to push them away, but they tugged at her sleeves and a whole deck of cards came flying out of the sleeve. The force blew her to one side of Brutalizer's back, where she did her best to hold on. Her top hat slipped off of her head, and a rabbit fell out. She tried to catch the rabbit with her hands and the hat with her foot, but she must have hit a secret compartment, because a huge cloud of glitter flew out and enveloped them.

Coughing, Gadzooks tried not to lose her grip, but in the scramble, she ripped her collar on the back of Brutalizer's antler, and a long rope of multicoloured handkerchiefs flew out. The rabbit grabbed on to the handkerchiefs and swung along beside them.

"MY SECRETS!" she yelled as a magic wand sprung out of her sleeve and hit one of the squawking birds. "I SWORE NEVER TO REVEAL THESE!" She was falling, but she whistled and all her birds flew down and grabbed her clothes, gently gliding her to the ground. Brutalizer finished up the course, then landed as well.

"I'm sorry, Gadzooks." I went over and gave her a hug.

She shrugged. "I bamboozled myself on this one, good pal. You didn't spy too many of my secrets, did you?"

I shook my head. "We barely even understood what happened. Your secrets are safe."

"Splendid." Gadzooks bowed and tipped her hat. "Good luck with the rest of the competition. I'll be rooting for you."

She reached out to shake my hand, but when I extended mine, there was a pigeon on it.

When I looked up, Gadzooks was gone. The pigeon cooed.

Chapter 17

DAY SIX: NEXT TOP NUTCRACKER

"Five, six, seven, eight!" Frosty clapped his squishy hands and demonstrated the choreography for us. I tripped on my own feet during a grapevine step and had to slow down to get my bearings.

"Ollie! Did you hear me holler 'stop'?" Frosty stopped dancing and frowned down at me. The way his snow face rearranged to frown was actually kind of unsettling. His dark coal-eyes pierced right through me.

"I only paused a moment, sir!"

"Let's try it again. Look alive, people! Alive as you can be!"

I watched him closely as he repeated the choreography for the sugar plum fairies. Our challenge today was to each do a one-person abridged performance of *The Nutcracker*, playing all the roles and dancing all the parts. Everyone was *so tired*, though, on the sixth day. And it was *so early*. But Frosty didn't slow down.

Frosty wasn't good at *taking* direction (from traffic cops, choreographers, or whoever), so he *became* a director. He was there to teach us some of the dances and also to judge. I had never met him in person before, and I guess I expected him to be less . . . creepy to look at. He wasn't a snowman like you'd make for fun in your yard – the nanobots or whatever that were making him animate gave him the shape of a regular human person, just pure white and snowy. As soon as that hat was on his head, he started dancing around, and he hadn't stopped dancing since.

He dismissed us to practise on our own, and Andrea sleepily stumbled toward me. I had to muster up a lot of positive vibes not to ignore her.

"I'm sorry we haven't got along." She started practising one of the Mouse King's clap-dances while she was talking, so I did as well. "Klaus over there convinced me to try to knock you out of the competition. He's very convincing. Did you know he's very smart?" She started to tilt over, so I helped her stand back up.

"Yeah, I know. But your tricks in the race still weren't OK."

She wiggled her shoulders and sighed. "I know it wasn't. You promise not to hate me if you become Santa?"

She sounds so sincere, I thought.

She always sounds like she's telling the truth, I thought back. *And then she fools you into messing yourself up.*

I don't think that's what she's doing this time.

Whatever. It's your funeral.

It's your funeral, too.

Pecan brittle! I mentally swore. *You're right!*

"Of course I don't hate you. I just don't think I can trust you any more, you know?"

She nodded while yawning and also doing the running man. "I get that. Can we at least hug?"

"Uh, sure?" I was very confused. She gave me a hug and squeezed.

"Friends for ever," she said.

I am very uncomfortable.

"Yeah, uh, friends . . . uh, I guess—"

"HEL-*LO*, EVERYONE!" Maria Duende beamed her bright smile and posed at the entrance to the field. A few cameras swarmed around her to capture the moment, and then our expressions. She had shown up with a surprise: everybody's parents. Apparently she thought it would be a good idea to get some footage of them coming to support us when we were at our most exhausted, so she had a team of camerawomen flood the stadium alongside all the mums and dads.

"Can I get on your shoulders, Ollie?" Polly asked.

Mum shook her head. "He's busy, baby."

"No, it's fine." I hefted her up and set her on my shoulders. "Seeing you guys is making me feel better about this long week." I poked Polly's side, and she giggled. "You have to dance, though."

"OK!" She pumped her arms in the air and made a very serious kissy face.

"I meant to bring you some ice cream, Ollie Pop, but I left with the scoop instead." My dad held up an ice-cream scoop; he was always doing things like that. Once he left his laptop in the fridge. "You know my scattery brain!"

"You'd serve your head on a cone if it wasn't attached, Raleigh." Mum wiped a smudge off of his overalls.

"Daddy's name is Raleigh?" Polly asked. "Does Mummy have a name like ours, too?"

"No, honey. Your dad's family does that because they're very, very silly. My name's Elizabeth."

Polly looked disappointed. "Oh."

Maria rushed up with Seyi, her camerawoman, in tow. "Smile for the cameras!"

We all turned, smiled and waved. Maria moved on.

"We're very proud of you, but it is very early in the morning and Mummy hasn't had her coffee. You should go visit Celia's parents, too. They wanted to talk to you."

"Thanks, Mum. I will." I passed a struggling Polly back over to her.

Dad handed me the ice-cream scoop. "Just in case it was meant to be." He winked. "It's made out of an unbreakable alloy! And it's sharp. I use it to cut even the most frozen chunks of ice cream." Unsure what to do, I winked back and tucked it into one of my suit pockets.

"Thanks, Dad." I waved while they walked away. Celia's parents were fussing over her a few feet away.

"My suit's fine." Celia was trying to slip away from her mother, who was poking at her Big Red Suit. "Ollie made it for me."

"You're wearing it sloppily," Mrs Pixie said. "It should be tucked in."

"Actually, my suit is at an optimal, *scientifically proven* tuckedness precisely where functionality, beauty and comfort intersect."

"Always with the *science*. It's too loose." Her tone made it clear there was no more room for argument.

"What are you doing, Dad?"

Mr Pixie was writing with a pencil on a notepad. "I want to remember everything about this moment."

Mrs Pixie was an accountant who liked everything a certain

way, and Mr Pixie was a poet who liked to throw parties. Celia said that science was a natural balance of the two.

"Ollie, save me!" Celia noticed me watching and waved me over. Her parents both turned around to give me hugs.

"There's our sweet little boy!" Mrs Pixie gave me a kiss on the forehead.

Mr Pixie shook me by the shoulders lightly. "A fantastic job, really. You've done a great job."

"They like you more than me, Ollie." Celia smiled at me to show she was joking, but Mrs Pixie apparently didn't realize and clicked her tongue.

"You know that's not true. We just never see him! It's always right out of the house with you two, off to do your 'science.' I feel like you've been on TV more than you've been at home!"

"You don't have to do air quotes when you say science, Mum. I'm a serious scientist."

"Well, how would I know? You never invent anything to help around the house!"

They had this fight a lot. My attention started wandering while they argued. I saw Klaus talking to Mrs Claus – I guess Santa hadn't come – and I saw Maria Duende toward the back of the dance floor, interviewing Andrea, who was practising the Charleston by herself.

I started to back away from the Pixies. "I'll be right back, you guys."

"Science is about way more important stuff than *vacuuming*, Mum!"

"Who cares about robots if your house is a wreck?"

They didn't seem like they'd be slowing down any time soon, and Mr Pixie was still just watching them and taking notes, so I headed over to Andrea, who was holding an opened envelope and reading a letter to the camera.

"'. . . so happy and proud of you. Your cousin even set up a wifi' – she spelled it like 'wife-eye' – 'so we could watch you compete on the news.' Hi, Mum!" Andrea waved at the camera and laughed in the way people laugh when they're trying not to cry.

I waited off to the side until Maria moved on, then awkwardly sidestepped over to Andrea.

"Your parents couldn't come?" I asked.

She shrugged. "Plane tickets are expensive. They had to use most of our savings to send me here. Farming is hard."

"Yeah, I bet." I gestured to Ramp, who was flopping around, struggling with the fast choreography. "He could be your dad, if you want."

She laughed. "More like my grandpa."

"Your great-great-great-grandpa." I laughed, too, and because we were both so exhausted, it felt like it was *way* funnier than it actually was. We kept looking at each other and starting up again every time we thought it was over.

Finally, when we were down to just hiccups, she nudged me. "Doesn't he look kind of familiar, though?"

"Who? Ramp?"

"Yeah. With the Santa suit and everything."

I squinted and cocked my head to the side, watching Ramp's head toss forward and back. I just saw the toupee, the too-big trousers. His red face, his long beard. I thought about that time he jumped crazy high in the mailroom.

"I don't think I recognize him from anywhere before the competition."

"OK, imagine him with, like, little spectacles. And a little fatter. And then imagine him saying, 'HO, HO, HO!'" She boomed it out.

I did. "I get what you mean. He kinda looks like Kris Kringle. Like in the old paintings."

"Yeah, totally. Weird, huh?"

"Pretty weird." I looked at her. "You really want to win, huh? For your family?"

She shook her head. "I don't know. I don't think so." Andrea tied her red hair back in a bun while she talked. "When I left, my dad said, 'You're going to go out there and you're going to *do anything it takes to win*. You're a Claus, and you're going to prove it. We deserve to be in that castle just as much as any of them.' And so I got here and couldn't stop thinking about that. *'Do anything it takes.'* So I have been. Speaking of which – " She reached behind my back and popped something off of my suit.

"A smiley-face button!" My mouth fell open. "You tricked me *again*!"

She nodded. "When we hugged earlier. But that's what I mean: I don't want to be Santa. Not if it means I have to act like this for ever." She fixed the smiley face to her shirt and handed me a remote control with only one button.

"I don't understand."

"I can't look like I quit, but I have to. Use this on me, during the competition. My suit's got loads of electronics in it – the pulse will freeze it up so bad that I won't even be able to move, let alone dance. It'll look like a malfunction, and I'll be disqualified."

"But your family – and what your dad said—"

"Please. This is what *I* want. Remember Sally?"

I did remember. Finally I nodded, and put the remote control in my jacket.

If this is what she wants.

* *❄* *

Frosty explained that Santa needed to have physical endurance and "effortless grace," both of which were best tested with dancing for hours straight. For act 1, we had to be Clara, the main character, but then also Clara's dad, and Drosselmeyer (who gives her the Nutcracker), and the Nutcracker. *Then* we had to fight ourselves as the Mouse King!

Klaus, Celia and I stuck pretty closely to Frosty's traditional choreography. We didn't change anyone's lives or anything, but I think we put on pretty good shows. Ramp's Big Red Suit did all the work for him. He told us that his tailor had put a full skeleton in the suit: Once it had learned the choreography, it led Ramp's body around for a perfect performance. Buzz put his own spin on the choreography and blew everyone out of the water by mixing his ballet in with more modern influences, like hip-hop and also some twisty-flowy-artsy moves I didn't know the name of. Andrea actually rewrote the story some; in her version, Clara didn't save the Nutcracker after he was injured.

"In my version, Clara marries the Mouse King," she explained at intermission. "And then she becomes Mouse Queen, kills the king, and takes control of the entire rodent empire. In act 2, she leads an army through the Land of Sweets and steals the magic of the Sugar Plum Fairy. Clara lives the rest of her life ruling both kingdoms with an iron pointe shoe. Unless" – Andrea winked at me – "something were to happen" – she winked at me again – "to" – wink – "her . . ." *Wink, wink, wink, wink, wink.*

Celia looked at me for explanation. I stared at the ground.

Act 2 was even more exhausting. We had to play the sweet-bearers from all over the world giving presents to ourselves, then be the Sugar Plum Fairy, Clara and the Nutcracker all at once during the last scene. I built an outfit with pieces of all their looks (Clara's dress, the Sugar Plum Fairy's wings and the Nutcracker's silly hat) so that I could convincingly play all three roles.

Klaus hated every second he had to dance in front of the crowd. Maybe inspired by Andrea's act 1, he changed his script so the Mouse King came back and ruined the party, cutting the act short with one intense fight-dance where he duelled himself with two different swords.

Ramp napped through the whole show, but his form was so good (thanks to the suit) that no one could really complain.

Celia added a lot of cool tech to her set. She flew around the stage, fire leapt from the wings, and a cannon shot actual candies out to the audience. The spectacle made up for her lack of dance experience.

Buzz totally destroyed us all, *again*, because it was obvious he was the best dancer onstage. I laughed, I cried, and the entire crowd gave a standing ovation when he did a 720-degree pirouette in the air and landed straight into a double somersault pop-and-lock salsa kick-flip hip shimmy.

Then it was Andrea's turn. She, as Clara, led herself as the late Mouse King's army into battle against herself as the citizens of the

Land of Sweets. It was very bloody, and swords were flying around everywhere. During a quick costume change, she looked at me in the side of the audience and secretly mouthed, *Now!* behind her hand. She mimed pressing a button.

I don't know if I can do this. She ran back centre stage and threw sabers around. *What if she gets hurt?* I watched her jump and twirl with a rapier. As a knight, she stabbed herself as an innocent townsperson and threw fake blood all over the front row of the audience while making dramatic crying noises. During the distraction, she tapped her wrist in my direction like she was waiting on me.

Fine. I pulled the remote out of my jacket and looked at it, and then back at her. I wiggled in my seat at the edge of the audience.

I don't want to do this. It feels like cheating.

But she asked me to. And she has to lose sometime.

I held my breath and pushed the button while she juggled butcher knives. Nothing happened. *Maybe I have to get closer?*

I slid out of my seat and tried to move to the front of the stage without attracting attention – lucky her performance was so interesting – and held my breath again. I pushed the button.

A visible jolt of blue energy spread around her costume and froze up. Three – no, four – swords were airborne as her suit short-circuited, and she fell to the ground on her back. The swords turned and fell to the ground as the audience gasped. A little boy behind me asked his mum if this was part of the show. I covered my eyes with my hands but peeked out through my fingers anyway.

The swords stabbed into the ground around her, but none of them hurt her, thankfully. The audience waited for a few minutes to see if it was part of the show, but the music kept going and Andrea just wiggled in her frozen suit.

Frosty stopped the show and a team of elves marched onstage with a stretcher. They picked her up and led her off the stage toward where I was standing.

As she passed she whispered, "Thanks, Ollie. You're a good friend."

Phew, I thought. I instantly felt so much better. *I'm glad I was able to help her.*

The awards ceremony was pretty much unnecessary. Buzz won – he was the only person to win two challenges already – and Andrea was eliminated.

As soon as it was over, Celia and I ran as fast as we could back home.

"Must . . . sleep!" Celia yelled.

I groaned like a zombie. "We just have to make it through one more day!"

Chapter 18

DAY SEVEN: HEATMISER AND SNOWMISER'S AROUND THE WORLD IN EIGHTY MINUTES

Compared to all the other challenges, doing anything for only eighty minutes sounded like a breeze. Even with the crazy Miser twins in charge.

Heatmiser and Snowmiser were AI programs with full control over the North Pole's air-conditioning and climate-control systems. They were also responsible for maintaining the fog that obscured our location to regular humans; anybody exploring the area would get lost in it and then blown by seriously strong winds away from the city perimeter. They kept us safe and kept our buildings warm and comfortable.

The key to their success was that they had been built to balance each other. Heatmiser always wanted things hotter, and Snowmiser always wanted things colder. Since they were able to move around inside of any technology connected to the North Pole's network, their fights would sometimes have real-world consequences.

Every computer in my neighbourhood overheated to the point of catching on fire once because Heatmiser lost a best two hundred out of three hundred chequers match. One time Heatmiser didn't laugh at one of Snowmiser's jokes, and he pouted so hard *all* the food in the kitchens became frozen food. I had a lot of ice lollies that week, and some of the ice lollies were hot dogs.

When we arrived on the field, we were greeted with an enormous metal dome taking up the entire non-spa half of the stadium. There was only one door, so all five of us walked inside and it slid closed on its own.

"I can't even see my hands," I heard Celia say. She was right; the whole dome was in pitch black.

Klaus called out from beside us. "Heaty? Snowbro?"

I heard Buzz snort, then put on a fake baby voice: "Help me, Snowbwo! The darkness is soooo scawy!!"

"Shut up."

"Heatyyyyy! Whewe aaaaawe you?!"

"I said *shut up*."

"*KLAUS!*" Up in the dark sky, a huge sun appeared and started beaming warmth down at us. It had a big white smile and was wearing sunglasses, which I thought was very funny. "How's my best little buddy?" Heatmiser's voice was loud and quick, like a crackling fire. "You might not recognize me because I'm a hologram, but it's your favourite uncle, Heatmiser!"

Klaus rolled his eyes, but I could tell he was smiling just a little. "I know it's you, Heaty."

"'Favourite uncle' my switchboard." A huge icy moon eclipsed the sun, and a thin smile spread among its craters. The moon was also wearing sunglasses, and it was still funny. "Everyone knows I'm Klaus's favourite." Snowmiser always sounded a little bored, even when he was freaking out. "And you've got so tall, Klaus darling!"

"You saw me last week, Snowbro." Klaus was staring at the ground and smirking.

I put my hands on my cheeks and opened my mouth in shock at Celia.

This is the cutest thing I have ever seen, I mouthed. She stuck out her tongue like she was grossed out by it.

"Could you give us a floor or something, guys?" Klaus asked the brothers. "It's pretty weird to be standing on nothing."

"Duh. If ice brain here didn't move so slow, I would have done it ages ago." The sun bumped the moon out of the way, and his rays grew bigger and brighter. I could really feel the heat coming off of them, which I was surprised by.

As Heatmiser lit up the ground, a beautiful green field started growing around us. Suddenly there was thick, bright grass as far as we could see, with the occasional tree or animal running around it. I knelt down to touch the grass – it felt *real*. I saw Ramp pat a rabbit on the head. Buzz swung on a tree branch.

"Welcome, Klaus—"

"And the rest of you."

"—*and the rest of you*, to our state-of-the-art Holo-Chamber." Snowmiser swooped down to the horizon and blew. A wave of cold washed over us, and the grass shrunk and turned brown. Snow fell from the sky, and the leaves on the trees turned brown and then fell off.

Heatmiser frowned at having his field ruined but kept talking. "We've got full control of artificial reality in here. It's really very impressive."

Snowmiser sighed. "You don't *tell* people something is impressive, brother. You just let them *be* impressed."

"Oh, so now you're saying I'm a show-off."

"I didn't say that."

"But that's what you meant!"

"You are *so* immature." The sun and moon pressed up against each other, and the world around us started shifting in strange ways. The trees grew green leaves while snow fell on top of them. A tropical storm dumped on us and froze into an ice block as soon as it reached the ground.

"Guys!" Klaus yelled, drawing the brothers' attention. "Can we get started with the challenge, please?"

Heatmiser sucked the water off of our clothes and hair, leaving us dry again. "Of course, little buddy. Let's get going."

"We should explain the rules." Snowmiser looked to his right and a bulleted list appeared in the sky next to him. "This challenge will test how you could survive the harshest climates in the world, as Santa must every Christmas. To that end, there are a series of rules. Rule number one: In case of emergency, all contestants should—"

Heatmiser interrupted him with a growl. "Yeah, yeah, yeah. It's simple: Don't die and keep moving. *Readysetgo!*"

"Santa *clearly* said—"

Heatmiser interrupted him with a loud, extended fart sound effect. The floor below us started moving backwards, and the holo-world around us moved along with it. We all started walking to keep up.

"I'm first!" Heatmiser said. "Welcome to one of my favourite places on Earth: the *desert*."

"Which desert?" Celia asked.

"Doesn't matter."

I could feel all the moisture being sucked out of the world, and what was left of the grass and trees melted into growing dunes of sand. Soon we were struggling to keep moving with our feet slosh-ing through the loose grains.

"Ugh . . ." I groaned as I struggled not to fall on my face. "It's so *hot*."

Celia made a motion with her hands like she was fanning her-self, activating the air-conditioning I'd programmed in her suit. I shifted my suit to a pair of shorts and a tank top to cool down.

"Don't forget your hover jets!" I reminded Celia.

"Oh, *yeah*!" I was so excited about those when we put them in. She flattened her palms toward the floor and powerful jets of air started shooting out of her sleeves and trousers. She sprayed sand everywhere but lifted up above the ground and didn't have to trod on the hot surface any more.

"Nice to have a challenge where we can actually use our suits," Buzz said. His shoes turned into little sleds with tiny rockets on the back, and he skated along the sand.

"You think you're so tough." Heatmiser chuckled above us. "Let's see how you fare against my *sand worm*!"

The ground rumbled below us, and we saw a cloud of sand being spewed up into the air as something burrowed toward us at an extreme speed.

Within seconds, an enormous monster burst out of the ground in front of us, covered in scales and with six rows of sharp teeth spinning around inside a circular mouth. It roared in our faces, dived at me – and then froze completely solid.

"My turn!" Snowmiser singsonged. The moving ground quickly ushered the frozen worm behind us and away. The sand started levelling out into a huge frozen lake. Celia stayed in the air, and Buzz stayed on his sleds. Klaus's shoes grew blades on the bottom for ice skating, and Ramp scooted along on his butt. I focused and elongated my shoes into skis.

Celia rubbed her shoulders like she was cold to activate her heating system. My suit grew into a big, fluffy coat.

"What? But I barely got a turn!" The water started melting as Heatmiser got angry, but Snowmiser eclipsed him again and froze it back over before it got too thin. "That's not fair!"

"Those are the rules." Snowmiser flew across the sky, and the lake in front of us lit up in a series of squares, like a chequerboard. Each square had a number inside it, starting with one where we were and gradually escalating into the distance. "Speaking of rules: Some of this ice is safe to pass over, and some is *very* dangerous. If you would like to stay alive, you must stay away from: prime numbers; numbers divisible by 91; numbers that appear in any movie released between October 22, 1991, and November 22, 1992; any number that's the same backwards and forwards; numbers I don't like; my favourite number; any number that—"

"Alright, alright, you've tortured them enough. Let's pull you out of Snoozeville, kids. *MY TURN!*" Heatmiser spread his light, and the ice started melting. Clouds formed above us, and rain started pouring down, replacing the frozen lake with a vast ocean. A storm whipped up around us with lightning and thunder while the waves grew and smashed against each other.

I saw Celia try to fly, but apparently water was not good for the suit's air jets. I tried to think of what else my suit could do. *What could I make?*

It clicked. I shifted my shoes into big flippers, and my hat expanded around my head and sealed at my neck. The hat's colour faded until it was totally see-through.

Now that I could breathe and see, I swam deeper into the water to get away from the crazy storm up above. I saw Klaus sail by in a comfy-looking submarine. I looked up above and saw the bottom of a surfboard that said *BUZZ BROWNIE*, and the kicking legs of what must have been Ramp clinging to the back of it. Celia made use of the oxygen I had built into her hat.

A huge stream of bubbles and a muffled slurping sound rose from below. I felt myself being tugged deeper underwater and tried to swim against the current with very little success. Klaus's submarine came flying backwards toward me, and I grabbed on to a tube jutting off the side. Buzz and Ramp slammed against the top and their surfboard went flying down into the depths. They held on to other pieces of the submarine, too.

Klaus was banging on the glass from the inside, and I think was yelling *"get off!"* But his voice was muffled by the water and metal. I felt something grab my foot and looked down; it was Celia. She climbed up my leg and took the same handhold as me as we were sucked down to the bottom of the ocean. The submarine *thunk*ed on to the ground, and then the current dragged us toward a giant pit swallowing all the water.

Then we were in a tube, pulling us down and in all sorts of directions – ending straight up. The water pushed us higher, higher, and then out of a geyser. I looked at the landscape around us.

"How pretty!" I yelled now that we were out of the water. "A beautiful island! Black cracked ground, water all over, and then, oh, *a volcano full of lava that we are currently heading straight for!!!!*"

The four of us outside kicked off the submarine and tried to fight the direction we were falling. I shook the water out of my suit and pulled my hat off my face, while Celia kicked on her hover jets. I – and Ramp, somehow – grabbed hold of her suit and dragged her down, but we would at least make it to the rim of the volcano. Buzz was using his rocket-sled shoes as a poorly balanced upside-down steering for his fall, and kept having to push his shirt out of his face.

The glass front of the submarine popped up, and Klaus's seat ejected. He flew out of the way of the volcano's mouth, and a parachute shot out of his chair to carry him gently to the edge.

The five of us collapsed on the ground and groaned. We had barely started complaining when the ground started rumbling.

"The volcano is erupting!" Celia yelled.

"Can we get a break, please, Heaty?" Klaus yelled. The sun didn't answer. "Snowbro?" The moon didn't answer, either. The two circles in the sky were too busy bashing into each other.

Ramp was lying on the ground with his eyes closed. "What, you kids can't – *nnngh* – take it? Back in my day, we—"

"Shut *up*!" Klaus yelled. "You're so terrible at pretending to be a kid that it isn't even funny any more."

"I *am* a kid," Ramp protested. "See, listen: 'Saturday morning cartoons!'" Ramp spread his arms out wide like the argument was over. "Couldn't say that if I was an adult, could I? That's a kid-only secret, that is."

Celia smirked at Klaus. "Looks like he's got you with that one."

I nodded. *It's nice to see Ramp frustrating someone else for a change.* "A hundred percent for sure a kid, I guess."

Klaus took a deep breath and pushed on his forehead with his hands. "OK, look, I hate him, and I think I might actually hate all of you a little bit, but the last time they got in a huge fight it lasted *three weeks*."

The volcano rumbled again.

"So?" Ramp asked.

"Yeah, so?" Celia said.

"*SO*, since they never got around to telling us what to do in case of emergency, we don't know how to get to the exit. It might just keep rolling random settings and trap us in this stupid dome for ever. And I don't know if you've figured this out, but" – he was interrupted by another, much more urgent, rumble from the volcano – "if you die in a Big Red Suit, you die in *real life*."

"Oh, I thought . . ." I decided correcting him was no longer important to me, but everyone got quiet, so I had to keep going. "I thought maybe you were going to say if we die in, like, this simulation. I think we're all pretty sure that clothes don't make a big difference."

Buzz nodded. "That's a good point, Ollie. I think maybe Klaus got swept up in the drama of the moment."

"*This is why I said I hated all of you.* Can you take anything seriously for five seconds, please?"

"Maybe you need to, like, take stuff a little *less* seriously, Klaus." Celia raised an eyebrow at him. "People might like you more."

Ramp snorted. "Kids like us might call that one a *sick burn*."

"I don't care if people like me! Right now I don't want to get *third-degree* burns from *an effectively real* volcano!"

"Oh, right," I said. "I totally forgot about the—"

At this moment, the volcano chose to erupt. I braced myself to melt. *Klaus was right*, I thought. *We weren't taking it*

seriously enough and now we're all going to be cooked like a bunch of
delicious hams.

I thought about how hams used to be pigs and felt pretty sad about that for a second. *I hope nobody is throwing any pigs into a volcano.*

No, I don't think that's how it works.

You're probably right about that, me. Wait, how do we have so much time to think about this? Are we dead?

I nervously opened my eyes and saw pure white all around me. I patted my body, and it was still there. The white was moving. And *very cold.*

"A blizzard?" I yelled. "The volcano erupted a blizzard?!"

"I have an idea!" Celia yelled. I moved through the white toward her voice and saw the rest of the contestants doing that, too. "We need to get to the edge of the dome."

"It won't let us." Klaus's suit was glowing, and snow was melting as it landed on him. "It's going to keep moving the landscape and creating things to keep us in the centre."

"What if someone loses the challenge?" Buzz interrupted. "What if one group starts moving, so the landscape moves with them, and someone stays here? Eventually it'll have to bump them to the edge of the dome, right?"

"I'm not doing that." Klaus immediately made sure there was no question. "No way."

"Well, luckily I wasn't asking you to, jerk." Buzz looked at me as the snow thinned. "I can't do it, Ollie. I can't be Santa."

"What?" I yelled. "You won two challenges – you can't give up!"

"Actually, I totally can?"

"I thought you wanted to be Santa."

"Nah." Buzz sat down on the ground but raised his hand up to give me a fist bump. "You gotta win, Ollie. You or Celia would be great. I mean it."

My eyes filled with tears while I fist-bumped him. "I'll never forget you, Buzz!"

"I'm not dying, Ollie. You'll see me in, like, fifteen minutes, tops."

Buzz's surfboard flew out of the volcano and he snatched it from the air. He ripped the fin off it. "Check it out. Snowboard."

I took it from him. Celia and I got on it. Buzz untied his sled-shoes and handed them to Ramp.

"Wait, where's Klaus?" I looked down the side of the volcano and saw him speeding away on skis.

"Go!" Buzz said. "Don't let him get too far ahead!"

We kicked off and zoomed down the mountain. Before long, we weren't even *on* a mountain any more; we were in the middle of a snowy forest where all the trees were on fire. A few seconds later and we were in a messed-up version of the savanna, where several confused lions were interacting with polar bears standing on an iceberg.

A bunch of mountain goats jumped around a boat sinking in the ocean, and then a rain forest grew in the middle of a city. We passed a moose standing on top of a moving river with a flaming skull for a head that stared straight at me and said, "*BUY LOW, SELL HIGH.*"

Kurt would have liked that, I thought. And also: *This computer is getting very confused.*

A loud horn blared for several long seconds while we navigated a beach covered in giraffes with only two legs.

"I bet that's Buzz losing." Celia looked up at the sky. "And it should get their attention."

She was right. The sun and moon stopped bashing into each other and rotated their faces toward us.

"Oh!" Snowmiser called down. "It looks like Buzz Brownie is out!"

"Really? I figured it would have been the tiny one."

"Hey!" I said, because I was the tiny one.

Heatmiser zoomed in to look closely at the landscape, and I had to shield my eyes from his rays. "Oh, yeesh. *That's* weird." A dolphin with two hairy human legs chirped happily as it ran in the sand.

Snowmiser turned up his nose. "If you had let me preprogram the challenge, like I *wanted* to do—"

"OH, WOULD YOU LOOK AT THE TIME," Heatmiser interrupted. "IT'S BEEN EIGHTY MINUTES. ALSO KNOWN AS: QUIT COMPLAINING O'CLOCK."

"Your point, while immature, is correct. Buzz Brownie is eliminated. The challenge is over. I need to get away from *you*." The moon flew away and blinked out of existence.

The sun grew bright red with anger. "Oh, no. You're not getting away from me that easy." The sun flew off after the moon, probably to make some toasters malfunction somewhere.

Around us, the simulation flickered, sputtered and then disappeared. We fell a few inches on to the real ground and were back in the surprisingly small dome, dimly lit this time.

Buzz waved to us from against the other wall. "The door's over here, guys."

"Good job, everybody!" I said.

Celia and I high-fived. Ramp nodded. Klaus ignored us and walked straight past Buzz and out the door.

"I'm sorry," I said to Buzz when we made it to him.

He bonked me on the top of my head. "Don't worry about it."

"We made it!" Celia led us out into the real sunlight and immediately fell to the ground. I collapsed next to her.

Ramp was already snoring, and he didn't even lie down.

Celia laughed. "He's got the right idea."

I couldn't keep in a little cheer. "We're in the top four!"

She gave me a thumbs-up. "Let's celebrate! After a short nap."

"Maybe a long nap."

"Honestly, celebrating sounds like a lot of work."

"A *very* long nap."

I hope it'll be enough, I thought. *I have a feeling this wasn't even the hard part.*

Chapter 19

The main entrance to Claus Castle is through two doors that are at least three times as tall as a human adult and probably eight times as wide. Pushing the very heavy wood requires a whole team of elves all working together, and even then they're fighting against years of the doors being mostly immobile. There are a lot of side entrances, including one right next to the main doors. There really isn't any need to use the doors except for the ceremony, to make Claus Castle look impressive and regal.

So I felt very uncomfortable not helping.

"Are you sure I can't—"

"No! *Nnnggggggghhhhhhaaaaauuuuughhhhh!!!!* No, sir! This is our job! We got it! *Hnnnnnnggghhhhhhraaaaarrrrrghhh!!!!!!!*" An elf near the centre of the right door pushed even harder than he had before, maybe to prove to us that everything was OK. His eyes looked like they were going to pop out of his head.

The doors had opened less than an inch.

"The other door is right over there," Celia pointed out, "so it's really no trouble at all."

"Wouldn't – *graarunnnnkkkkk* – dream of it, Miss Pixie! This is an official meeting between Santa Claus and his successor!"

"He's right." Klaus looked up from his mobile phone and waved his hand toward the team of elves. "Let them have their fun. It's tradition. Makes them feel special."

Ramp ran his fingers through his beard. "What makes this meeting so official? Why are we here?"

Celia sat down in the snow. "I guess because we're the finalists. One of the four of us is definitely Santa."

Klaus huffed. "How lucky for the North Pole. An old man, a crybaby, a mad scientist—"

"And a spoiled brat," Ramp finished. *Boom.* "And who're you calling an old man? I'm sixteen and three-quarters!"

"I'm not a crybaby!" I said, tears welling up in my eyes.

"And the only person I'm mad at is *you*." Celia glared at Klaus. "So *watch it*."

The door had only opened two inches now. I decided to go help.

"You don't have to – *graagh! GRAAAAGH!* – do that, Mr Gnome!" The elf man looked like if you turned a stick bug into a person, but he never stopped smiling pleasantly, even when he was yelling under the strain.

"It's really OK. They're about to start fighting, and I didn't – *oh geez, this is heavy. Harrrrrrghhhhh!!* – I didn't really want to be part of the fight, you know?"

The stick man nodded, which made his hat slide off his sweaty head and plop into the snow. "I hope you don't mind me saying so, Mr Gnome, but I think – *kkkkkkkk* – you'd make a *wonderful* Santa."

"You think so?"

"I do. Santa should be someone truly kind. And it's high time an elf is in charge."

"Maybe. But Celia's smarter and good at making plans. And Klaus is a natural leader who has trained for this his whole life. And Ramp . . . well, Ramp's not going to win, right?"

"Even so. You've got my support."

I felt all warm and fuzzy. Even when Celia and I had been throwing parties and doing charity work before the merry-thon, no one had been so direct and kind. Even people who liked me seemed to believe Santa was making a mistake changing the tradition. Having someone who worked *in the castle* say I would be wonderful meant a lot. I felt ready to take on the world.

Celia walked up and pushed on the other door. "Klaus is in – *who made this so heavy? oh my gosh* – a bad mood. Like always."

"He's probably nervous – *I don't know but they should be fired from ever making any doors again* – about seeing Santa. I wonder if they've talked at all since the conference room."

"I don't think so. This is good enough." She meant the door, and I looked at the crack we had made, which was now an opening a couple feet wide. The team of elves collapsed to the ground, and I took deep breaths to try to calm my heartbeat.

Klaus immediately breezed past us and through the opening, practically dropping his coat on the floor before he'd even made it through the doors. Ramp slowly hobbled after him, and I followed Celia in after giving the stick man a hug.

The entrance to Claus Castle has got to be the most beautiful thing at the North Pole, and there are a lot of *really beautiful things* at the North Pole. Coming in through the double doors put us right in the centre of two lush red-carpeted staircases mirroring each other in gentle curves up to the second floor. Below the balcony at the top, a hallway stretched for what felt like for ever, a gorgeous red carpet down the centre.

A whole separate team of elves took our coats. I ran in past everyone and spun around. Portraits of various sizes hung everywhere with different Santas and their families. Directly above the entrance doors, bigger than all of them, was a portrait of the original Kris Kringle playing with what could have been the very first model train. He wasn't in his traditional suit for this portrait, either; he looked more like Kris Kringle the *inventor*. He had goggles on his forehead like Celia did when she was busy at work. He was wearing overalls with all sorts of tools sticking out of the pockets, but he wasn't using any of them. He was just grinning from ear to ear and pointing at the toy train spewing steam out of its smokestack.

"This portrait wasn't painted by anyone, you know." Santa appeared on the balcony up above us, smiled, and waved. As he descended the stairs, he continued, "Kris Kringle invented a machine that drew your portrait exactly like it saw you. He didn't know it then, but he was inventing an early version of something the rest of the world wouldn't have for hundreds of years: a camera.

"Kris Kringle was an inventor, a leader and a lover of toys. Most important, though, he was kind to everyone. He loved the world and everything in it. Santa needs all of these qualities."

"He wasn't that great," Ramp snapped. "I mean, we don't really know. All we have are stories. Stories that are too good to be true."

Santa laughed. "Maybe so. But his legacy, at least, speaks for itself."

"Yeah, because he threw out everything that didn't work." Ramp looked really angry, and I had no idea why. I remembered what Andrea had said, and glanced between him and the portrait. They *did* look alike.

"Wait a second." Celia didn't notice what was going on with Ramp because she was still staring at the portrait. "If this was made when Kris Kringle was alive . . . that can't just be the first model train. That must be the first *train*. Full stop."

Santa's grin got even wider, and he clapped both hands down on Celia's shoulders. I tried not to feel sad seeing Klaus bristle with jealousy.

"That's exactly right. But he believed in letting the rest of the world discover things for themselves when they were ready. A belief we share even today."

"Can we get on with this?" Klaus spoke just a little too loud, and his voice echoed through the castle's halls. "Everybody already knows this stuff. Why are we even here?"

Santa looked down at the ground for a moment, his smile gone. "Of course. Follow me." The heels of his dress shoes clicked on the ground as he headed back to the banister, where he grabbed a small reindeer statue at the bottom of the rail and twisted it. The left staircase rumbled and folded up, revealing another set of stairs going underground. I looked at Celia, but she seemed just as lost as I was.

"No." Klaus charged forward at his dad, a bundle of furious energy. "This isn't theirs. This isn't for *them*." He spat the word, and glared back at us. "You've never even let me in there before."

"Klaus, please. I know what I'm doing."

"I'm out of here." He turned and headed down the centre hallway, probably to his room. "I'll go in there when I'm Santa, and not one second before. I refuse to be a part of this."

Santa followed him for a few steps. "Klaus, if you would just—"

"I don't want to hear it."

A door slammed, and Santa winced. We all held our breath while Santa rubbed his tired eyes.

"I'm sorry about that, you three. Let's continue." He flipped a switch inside the new stairwell, and electric lights built to look like torches lit up and flickered all the way down. It was a long way.

"Down here is where we keep Kris Kringle's legacy safe." Santa led us to the bottom of the stairs, a dead end. In front of the wall was a little snow globe of the North Pole, displayed on a pedestal. Santa wrapped his fingers around the globe, and it glowed with a blue light that moved up and down, scanning his hand.

"This only recognizes someone who has been sworn in as Santa," he said, then winked. "So don't get any funny ideas about coming down here by yourself."

The blue light died, and jingle bells chimed. The stone wall rumbled and lifted, revealing a clean white corridor with indentations along the walls, each holding a different invention.

"There's the train!" Celia pointed, already running ahead of us down the hall. "And the first Big Red Suit! And his original notes on reindeer genetics! *Kris Kringle did this science and wrote it down, Ollie!*"

"Whoa!!" I said. I wasn't as excited as she was, but I knew that was the response she wanted to hear. There's nothing better than when your friends get excited about things they love. Ramp, however, was standing at the entrance wringing his hands. His face was sweaty and twisted into an uncomfortable expression.

"Are you OK?" I whispered.

"I'm fine!" he practically growled. "Let's keep moving."

"I understand how you feel," Santa said. "I was nervous, too, my first time here. It's a lot to take in. We have his notes for every invention we know of – except one."

"If we have these notes, why haven't we used them?" Celia asked. "I thought we couldn't replicate anything."

"We can't." Santa kept walking down the hall, and we followed. "Everything we have is missing something. Something crucial. Like he went through the cookbook and tore a whole page out of every recipe."

"But still, with this as a springboard—"

"Trust me, we've tried. For hundreds of years. None of our scientists can replicate anything."

I said, "Until Bertrand."

Santa gave me a confused look, which I didn't expect. "What do you mean?"

Celia looked at me, wide-eyed. *He hasn't told them? How do they not know?*

"Uh, nevermind. I just mean, I bet Bertrand could."

"Oh. Could be! Smart kid. He hasn't been talking to us lately. Losing the race got him pretty down."

Yikes. "Have you . . . uh, seen his sleigh?"

"He won't show us. Why?"

Double yikes! "No reason. Never mind."

We reached the end of the walkway – this time with a microphone in front of it.

Santa cleared his throat and said, *"Ho, ho, ho! Merry Christmas!"*

Jingle bells chimed. A robotic voice said, "SANTA RECOGNIZED. WELCOME, MATTHEW CLAUS."

"Kris Kringle actually built all this, too. Originally it was his private workshop." The wall rumbled and slid up again, revealing a simple circular room with various half-finished projects scattered around it. "Now it's mine. And one day, it will be one of yours."

Santa gestured to the centre of the room, where the Quantum Kringle floated, suspended in midair by some kind of energy coming from the ceiling and the floor. He gently plucked it from the air and held it out to us. "Would you like to touch it?"

Celia and I stared at the swirling galaxy of snow. We reached out together and rested our hands on it. It felt warm and alive. It vibrated like it was humming.

Ramp's hands were clenched into the fabric of his shirt, tugging at it too hard. He looked like he was having trouble keeping it together.

"It's OK." Santa gently nudged it toward him. "You're not going to hurt it."

Ramp reached one shaky hand out and touched it. Immediately, his body calmed down. Ramp stared deeply into it and I watched the swirling galaxy reflected in his eyes.

"It's beautiful," he said.

Santa pulled it away from us and put it back in its place, but Ramp kept his eyes on it.

"The Quantum Kringle is what makes Santa *Santa*. This is what makes Christmas possible. Without it, Santa couldn't get all around the world. We couldn't keep inspiring all those kids to make wishes, so we'd have no power. All the elves and humans at the North Pole would have to go back to living with everyone else. We wouldn't be able to do the good we do without this one thing. And it's also the only thing for which Kris Kringle left no notes. Not a single hint on how to make another one."

Santa adjusted his tie and tugged at his suit jacket. "I wanted to remind you what you're competing for. This job comes with beauty, but also centuries of responsibility and power you need to be gentle with. Imagine what havoc the Quantum Kringle could cause if it was used as a weapon! Faster-than-light travel is dangerous. Do you understand?"

Celia and I nodded. Ramp just stared.

"Good. Let's go." Santa led us back out of the little workshop, and the wall with the microphone closed behind us. He led us down the hallway and the wall with the hand scanner closed behind us. He led us up the stairs and twisted the reindeer statue, closing the stairs. No one would even know there was a hallway if they weren't looking for it.

Celia and I let out a deep breath we had both been holding. Ramp stared at the statue.

Santa continued, "Your next challenge is to prove you can use it. Santa has to travel around the world, so you have to *know* the world. All of it. Every continent, every country, every street, every chimney. You have to be able to navigate even if every computer fails. And you have to think on your feet. To that end, we're going to have a quiz competition. So study up." He gave us each a hug. "And if any of you decides this is too much for you, now is the time to back out. I want the winner to come with me on my delivery route this year, so we'll hold the final round on the morning of Christmas Eve. You have until then to decide."

"I don't meant to argue, but isn't that, maybe, a bad idea?" Celia asked. "Everyone will be doing last-minute preparations for that night, and—"

Santa grinned. "Sure, but it's dramatic, right?"

"I guess so."

He clapped his hands once. "Great. Then it's settled. I'll see you then. I've got to go talk to my son."

The elves at the door hadn't even tried to shut the main doors yet, so we walked straight outside. Ramp powered ahead of us and kept walking, not even stopping to say goodbye.

"What's up with him?" Celia asked.

I shrugged. "What's ever up with him?"

We turned and looked back at Claus Castle. It felt so big up close. Scary big. I grabbed Celia's hand and squeezed. She squeezed back. We could handle it. We could win this thing. I thought about the stick man: *You've got my support.*

My phone buzzed. It was a text message from my Mum.

Have you seen the news?

I texted back: **No???**

You need to come home. NOW.

Chapter 20

My whole family was crowded around the TV when we got back to my house. Maria Duende had a countdown on NPNN to the unveiling of a "breaking news" story about "Ollie Gnome's Shocking Secret."

I was so sick of countdowns.

"We're verifying our information currently, but if our source is telling the truth . . . Ollie Gnome might not be the elf we all thought he was. More on this story after we get a statement from Santa Claus – tonight at seven on the *North Pole Nightly News*! Available only on the North Pole News Network."

"I don't think I have a shocking secret. Do I?" I asked.

Celia shook her head. "No way. I'd know if you had a shocking secret."

My mum crossed her arms. "That's what we thought. Ollie's an open book. Still, Maria wouldn't make such a big deal out of this if it wasn't something real. Everybody at the North Pole is going to be watching this tonight."

My dad started cleaning the living room, which he always did when he was nervous. "All we can do is wait until then. No use getting all worked up." He handed Polly a plate to take to the kitchen, and she stopped on the way to give me a hug.

"I'm sorry you have a shocking secret."

"Me too, Polly."

"I made a casserole," my dad said. "It has jelly beans in it! You'll feel better after eating."

＊　＊　＊

But I didn't feel better after eating. I felt like I was going to throw up. The timer on the TV just kept ticking down to the "BREAKING NEWS" and the "SHOCKING SECRET."

"No matter who wins, no matter what happens on Maria's show, we're partners. Deal?" Celia stuck her hand up for me to shake.

I reached my hand out and shook. "Deal."

"It's coming on!" Mum said.

When Andrea's face was the first thing to appear, I knew I was in trouble. Her eyes were red, like she'd been crying, and her long hair was messy . . . but a perfect kind of messy. A lock of bright red kept falling in front of her face, but she acted like she was so emotional she didn't notice.

It would have been heartbreaking if it wasn't all a lie.

"I hate to do this," she said. "But I've thought about it for a while and I know now I have to talk about it: I lost the Next Top Nutcracker challenge, and was kicked out of the Santa Trials, because Ollie Gnome intentionally sabotaged my Santa suit."

No way.

"That's a serious accusation." Maria was making the face she made when she had to look serious but knew she was nailing a really good story. "Can you tell us how?"

"I don't know exactly how it works. But he gave me this button and said it was 'for good luck.' He was lying; the button electrocuted my suit and froze me completely, right when I was in the most danger."

This can't be happening. Seriously? Again?

"Hard to believe?" Maria Duende's face was back on-screen, looking Very Serious. "We thought so, too, until we saw for ourselves."

Footage started playing from somebody's phone camera, which clearly showed me leaving my seat and moving closer to the stage. Andrea was throwing her swords around. I pulled out the remote and very clearly looked from it, to her, and back to it. I pushed the button, and her suit immediately seized up. The swords fell all around her.

It was only a few seconds of footage because everything happened so fast. Maria made sure to slow it down for clarity. And then slow it down even more. And then play it again. And then zoom in on the remote control and mark it with a red circle, connecting that circle with an arrow to another circle surrounding Andrea falling, like a play-by-play.

"He didn't know my choreography." Andrea's voice played over the video. "He froze my suit knowing I could get hurt by the swords." She came back on screen, rubbing tears away from her eyes. "Sorry. This is hard to watch again."

"It's alright." Maria smiled and handed her a handkerchief. "Take your time."

"I kept this, to show you." She pulled the smiley-face button out of her pocket, the smile smudged by a black mark from the electricity discharge.

"Andrea, would it surprise you to know that he's used these buttons in the competition before?"

"It wouldn't surprise me at all. Nothing would, at this point. Who knows what he's capable of."

"Well, we have more footage to show you."

Now it was one of Maria's floating cameras that flew around during the race. It showed me climb the leg of Goldie's sleigh and pull the smiley button off my shirt. It showed me shove the button into the crack at the top of the leg, and the electric burst that followed. Goldie's sleigh tumbled to the ground.

"This is so stupid!" Celia yelled at the TV. "You thought it was just a regular button! And she *gave* it to you!"

But they don't know that, I thought, and curled up tighter on the couch. I tried to remember if any of my conversations with Andrea had been caught on camera, and couldn't think of any. There were no cameras in the Stable. There was no camera when she gave me the first button. Maria Duende had just stopped recording her when we talked about the second button.

"Even later in the race," Andrea continued, "he tried to completely destroy my sleigh after he had already passed me on the track."

A video played of me screaming "Jingle Bells" like a maniac while flinging the growing marbles at her sleigh. I looked furious. Scary.

When the camera cut back to Andrea, she did a cartoonish shiver. "I'm lucky I didn't get seriously injured."

"Very lucky." Maria nodded. "We've given all this information to Santa and Mrs Claus. They're with us now, live from Claus Castle. Hello, Santa?"

"Hello, Maria." The camera split to show Santa and Mrs Claus looking tired and sad at a desk together on one half of the screen, and Maria on the other.

"How are you two feeling?"

"We – " Santa choked up and rubbed his eyes.

I immediately started sobbing. My parents came and wrapped their arms around both my shoulders.

Mrs Claus rubbed Santa's back and finished the sentence. "We're disappointed. Santa and I truly believed this was a good group of kids. We couldn't imagine such direct sabotage would be occurring in a competition meant to build a better Christmas."

They hate me. I ruined everything.

"Have you reviewed the evidence?"

"We have." Mrs Claus patted Santa, who put his hands down and addressed the camera.

"Given that this behaviour was not directly covered in the rules, Andrea is still out of the competition. Her suit should have been prepared for *anything*, even electrical failure."

Maria nodded. "That seems fair. And Ollie?"

Santa took a deep breath and let it out with a long sigh. "Mrs Claus and I consider his behaviour completely against the spirit of both this competition and Christmas." He paused for a long moment. "This is hard to say, Maria. I was *just this morning* welcoming him into my home."

"I understand, Santa." Maria glanced down at the floor and shook her head. "This is difficult for all of us."

Santa cleared his throat and looked directly at the camera. At me. I could see the strain, the hurt in his eyes. *I did that. I made Santa cry.*

My whole family was dead silent, even Polly. Celia glared at the screen like she was going to burn a hole through it. It felt like a hundred years before Santa finally spoke again, and I wished it really was.

"Ollie Gnome is disqualified."

Chapter 21

The next few days were like sludge. I felt like I was sick. I couldn't leave the house without being swarmed by cameras and reporters from NPNN, but I didn't want to leave the house anyway.

I don't know how many days it was. Maybe it was a whole week. Maybe even two weeks. I would eat food when my dad brought it to me, and talk if Mum asked me to talk. Polly would bring books and make me read to her. I couldn't bear to think about what everyone was saying about me, so I didn't think at all.

Until the doorbell rang.

"Dad!" I yelled from my room. "The doorbell rang!"

Nobody answered.

"Mum??"

Nothing. The doorbell rang again.

"Polly?????"

Still nothing. I guessed they'd gone out for lunch without me. When the doorbell rang a third time, I rolled to the floor. I brought the covers down with me, so I was wrapped up like a caterpillar. I inchwormed my way along the floor to the door of my room and nudged it open with my nose.

The hallway was wider, so I was able to roll in my bundle all the way down it toward the entryway. When I got to the front door, I lifted my legs up and flicked the lock on the door with my toes. Without waiting for me to even *try* to open it the rest of the way, Celia burst in and stepped over me, carrying a huge covered tray.

"Get up!" she said, and kept walking to the kitchen.

"You left the door open," I mumbled, but didn't make any move to fix it.

"Because you have company!"

"Company?"

"That's what I said!"

I turned to look at the open door, and Buzz was standing in it with two big boxes of sodas in one arm and a box wrapped in colourful Christmas wrapping paper in the other.

"Oh, hey, Ollie." Buzz stepped over me and headed to the kitchen as well. "What are you doing on the floor?"

"What are *you* doing in my house?" I responded. He didn't answer, and suddenly Bertrand was in the doorway. I sat up but didn't unwrap the covers.

Bertrand was wearing one of his signature bow ties and smiling real big. "Where do I put these?" he asked, and held up a basket of cupcakes with one hand. "Or this?" He held up a very tiny wrapped box in the other.

"That depends," I answered, "on what is even going on right now."

"We're in here, Bertrand!" Celia called from the kitchen.

"Marvellous." He squeezed around me and kept walking.

Sally was in the doorway now, pizza boxes in one hand and a

book in the other. She didn't even look up from the book, just walked past me to the kitchen.

"Hey, wait, what are you—"

I stood up and started to follow her.

"Oh, cool. You're doing, like, a cocoon thing? That's cool. Cocoons are pretty deep." Kurt was in the doorway now with a box of donuts and a wrapped cylinder. "The donuts are actually in this one," he said, shaking the wrapped box. "I thought it would be funny."

"It's totally funny!" I said, because it was. "But, uh, why did you bring donuts?"

Kurt laughed and walked to the kitchen. In the doorway now was a wrapped box that Gadzooks rose out of, carrying a tray of poached eggs and an even larger wrapped box.

"How did you fit that box in that box?" I asked. "How did you fit *you* in that box?"

"Oh, hush. This day is for celebration!" She looked me up and down. "You're hardly dressed for the occasion. We'll have to fix that." She bumped into me as she walked toward the kitchen.

I reached to grab the box from the doorway, but the box was gone. I realized my hands weren't restricted by the blanket, so I looked down. I was wearing a tuxedo. I touched my hair, and it was washed and gelled. I coughed and felt something stuck in my throat. I coughed a few more times, stuck my hand in my mouth, and drew out a feather. *Got me again, Gadzooks.*

No one appeared for a few seconds, so I started to close the door. A wrinkly hand stopped it from shutting and pushed it back open.

"This is how you treat your guests?" Ramp grumbled. "Slam the door in their faces?"

"Sorry, Ramp. I didn't mean to—"

"Yeah, yeah, yeah." He wasn't carrying anything but started pushing past me anyway. "I heard there was a party. Where's the grub?"

"A *party*???" I said it all surprised, even though I had basically figured that out by now. The door shut this time, and I followed Ramp into the kitchen. "For what?"

Food was now piled all over the counters in the kitchen. The dining room table had a bunch of wrapped boxes piled high on it.

"Don't tell me you forgot!" Celia put her hands on her hips and smirked at me.

"Forgot what?"

"It's December 11th! Exactly two weeks before Christmas!" She grabbed her covered tray and walked to the centre of the room. Kurt, who had apparently brought his guitar, strummed a chord.

Everybody sang, *"Happy—"*

"Wait one second!" Kurt interrupted. He plucked at a string and tuned it up a little. "OK, now." He played the chord again.

"Happy birthday to you!" Celia lifted the tall cover off of her tray and revealed a cake decorated like a little North Pole.

"Happy birthday to you!" Little toy elves lit the candles, and little cars drove around the North Pole streets. Claus Castle lit up and sparkled.

"Happy birthday, dear Ollie . . ." A little elf – *who looked just like me!!* – shot a little tiny firework and waved.

"Happy birthday to you!"

"The big one-two! Make a wish!" Celia said.

I leaned over and blew out the candles. I wished for the same thing I always wished for: *I wish for this Christmas to be the Best*

Christmas Ever . . . even though that seems unlikely. Especially because that seems unlikely.

Everybody cheered, and I was very embarrassed. "I can't believe I forgot my birthday!"

Before anyone could say anything, something heavy slammed into our back door, rattling the whole house. I glanced around at the other guests, and they all seemed surprised, too. Slowly, I crept over to the back door and grabbed the doorknob. I cracked it open.

"Happy birthday, Ollie! Sorry we're late!" It was Crasher, scrambling back to standing. Behind her, Snoozer, Truther, Rocker, Slammer, Jammer, and all three members of Treason 4 the Season were gently landing my empty sleigh on the ground in our backyard.

"We wanted to make sure we brought her!" Crasher motioned with her nose at H.O.R.S.E. while they unhooked from the sleigh.

"HAPPY BIRTHHORSE!" H.O.R.S.E. whinnied.

"Jet fuel can't melt birthdays," Truther mumbled as the reindeer walked inside.

"Thanks, I think?"

Over the next hour, more and more people rang the doorbell. Luther came, and his jacket shone *HAPPY BIRTHDAY, JERK.* Chef came and brought his own grill to cook reindeer nuggets for everybody. The stick man and his buddies from the castle door all came. Mum, Dad and Polly eventually came back, too. It was a huge group, and they were all there to see me!

"The only people who think you did it are the ones who don't know you," Buzz told me. "That's the kind of thing *I* would do. But not you."

"Still, I'm sorry I let you down, Buzz. You gave up to let us win!"

"I don't want to be in charge, doofus." He flicked my nose and made me laugh. "Don't get me wrong: I am very strong and smart and cool. But I didn't want to win."

"And now I can't."

"The way I see it" – Sally crunched on a nacho and didn't look up from her book, titled *How to Talk to People at Parties* – "you and Celia have always been a team, right? It doesn't matter who wins."

"That's what I said!" Celia hugged my shoulders and handed me some fruit punch. "We're partners."

"Dad's not going to change his mind." Kurt was setting up Treason's instruments for an impromptu show. "We tried talking to him, but he's a pretty stubborn dude."

"But now Celia has to win." Bertrand was hanging out with H.O.R.S.E., who we had disconnected from the sleigh and set on the table. "And she can't win without you."

"TWO HORSES ARE BETTER THAN ONE."

"We all present presents to participate in your perfect pal practice parties." Gadzooks waved at the pile of gifts.

Bertrand laughed. "She means this is all stuff to help you study."

Buzz grinned and posed. "Most of us will be busy preparing for Christmas, but we wanted to help. So we all brought something."

"I didn't." Ramp crunched on some hard candies. "Because I wasn't *actually* invited."

Sally held up *How to Talk to People at Parties*. "Do you need to borrow this, Ramp?"

Ramp's eyes glinted. "Cheeky!"

I loved hearing all my friends laugh. *It's gonna be OK*, I thought.

Chapter 22

"You brought two presents each for brothers Mozart and Beethoven. When you arrive at their house, however, there's a new baby we didn't know about. What do you do?"

Celia thought for a second. "Take one present from each of them for the baby. They can't stay mad at it; it's a baby."

Buzz's present was a kind of flare gun that could build and shoot fireworks. I fired a tiny one that spelled out *I'M SO IMPRESSED!* in bright green lights.

"OK, next one." I flipped to a random page in the giant *Santa Manual*. Sally said Celia had no chance of winning without a copy, so it was her gift.

"You go into the apartment of a married couple with two kids. They have a stocking up for their dog. What do you put in it?"

"Nothing. It's a dog."

I fired the red firework that said *SORRY DUDE!*

"It's amazing and beautiful that they love their dog so much," I explained. "Put one of your emergency dog treats in the stocking."

"But what if I run out? Without those treats, a dog could wake up a whole family!"

"Bring a lot of treats, I guess."

H.O.R.S.E., who was still sitting on our dining room table, lit up her eyes. "INSTALLATION HORSEPLETE." A tiny compartment opened in her metal neck, and a flash drive spat out. That was Bertrand's gift: a copy of the entire up-to-date Naughty/Nice database.

"It's a lot of data, but you might be able to use it for something," he had said at the party. "Klaus will have access to it, so it's only fair."

It was the day before Christmas Eve, though, and it had taken H.O.R.S.E. the full two weeks to download everything. *So much for that.*

"She could at least update our map," Celia said. "I can study her updates tonight. You should get some sleep."

I interrupted my own yawn to laugh. "No one's sleeping tonight," I said. "It's the night before the night before Christmas. Everyone else is at The Workshop, even Santa. I'm not going to leave you alone now. We just need to get energized."

I pushed the only button on Kurt's gift – a cube only a few inches tall. "Play a fun song."

"Grandma Got Run Over by a Reindeer" started playing, and I felt like I was trapped in a nightmare.

"A different song." It switched to something else upbeat and dancey.

"I figured you'd need a good study soundtrack," Kurt had said. "So I got you *every song*. It gets way louder than it looks like it would, too."

My phone and Celia's phone buzzed at the same time. I checked mine first.

"It's an email to everybody in The Workshop." My voice rose in pitch as I read further down the message. *"Asking if anyone knows where Santa is???"*

Celia was reading now, too. "He's missed four inspections, starting two hours ago. Last seen at the Stable. Mrs Claus is safe, but she has to stay with the Wish Generator to make sure it doesn't malfunction tonight, since we're using so much power to finish preparations."

"We have to help. The whole North Pole can't take a break right now, even to find him."

Celia nodded. "I won't be able to focus on studying now, anyway."

We threw on our coats and shoes and headed outside.

"I'll start looking in town and check what's happening at The Workshop," she said. "You check the Stable and Claus Castle, deal?"

"Deal." We took off running in opposite directions. I pulled out my phone, found Crasher in my contacts, and dialled.

She answered immediately. "'Sup, Cap'n?"

"Are you at the stable?"

"Nope. I'm helpin' get the Big Nine ready for tomorrow night. It's borin', you know, but important. They don't ask just anybody to do it. Life-or-death stuff."

"Oh. I was going to ask for your help finding Santa, but if you're busy—"

"Are you kidding? That sounds *way* more fun. I'll be right there. Sorry, XII!"

"You really don't have t—" The phone went dead. *Cool.*

I turned a corner on the edge of town and could finally see the whole Stable, all four glass towers even prettier at night thanks to lights shining out of the dome. I paused for a second to admire how beautiful it was, and Crasher slammed into my back.

"Sorry, Cap'n!" she yelled, not slowing down at all.

I was tossed up and over her head, on to her back. I wrapped my arms around her neck, and she lifted us up toward a tower entrance.

"What's goin' on?" she yelled over the wind.

"Santa's missing!" I yelled back. "He had a meeting with Dreamer before he disappeared!"

"Got it." Crasher didn't set me down when we reached the tower like before – she just yelled "DUCK!" and flew down the spiral stairs at lightning speed. I squeezed my eyes closed so I wouldn't think about how much it would hurt if we crashed into one of the walls.

We burst through the entrance, and Crasher tried to slow down before heading straight toward a clump of trees. I reached my arms up and grabbed a branch, pulling myself off her before she tumbled into the trees and flopped on to the tall grass between them.

"That was amazin'!" she yelled.

I let go and dropped to the ground – right in front of Maria Duende.

"Hi, Maria." I tried not to sound angry.

"Why are you here, Ollie Gnome?" She thrust a microphone in front of my face.

"I'm trying to find out what happened to Santa."

"Is that true—"

"Yes."

"—or are you *returning to the scene of the crime*?" In her excitement, she pushed the microphone too far and crumpled my nose.

I stepped back in surprise, and she gasped. "Seems I've caught you off guard! Weren't expecting to be seen through so quickly?"

"I definitely didn't kidnap Santa," I said, irritated that this was even being suggested. "And I didn't sabotage Andrea, either. Everyone knows that but you."

Maria paused, and after a moment motioned for Seyi to turn off her camera.

"We came here to interview Dreamer, but he won't see me. He likes you, right? He gave you reindeer."

"Uh, I wouldn't say that he *likes* me. But I think I know how to talk to him."

Crasher was finally fully upright and off the ground – we left Maria and walked through the Stable, which had a much different feel than it had the last time I'd been there. Fewer reindeer were around; many were probably at the takeoff zone helping Santa's team, the Big Nine, get ready. The rest were mostly sticking to the ground and talking in hushed tones. They watched me and Crasher pass by and whispered things about us.

It's already spreading, I thought. *They're worried about Christmas.*

Crasher waited at the entrance to Dreamer's grove, and I held my breath as I walked through the tree tunnel.

"Why did the chicken cross the playground?" Dreamer's gentle, regal voice began before I had crossed all the way into the clearing. I looked around; it was hard to spot him with his voice coming from everywhere. Eventually I found him, floating up high, reading a book nestled between branches on a tree.

"Dreamer, Santa's missing, and this was—"

"To get to the other slide." He turned and looked me directly in the eyes from way above. His face didn't move at all. "Ha."

"Is that . . . a joke book?"

"I requested one after our last meeting. I hated yours, of course, but I saw the potential."

"Uh . . . great! I'm glad you're enjoying them."

"Yes." He floated down and stared at me with his huge reindeer eyes. Nothing about his expression shifted even a little bit. "They are hilarious. For example: What happens when you cross a vampire . . . with a snowman?"

I knew this one. "Frostbite!"

Dreamer reared back in the air and glared down his nose at me. "You interrupted me."

"Sorry, I mean, 'What?'"

"Frostbite. Ha. Ha. Ha. Now hurry up and explain why you're here. I don't have time to talk to all of you."

"All of us?"

"Yes. Complainer was here, then the Great Gift-Giver himself, and then Pesterer, the one who is like a fly, always buzzing those cameras in places she doesn't belong. And now you. Must I entertain every two-leg tonight?"

"'Complainer'?"

Dreamer shook his antlers and caught a falling ornament fruit in his mouth. "Yes, your friend. I believe you gave him that name."

So Ramp came to the stable.

"What did he want?"

"He told me Gift-Giver sent him to borrow three extra reindeer. I gave him the same three he used in the race. I mentioned it to Gift-Giver when he arrived for our formal meeting, and he knew nothing about it. You are such poor communicators."

"Do you know where he went after he left you?"

"Of course not."

So that was it. I bowed, said thank you, and left. I didn't tell Maria about Ramp – I didn't want her to broadcast anything until we had all the facts. I hopped on Crasher's back, and we set off toward Claus Castle.

I checked the time on my phone – past midnight. As I was putting it back in my pocket, I got a text from Celia. **Ramp's sleigh is gone. It's not in The Workshop.**

He has reindeer, too, I sent back. **Santa told us to think about whether we really wanted it. Maybe he's quitting?**

Maybe. No sign of Santa?

Nope. Just now getting to Claus Castle.

Crasher skid along the snow in front of the main doors, spraying snow all over the stick man, who had been snoozing on a stool.

"Oh no." He looked around, eyes wide. "I've been working more shifts lately – and I didn't get much sleep last night – and—"

"It's OK, sti – wait, what's your name?"

"Karl Kobold."

"Karl. Did you know Santa's missing?"

His hands drifted up to his face, and he pushed his features around in surprise. *"What?!"*

"How long have you been asleep?"

"I don't know. I haven't seen anybody, but – " He looked at the time on his watch and his face drained all its colour. "A long time. I think the answer is a very long time. *Oh no. What have I done?? Santa is missing, and it's my fault!!!!"*

"It's OK. Calm down. I know where we should check."

"I'll wait out here, Cap'n." Crasher glanced around nervously.

"In case Santa comes back. I'm not really into spooky castles, ya know?"

I walked to one of the side doors, and Karl followed. Claus Castle *was* a lot spookier in the dark. It was old, and the walls were covered with paintings that seemed to move in the shadows. Even the plush carpet felt too squishy and weird to be safe.

"Ramp?" I called. Nobody answered. "Santa?"

"Even the kids are out," Karl told me. "Bertrand is with his mum, Sally's at The Workshop . . . who knows, with the older boys. How long has he been missing?"

"Almost three hours."

Karl nodded. "We can't even call an official emergency yet. He could just be off working on his sleigh somewhere and thought we knew about it."

"Maybe." I got to the reindeer statue on the staircase and turned it ninety degrees. The stairs folded up and revealed the *other* stairs, but the hole was so dark I couldn't see the bottom.

"Here you go." Karl handed me a big, heavy torch that felt like a club. "Everybody on the security team's got one of these."

"Thanks." I clicked it on and pointed the light into the hole. Stone stairs, scurrying spiders, the hand-scanner snow globe, and—

Oh no.

Curled at the bottom was a body with no suit and a very jolly face.

❄ ❄ ❄

"He's asleep." Celia checked his pulse and breath. "He's even snoring a little bit. Why haven't you guys turned on the lights yet?"

"Oh, right." Karl sheepishly crossed over the carpet to the door and flicked a switch, lighting the big electric chandelier and several smaller lights around the main hall. With the lights on, Santa was obviously breathing – his body was moving up and down.

"We shouldn't tell Maria yet." Celia gently shifted Santa into a more comfortable position. "Everyone will panic."

"*I'm* panicking!" I whisper-yelled. "What are we going to do about Christmas?"

Celia smacked Santa's face gently. "Santa, wake up. Wake *up*, Santa."

Santa just kept snoring.

"Hopefully he'll wake up by Christmas. Karl, could you call any Secret Helpers to carry him to his bed?"

Karl nodded and walked away to say something into a walkie-talkie. Celia and I decided to investigate farther into the secret hallway.

"The walls were already up when we got here, so someone's been back here," Celia observed. "Santa's the only one who can open the doors, though. So did someone follow him in, knock him out, and then drag him all the way back down the hallway just to leave him there? That doesn't make sense."

Celia walked ahead to the next room and froze in the doorway. "The Quantum Kringle is gone. And this room is a wreck. Everything's been thrown around everywhere."

We immediately ran back down the hallway, where two Secret Helpers were lifting Santa up and carrying him toward the master bedroom.

"So someone took the Kringle and Santa's clothes, and then left. But they either dragged Santa back to the stairs for no reason, or Santa let them in himself and they waited to knock him out until they were on their way back out."

"What if it was Klaus?" I asked. "I don't want to believe it, but . . . maybe he was worried he wouldn't win. He's been really mad at Santa lately, too."

"Or Andrea. I wouldn't put anything past her at this point."

"Or anyone else who lost the competition and doesn't think they should have." I put my face in my hands. "My head hurts."

"It's not going to do any good to keep guessing. I wish there were *cameras*."

Karl gasped and whirled around. "There *are*!"

"Wait – really?"

"Of course there are! I'm sorry I didn't think of it already. Look!" He pointed to a corner inside the stairwell, where a little metallic glint shone inside all the stone. "I mean, this is *where Santa lives*. He's got the best security team in the business! Even the secret rooms have cameras."

Karl led us outside and walked us around the back of the castle. He looked around the snow until he found what he was looking for – fake clay snow blending in with the real stuff. He pushed down on the snow twice, and it rose up, revealing a hatch in the ground. We all jumped down.

It was a room small enough that we three elves were cramped standing in it together. Lots of monitors were all over the walls, showing live camera feeds of every inch of Claus Castle.

"Somebody comes in and reviews the footage every day just in case, but we haven't had a real security issue in . . . well, ever. Only real excitement we get is Kurt sneaking out at night." Karl rotated us so that he was in front of the large keyboard, and he hit a few buttons to pull up the entrance to Claus Castle, where Karl was snoozing on the stool. "And I'll rewind until we see something." He pressed an arrow key, and the video started rewinding. Nothing happened for a while – so much so that it was practically a still image – until we saw a blip of something exit the castle backwards and walk up to Karl. It happened too fast to understand, so he played it more slowly.

Karl was awake. A figure totally covered in a hood and cloak walked directly up to him, held out a bundle of sticks, and shook them in Karl's face. He immediately fell asleep.

"It wasn't your fault!" I said. "They put you to sleep!"

"I smiled like I knew him, too. But I don't remember that at all." He pushed a button that switched to a camera over the main hall.

The cloaked person twisted the reindeer statue, opening the stairway. At the bottom of the stairway was the hand-recognizing snow globe – he put his hand over it, and it glowed with a blue light. After the scan was complete, the wall rose off the ground.

Celia frowned. "Santa said it only recognized Santas, though."

"Could it be Santa's dad? The last Santa?"

"I think he's still in California. But maybe."

The cloaked person walked down the white hallway to the microphone. He took a deep breath and said something, causing the door to open. He walked through.

"Wait a second. Go back."

Karl rewound a few seconds.

"Is there sound?" Celia asked.

"Yeah. Let me just . . ." Karl pushed a few buttons and clicked on a speaker. "That should do it."

Now we could hear the figure take a deep breath. He yelled in his best booming voice:

"Ho, ho, ho! Merry Christmas!"

Jingle bells chimed. A robotic voice said: "SANTA RECOGNIZED. WELCOME, KRISTOPHER KRINGLE."

"WHAT????" I yelled.

"WHAT????" Celia yelled at the same time.

"WHAT????" Karl was also yelling, I think. It was very loud in that tiny room.

"Maybe we heard it wrong." Celia reached over him and rewound a little.

The robotic voice said, "WELCOME, KRISTOPHER KRINGLE."

Karl, apparently in shock, pressed rewind over and over.

"KRISTOPHER KRINGLE. KRISTOPHER KRINGLE. KRISTOPHER KRINGLE."

"Kris is short for Kristopher?" I mumbled.

"OF COURSE IT'S SHORT FOR KRISTOPHER!" Celia shouted. "THE REAL ISSUE HERE IS THAT KRIS KRINGLE HAS BEEN DEAD FOR CENTURIES!"

"I know!" I huffed. "I was just surprised, is all."

Celia tried to pace but the room was too small, so she just circled in place. Karl clicked for the video feed to keep going. *Kris Kringle, I guess*, walked into the private workshop and went straight for the Quantum Kringle. He grabbed it, tossed it between both hands, then lifted it up into the air.

The snow galaxy within spun and grew until the snow started pouring out of the Kringle and whipping around the room. The snow created a strong wind that knocked papers on to the floor and tables over sideways. After just a few seconds, the whole room was the wreck Celia had seen a few minutes before.

"Can it do that? Did we know it could do that?"

Celia shook her head. "I've never heard about this. Santa said it was only an engine."

The wind, too, pushed the cloak away from *Kris Kringle???*'s body. At first it looked like a normal, thin body shape, like that of an old man. Below the waist, though, were thick furry legs with the knee bent the wrong way. At the ground, instead of feet, they ended in cloven hooves with sharp, curved claws.

As the snow shrunk and returned to the globe – which had no visible cracks anywhere we could see – the figure's hood was blown back, too, and we saw first tiny pointed horns on the top of a bald head . . . and a long white beard on a face that looked a lot like the Kris Kringle portrait.

"Ramp!" I yelled. "It *is* Ramp!"

A few seconds later, Ramp was back at the entrance, where Santa had just entered to investigate. Ramp waved the bundle of sticks, and this time a cloud of some kind of sleeping powder was visible as it settled over Santa's face. Santa fell to the ground, and Ramp twisted the Kringle in his fingers. Snow encircled Santa and Ramp, and when it dissipated, Ramp was wearing Santa's Big Red Suit and Santa was wearing long johns. Other than the little horns and feet, Ramp could have been *the* Kris Kringle.

"We have to go." I turned and pushed the hatch open, slipping on the snow as I dragged myself out of the hole on all fours. "He took a sleigh, reindeer *and* the Kringle. He's leaving. We need to – we need to tell someone, or stop him, or—"

Celia ran after me and grabbed me, which I was glad about

because I didn't really know where I was going. "There's no way we can catch him now. We need a plan."

I nodded, and tried to swallow my fear. *How was Ramp also Kris Kringle? Why was he stealing the Quantum Kringle? Why did no one tell me Kris was short for Kristopher? What if Christmas is over?* I felt like I was going to faint, but I focused and fought through it.

"I'll call our friends." I pulled out my phone.

"Which friends?"

"All of them. Everybody."

Celia nodded. "Tell them to meet us by the takeoff zone. I'll meet you there. I'm going to work on a plan."

"But the last trial!" I said. "You have to be there in just a few hours! You need to study and sleep."

Celia made a face at me that said, *Come on, dude.* "It kinda seems like we need to save Christmas, right?"

"Right, you're right. That's way more important. Let's *for sure* save Christmas."

Chapter 23

A few hours later and all my friends were assembled in a hangar near the takeoff zone. It was like my birthday party, except Ramp wasn't there, and no one was happy, and *it was nothing like my birthday party but it calmed me down to think about it like that, OK?* Thunder rumbled outside, because of course it was a stormy situation.

Celia arrived last, wearing her Santa suit like the rest of us who had them. "Did everyone bring what Ollie and I asked for?"

The group collectively turned from our long conference table and nodded.

"Great. Karl, tell them what you told me."

Karl stood up and clicked a button on a remote – a big TV someone had wheeled in clicked on and started playing a regular human news story somewhere in America. The headline read *SANTA PRANK? Sleigh spotted flying through the air above local neighbourhood.*

"About an hour ago, Ramp was spotted in Bellville, California."

He clicked the remote, and the news changed to a different station in America. "A few minutes later, this aired in Huntington, West Virginia."

EVIL SANTA INTERRUPTS ANNUAL COMEDY GATH-ERING.

He clicked quickly through several more. "He's already been to Warsaw in Poland, to Kabul in Afghanistan, to Trondheim in Norway, to Abuja in Nigeria . . . he doesn't seem to be following any particular pattern. And the humans are starting to put it together that something is wrong. I wasn't sure what he was doing, but then I saw this interview." He clicked again.

A little girl about Polly's age was crying on a German news station. Subtitles translated for us. "I wrote a letter to Santa asking for my goldfish to be able to talk. Santa came and used magic . . . and now my fish only says mean things!" The little girl lifted a goldfish bowl up in front of the camera.

A big bubble floated out of the fish's mouth, and when it popped at the top of the water, it said, "Your favourite movie is actually not very good." Another bubble popped. *"Those* shoes, with *that* scarf?"

"I'm not even wearing a scarf!" the girl cried.

H.O.R.S.E. whinnied. "HORSE-REFERENCED WITH WISH DATABASE. RAMP IS TARGETING AREAS WITH RECENT POWERFUL WISHES."

"Exactly." Bertrand nodded. "And look at the headline."

KRAMPUS GREIFT AN!

"Krampus?" I frowned. "I thought that was a myth."

Kurt laughed. "Yeah, and a lot of the world thinks *we're* a myth. Not for long, though."

"He's using the Quantum Kringle in *broad daylight* some places." Sally tapped her fingernails nervously on the table. "There are going to be a lot of questions."

"I have one: Why is he doing this?" Buzz wasn't even sitting down, he was so anxious. He'd even brought his axe and had it resting over his broad shoulders. "I thought he was just some harmless old dude trying to be the next Santa."

"I know why." Everyone turned and looked at Bertrand. "Well, I don't know *why* why, but I get what he's trying to do." He adjusted his bow tie and looked at the table, obviously uncomfortable with everyone staring at him. "The Wish Generator only works because those kids were making wishes. If he convinces enough people that Santa is going to *ruin* their wishes, and they tell their friends, and *those* friends tell *their* friends . . ."

"No one wishes at all." I put my head in my hands. "And if the Wish Generator doesn't work—"

"Then it's not just this Christmas that will be ruined. We use too much energy for traditional sources, like fossil fuels. The North Pole would have to shut down. Our inventions wouldn't work. We'd all have to move back into the real world."

The reindeer shifted uncomfortably. Crasher flattened her ears. "The Stable takes care of us with that energy. We'd have to go back to bein' wild animals. I don't think I could do that."

"Well, luckily I've got some good news." Celia tapped some buttons on her laptop and changed the TV screen to a map of the world with a bright red dot zipping around it, pausing for a moment before taking off again. "He took a sleigh I made, which means we can track it."

"How do you catch the old fogey, though?" Frank and her brothers were standing in the corner, like they weren't sure whether to trust us yet. "Nothin's as fast as the Kringle."

"I actually have an idea." Celia grinned. I was jealous she could find something to be excited about; we hadn't even started, and I already felt like we'd lost. The red dot on the screen was zipping all over the place – how were we supposed to compete with that?

"Bertrand," Celia continued, "did you bring your wish engine?"

"Yeah, but . . . you saw how it worked in the race. There's no way we could reach light speed on our own."

"You won't be on your own." Buzz started smiling as he figured out Celia's plan. "We could get everybody at the North Pole wishing."

Bertrand seemed less convinced. "I could work with my mum to see if we could transmit some wishes to you . . . but still, I don't know how fast we could get. The Kringle goes faster than light without breaking a sweat."

"For now, we should focus on trying to stop Ramp from doing any more damage to Santa's reputation." Celia was already grabbing Bertrand's engine and hooking it into my sleigh. "I think we should chase him, fix what he breaks, and deliver presents as we go."

"You want to deliver presents on Christmas Eve? During the day?" Sally crossed her arms and leaned back in her chair. "Are you sure that's a good idea?"

"I don't think we have a choice." I was starting to get pumped, too, the more I understood. "He's already pulled us into the spotlight. We have to make the best of it."

"And this will be quite a laborious activity, for we are good pals but not trained Santas." Gadzooks, who had been watching quietly with owls on either shoulder, finally chimed in. "More time is an *exemplary* idea."

"Great." Celia stood at the head of the table in her Big Red Suit, looking like she belonged in charge. It was awesome. "Karl and Bertrand have to stay behind as support, which leaves me, Ollie, Kurt, Sally, the triplets, Gadzooks and Buzz."

"The Big Nine only work with Santa." Rocker looked around at the other reindeer. "I think I speak for all of us when I say we'd be happy to help."

Slammer, Jammer and Treason 4 the Season all nodded silently. Snoozer snored in an affirmative way, and Truther flicked her tinfoil hat with her ears while darting her eyes around the room nervously, which I guess was as close to agreement as she would get.

"We'll be the Little Nine." Crasher snorted. "I'll take lead, like before."

Slammer didn't argue, and all of us seemed to be in agreement.

"Great." Celia gestured to our sleighs, which were already connected. "I built a replacement sleigh to connect to Ollie's, so we'll all fit. It looks like we're ready to go."

"Not quite yet."

My face turned red at the voice. The whole room turned and looked behind me at the hangar entrance, but I already knew who it was.

Andrea walked over to the table, putting her red hair in a knot on top of her head and sticking her Santa hat over it. "I want to help."

Lightning struck, and thunder rumbled. The whole table looked to me. I still couldn't make eye contact with her.

She sighed. "For real this time. I promise."

There was another long silent pause while I thought about all the different things I wanted to say. I settled on:

"Cool. *Cool* coolcool. That's cool, except, I think it probably isn't, because it seemed like it was for real *every time*? And all those times you were lying, which was pretty not cool. So it is probably safer for us to assume that this isn't cool, either. Probably not even a little, if that makes sense? Maybe not at all. I'm thinking most likely not at all."

"Ollie means no." Celia stared Andrea down. "Why would we trust you?"

"I only lied about Ollie because Klaus promised a home for my family at the North Pole. If the North Pole shuts down, none of it matters."

"And if Celia isn't even going to the trial, Klaus wins by default." Buzz shrugged. "It makes sense."

Myrle spat on the ground. "Doesn't sound fair to me. We're the ones tryin' to save Christmas out here while he's ignorin' all our phone calls."

Bertrand shook his head. "We didn't know Ramp was evil. What if she's trying to ruin Christmas, too?"

"She's telling the truth about the deal with Klaus." Sally looked at me apologetically. "He was bragging about it the other day."

"Celia and I would have helped you," I said quietly. "And we wouldn't have made you do anything."

"Well, now I know." Andrea looked at her watch. "Clock's ticking, though."

"I vote no." Celia looked at me. "But you get one and a half votes."

It didn't take me long to decide. "You can come. But everyone here heard you admit you lied. So after we save Christmas, you have to tell everybody else."

"Deal. Can we get a move on now?"

All of us split from the conference table and prepared for the day. Sally took the harpoon gun from her sleigh and attached it to ours. Buzz fit his giant wheels on to it in case we had to traverse more difficult terrain. I called Karl and told him to spread the word, and the rest of us went to gather toys from The Workshop's warehouse.

"Mum said to let you use The Bag," Bertrand explained while we headed down into the basement levels of The Workshop. "It's down here with the toys." The door opened, and Bertrand led me to an unassuming cloth bag hanging on a peg on the wall. "It looks old, but it's tough. It goes around your shoulder like this." He wrapped its ropey cord around one of my shoulders so The Bag rested against my hip.

I squeezed it, and it felt like there was nothing inside it at all. Bertrand took a huge dollhouse – one of the haunted ones I had made myself – and pushed it into The Bag, which opened wider than it looked like it would. He cinched it closed, and it still felt like there was nothing in it. He reached his hand back in, said, "Dollhouse," and showed me that he could pull the dollhouse back out.

"I've always wondered how it works," I said as everyone who came with us started grabbing toys and loading them into The Bag. "Is it, like, some kind of dimensional portal with a rudimentary AI that can hear what you ask it to find?"

Bertrand paused and looked at me, surprised. "I thought Celia was the science one."

"I design toys, too. I know stuff. Celia just knows *more* stuff, and learns it faster. I'm more about making things fun, and pretty."

"Well, you're right. The Bag was one of Kris Kringle's inventions, so we don't totally understand it, but that's the best I've come up with, too. You can be as general as you want with it; it's smart. Also, don't be afraid to ask it for things we didn't put in there. You never know what might have got left behind."

The triplets, Kurt and Gadzooks started making it a game – throwing huge toys at me to catch with The Bag. It never got any heavier, even when loaded full of thousands of presents. *Amazing.* It was slow going on our own, though, and a bunch of elves who worked in the warehouse helped us fill it just like they would have with Santa.

Bertrand split with us to meet Mrs Claus at the Wish Generator. Back at the hangar, we all piled into the sleigh, and Celia hit a few buttons to start the engine powering up.

Bertrand spoke on our SweetTooth headsets. "Alright. Karl's got a crowd of North Pole residents gathering outside to start making wishes. Make sure your personal gravity field is on – otherwise you could all get knocked out by the g-force. I'm locking on to the portable generator . . . you should receive a burst of energy starting . . . now!"

The sleigh sputtered and jostled, but the engine didn't kick all the way on.

"One second – Mum's checking my maths." Bertrand covered the microphone with his hand, but we could still hear his muffled voice. "I'm telling you, I looked at it! All the numbers are *exactly, perfectly* . . . oh, you're right. I did miss that. Thanks, Mum." His hand moved away from the microphone. "OK, get ready. It should really work . . . *now*."

The sleigh sped forward so fast the reindeer team had trouble keeping up. Thunder rumbled, and we would have been drenched if the personal gravity field didn't have the added benefit of deflecting the droplets.

Celia checked the map. "Looks like he's in San José, Costa Rica. We'll head there first."

I didn't know what light speed looked like, but this definitely wasn't it. We were flying fast – so fast it was hard to focus on the ground. But I could still comprehend what was going on.

"Where's the music?" Kurt leaned over and pushed his music box, which he had installed into the dashboard. "I've got the perfect song for this." The box started playing "Play This Song While You're Saving Christmas," one of LDB's biggest hits from his first album. It was OK; his new album was better.

We arrived at a house on the outskirts of San José just in time to see a crackle of light and vanishing snow in the space where Ramp was. A girl was crying from atop a huge pile of books in her yard. Our onboard computer translated her Spanish so I could understand what she was saying.

"I wished for new books, and Santa gave me two hundred copies of this boring book *The Fountainhead*!"

"HORSE RECOGNIZED: SOFIA VILLALOBOS. PRESENT: *AN ILLUSTRATED HISTORY OF MONSTER TRUCKS*."

"That wasn't Santa. That was a bad guy." I reached into The Bag and handed her the book. "Don't ever stop making wishes."

She stopped crying and hugged it. "Thank you, little Santas. My favourite is when Gravedigger CRUSHES the competition on *SUNDAY, SUNDAY, SUNDAY.*" She had a very good scary announcer voice.

I opened The Bag and scooped all the copies of *The Fountainhead* into it, then hopped back on to the sleigh.

"Now what? Do we deliver presents here?"

"I believe I may be of assistance!" Gadzooks flourished a plastic wand and whistled. Within moments, a huge flock of all different kinds of birds was flapping above us. "Kindly throw them the presents, Ollie!"

I stuck my hand in The Bag and said, "San José presents!" One by one they appeared in my hand, and one by one I flung them up into the crowd of birds. One or several would catch each present and then fly off to the address H.O.R.S.E. called out.

Celia asked, "Could that work while we're flying, Gadzooks?"

"Absolutely, my dear friend!" she answered. "There are birds to help us everywhere."

"Ramp – I mean, Krampus? – is moving *so fast*. It looks like he's in . . . Atlanta, Georgia." Celia kicked on the engine, and we took off again.

I held The Bag upside down off the side of the sleigh and yelled, "PRESENTS BELOW US!" As we flew north into the United States, presents streamed out of The Bag and were caught by birds to be dropped down the right chimneys or left on the right porches. It must have looked *very strange* to normal humans – getting their presents not just early, but from birds. I tried not to worry about it, or worry about all the attention we were going to get when we made stops. *Right now we just have to catch Ramp. The rest can come later.*

This time Celia stopped us several floors up by an apartment building. Ramp was already gone, but I could see a teenage boy inside staring at a video on an old computer and looking petrified. I knocked on the window, and he opened the door.

"Who are you?"

"We're Santa. Sort of."

"That man with the big horns said *he* was Santa."

BIG horns? What? "Well, he lied. What did he do?"

"I wrote a letter to Santa – I didn't even really know for sure there was *one* Santa – and asked to be famous. That guy with the horns came in and did something to my computer. Now this video of me farting in public is *everywhere*."

Kurt snorted. "That's awesome."

"It's *not* awesome!"

"It's all about perspective, bro." Kurt reached into The Bag and said, "Laptop." He pulled out a fancy new laptop and handed it to the teenager. "Farts are funny. There's sound-editing software on this – auto-tune your toots into a song or something. And don't take yourself so seriously."

The teenager took the laptop and stared at Kurt. "Uh, thanks. I guess you're right."

"No prob." Kurt winked and turned back to Celia. "We're done here."

Near London there was a boy with a star-shaped scar on his forehead sitting on a street where every house looked just like every other house.

"I wanted to get away from my evil aunt and uncle, so I wished for a letter from a magical school. Santa gave me this!" The boy showed us a very polite rejection letter from a nearby boarding school for sorcerers.

"Oh, I went to that school! I was spelledictorian!" Gadzooks stepped off the sleigh. "I'm going to make some calls to be sure he gets there. Don't worry, the birds will keep helping distribute presents. Stop that mean old man Krampus for me! Toodle-oo!"

"Thank you!" the boy yelled as we lifted off.

"Try not to get ex-SPELLed!" I yelled back, and giggled. The triplets flicked me in the head.

In Seoul, a girl wished for a statue of herself in the city, and Ramp had created a giant marble version of her picking her nose. We shot the harpoon gun Sally had added to the sleigh in to the statue and pulled it to the ground, where it crumbled safely on to a street we evacuated. I scooped up the rubble with The Bag.

"I don't know what you're doing, but it's working," Bertrand said to us over our headsets. "More people are making wishes – but we still don't have enough power to catch up."

Karl chimed in. "The public are starting to get it. Some people thought at first it was a carefully constructed prank, but too much is happening for that to still be believable. He's doing more damage than you guys can fix right now, but he doesn't represent Santa alone."

In Johannesburg, a kid wished for their family to "stop moving" because they had switched schools three times in two years. Ramp froze them in ice, and we left the triplets behind with blow-dryers to thaw them out.

In Portland a three-year-old girl wished to be a firefighter when she grew up and suddenly found herself trying to drive a fire truck down the road in the middle of a huge fire that sprung up out of nowhere in the city. Buzz stayed behind with an arsenal of heavy-duty water guns he pulled from The Bag.

When we arrived in Tokyo, we saw a bed rocketing into the sky. Celia slowed us down, and Crasher steered us to it. On top was a boy clinging for dear life to his pillow and screaming. He wouldn't move to grab my hand, so Sally grabbed my leg and Kurt grabbed Sally's leg and I jumped on to the bed. I held on tight to the boy and his pillow and Kurt dragged us back on to the sleigh.

The bed continued up into the upper atmosphere, and I watched the four rockets on each leg sputter out as it got farther and farther away.

"What did you wish for?" I asked, breathless.

The screen translated his Japanese: "I wanted to go to space."

In Sydney, a girl wished to sing at the opera house one day and suddenly found herself with a gig that night and no plan on what to do. Kurt stayed behind to help her plan her set list.

In Cairo, a boy had wished for new video games, and Ramp had turned all the video games he already had into only *Pong*.

"He said, 'Back in my day, this is the only video game we had, and we *liked it*!' I just wanted to catch some monsters!!!"

We gave him some new ones. Sally got him a laptop, too, and stayed behind to teach him how to make his own video games. I scooped up all the copies of *Pong*.

In Miami, an adult woman had wished for less paperwork in her job so she could spend more time on holiday with her kids. Instead, her entire hotel room was full of stacks of paperwork.

"I'll take this one." The boy with the beige sweater stepped off of our sleigh and into the woman's hotel room. "I'm pretty good at this kind of stuff. Thanks for letting me come on your adventure for a little while, guys. It's been great." He pointed at me. "Special thanks to you for texting me that invite, *best friend*."

I had lots of questions, like: *When did I invite him? When did he get here?? How would his name be in my phone when I don't even know it???? How can we be best friends when I don't even know who he is????????????*

But I just said, "Yeah, totally. Thanks for coming? We'll come back and get you later."

I was also pleasantly surprised with Florida. It wasn't nearly as bad as I had imagined.

"Hey, guys?" Bertrand sounded freaked out over our headsets. "Something crazy is going on at the White House."

"What's the White House?" I asked. "Like an igloo?"

Andrea looked at me like I was crazy. "Are you serious? That's where the president of the United States lives!"

"Is a president like . . . a king?" I asked.

Celia nodded. "Yeah, I think it's like a king."

Andrea pointed as the sleigh slowed to a stop above a rose garden. "*That's* the White House."

"It's just a big white house."

She threw her arms in the air, exasperated. "Exactly!"

At least two hundred kids were in the gated yard in front of the White House, handcuffed and surrounded by policemen.

"They all wished to live in the White House," Bertrand told us, "so Krampus just dropped them off. Now they're all arrested for breaking in."

"Let me handle this." Andrea cracked her neck and her knuckles. "I can talk anyone out of anything."

"Thanks, Andrea." I smiled at her.

She smiled back, said, "Go get the old guy," and left Celia and I alone on the sleigh.

"How're we doing on power?" Celia asked while steering us away. "We haven't even been going fast enough to *see* Krampus."

Bertrand took a second to respond. "I still don't think we're going to be able to break past light speed. You've got a *lot* of power, and Karl is doing a good job getting more people to make wishes—"

"Stop CHASING ME!" A terrifying growl came up from behind us. Before I could even turn around to see what it was, something slammed into our sleigh and disappeared in a puff of sparks. A second later, something slammed into us from the other side. The sleigh teetered over the ocean, and a little alarm beeped on the console.

"It's Krampus!" Celia yelled. "He's dropping in and out of light speed to attack us."

I pulled out the only weapon I had to defend myself with – the firework gun Buzz gave us to help study. I shot the next time we were hit, but the firework sailed lazily out over the water and exploded.

I'M SO IMPRESSED! the firework said sarcastically.

We got bumped again, and I fired again. *SORRY, DUDE!*

Frustrated, I fired a shot off to the side when nothing was happening. Instead of flying out over the water, it bounced on a bubble – the force field protecting Ramp's terrifying black-and-red sleigh. For just a brief second, I could see him, and something was *very, very* wrong: His horns had grown huge and curved backwards, adding several feet to his height, which had also grown considerably. His body had grown hairy and huge, and his feet ended in hooves as big as my face. On top of it all was still an awkwardly overstuffed Santa suit, with the hat skewered by one of the horns.

And then he was gone again.

"The force field!" Celia turned to me and grinned. "The way I built the sleigh. When the force field is on, the engine can't run. Each individual hit will only stop him for a second, but if you can pelt him with lots of stuff at once, he won't be able to speed up at all."

The next time we saw him, though, he was charging us directly from the front.

"PULL UP!" I yelled. "PULL ALL THE WAY UP, OH MY GOSH!"

Crasher veered up and the other reindeer followed. I turned The Bag upside down and yelled, "*THE FOUNTAINHEADS*!" A bunch of copies of *The Fountainhead* tumbled down on to Ramp's sleigh, activated his force field, and then tumbled down into the ocean. "STATUE RUBBLE!" A ridiculous amount of marble came pouring out of The Bag, buying us even more time.

"What do we do now?" I asked while I poured the rubble, and Celia kept pace with the momentum Krampus was still moving with.

"I don't know!" Celia yelled over the splashing rocks. "I didn't really expect us to get to this point!"

Even in all the craziness, my head kept going back to one question: *Why was Ramp doing this?*

I needed to know the answer. And I knew what I had to do.

"I'll see you in a little bit, I hope!" I yelled. And then I yelled, "*PONGS*!" and leapt off our sleigh while several copies of *Pong* kept Ramp's force field going. I *ka-thunk*ed on to the bubble and started sliding off, but the sleigh must not register people as weapons because it popped and I was able to grab hold of one of Ramp's horns before his sleigh sped back up to break light speed.

"Get off! Get off of there!" Ramp growled. "Ouch!"

I was trying to pull my body in closer to the sleigh but kept accidentally kicking Ramp in the face in the process.

"Sorry!" I yelled. "I'm so sorry! I don't mean to – I can't seem to keep my body from floating, and—"

"Shut up!" Ramp raised up the Kringle, and the magic snow expanded from it and wrapped around me. I saw pure white, and then I was tied with rope to the back of Ramp's sleigh.

Instead of disappearing like it had in Santa's workshop, though, the snow . . . *glitched*? The snowflakes twitched and jumped in the air, like they couldn't settle on where they were supposed to be. A few of them touched Ramp, and he winced as his horns grew taller and his fur grew coarser. His tongue lolled out at least six inches past his lips.

"I can't believe thith," he lisped around his tongue. "Thith thould have been THO THIMPLE. But you and Thelia had to go and RUIN IT, HUH?"

"I didn't know it was going to be this beautiful." All around was a sea of colour – every colour I'd ever seen and some I hadn't. It flowed and shifted around itself like someone was mixing paint very slowly. "How can you be mad when you get to see this?"

"Thut up." He was staring intently at his centre console. When I leaned over all the way to one side in my ropes, I could see little snippets of text scrolling quickly up the screen.

Wishes, I thought. *He's picking which wishes to ruin.*

"It's not working, you know." I tried to quietly wiggle my hand back into my suit to look for something in the pockets I could use to escape. "People know you're not Santa. They're still making wishes."

"You can't fickth everything. And you can't chathe me for ever."

"You can't *do this* for ever."

"Yeth, I can."

What a strange thing to say. "How old *are* you, Ramp? I know you're not sixteen."

"I don't know," he mumbled. "I thtopped counting thenturieth ago."

"Centuries?!"

Ramp didn't answer. He dropped out of light speed in front of a window. Inside, a girl with very short brown hair and a flowery blue dress was tapping her foot impatiently.

"Are you the evil Santa?" she asked.

"I'm more of a chaotic neutral."

"Well, I've been waiting all day for you to show up."

What? I narrowed my eyes at the girl.

"I won't waste your time: I know a lot of lame nerds with a lot of dumb wishes. I can give you a list, and you can go goof 'em up. It'll be really funny."

Now Ramp narrowed his eyes. "Give me the litht."

"Seriously?" I squirmed in the ropes, loosening them just a little. I slipped my arm up my sleeve and dug around in my pockets.

"Quiet, Ollie." Ramp took the list from the girl and glanced over it. He raised the Quantum Kringle, which glowed and poured snow into the girl's room. When the snow returned to the globe – after the strange glitchy wiggling – her room was completely bare.

"What?! What did you *do*?" the girl screamed. "Where's all my stuff?"

"I thplit it between the people on thith litht." Ramp threw the list down at her feet. "You better hope they're kind enough to give it back." He twisted the Kringle, and we shot back into the tunnel of colour.

"That was pretty cool of you," I said. My hand finally found something – *the ice-cream scoop.* My dad had said it was indestructible and sharp. Maybe it would cut through the ropes. I started wiggling my hand out. "Standing up to that bully."

"I told her: I'm not evil. Evil ith for the young."

"You're *acting* pretty evil."

"You don't even know what real evil lookth like."

"I'm looking at a scary goat monster flying around the world ruining children's wishes."

Ramp let out a low, rumbly growl. "It'th complicated."

"I can handle it. I'm twelve now."

A loud screech ripped through the air and I clutched my ears. Ramp whipped around and I got a look at his bright red eyes with scary horizontal pupils.

"What? *How?*" he gasped.

"How what?" I wriggled against the ropes but couldn't turn all the way around. I finally slipped my arm back through my sleeve and started slowly sawing on the rope with the ice-cream scoop.

"I'm coming, Ollie!" *Celia's voice. They did it. She made it past light speed!*

Ramp slammed on the brakes, dropping us out of light speed somewhere with lots of trees. He nudged his reindeer – their skin was black and something was strange, but I couldn't see very well from the sleigh floor – and rotated the sleigh. He took off in another direction, and we were back in the tunnel.

"Why are we staying in light speed so long?" I asked, still sawing at the rope. "Can't you go around the world like seven times in a second?"

"I'm trying to throw her off my trail."

Another screeching noise as Celia broke into the light-speed tunnel, this time right next to us.

"Ollie, come on! Let's go!"

Crasher and the others were all wearing their goggles, visibly uncomfortable with the speed. Most reindeer trained for years to be in the Big Nine – it must have been really difficult the first time.

One of the ropes snapped, and I kept sawing at the other two. Ramp dropped out of light speed, but Celia mirrored him and appeared right beside us in time to catch up before Ramp shot us away at a different angle.

"I'm trying!" Another rope broke. One more.

Ramp bumped Celia with the side of his sleigh, and she dropped out of sight for just a second before appearing back beside us.

"Go away!" Ramp yelled. "Leave me alone!"

I snapped the final rope. I stood up and started moving toward Celia's sleigh, but Ramp pulled out his bundle of sticks and aimed it at her face.

Poof. A yellow powder popped out of berries at the end of the sticks and surrounded Celia's face – but she held her breath. She slammed into Ramp's sleigh this time, and we wobbled uncertainly.

"How ith Celia tracking me?" Ramp grabbed me by my collar with one hand and lifted me off the ground. "Tell me or I'll throw you off the thleigh."

"Your sleigh!" I said, because I *really, really* didn't want to die. "She built it, remember? It has a GPS that can track you anywhere on Earth."

"I thee." He jerked the sleigh sharply upward, and Celia disappeared from view. "Then we'll go thomewhere thee can't track us."

"What do you mean?" I asked.

Ramp kept his focus on his computer and the steering. He didn't answer.

"Where can't she track us?"

He still didn't answer, so I sat back down on the sleigh and sighed. Jumping off would be incredibly dangerous, even if I knew where we were. Which I didn't. *And what trip could take whole minutes at light speed?*

Something like ten minutes later, the sleigh landed gently on dusty red ground speckled with white. Ramp immediately jumped out of the sleigh and took several big jumps toward a small wooden hut in the distance, kicking up a cloud of red dust as he went.

I stepped out of the sleigh and looked around – on all sides and as far up as I could see, white swirly snow mixed with red dust. I caught some snow in the air, but it didn't melt – it was fake snow, like in snow globes, but bigger. I could make out the patterns in individual snowflakes. It spun and whirled in a predictable pattern, too – the snow would come close to the ground in a wide circle, then zoom into the middle, shoot to the top, and expand back out into the circle.

The edge of the circle was nearby, the opposite way from Ramp, and I walked over to inspect it. I found a glass wall gently sloping up and back toward the centre, where the snow met. *A snow globe.* Sort of. It was like the top half of a snow globe had been stuck on to the ground.

When I got back to the sleigh, I inspected Ramp's reindeer. All of them had black fur, coarser than it should be. Their antlers were sharper than normal, curved in angry ways, and there were so *many* of them – *because each reindeer had three heads.* I leapt backwards when I realized, and the closest one just stared at me.

He didn't have nine, I thought, *so he* made *nine.*

"Do you . . . uh, do y'all know where we are?"

They didn't say anything. Didn't even really acknowledge me except to stare. None of them moved.

"Uh, OK. Good talk." I backed away from the three-headed reindeer slowly, but they didn't move an inch. Eventually I turned around and walked through the red dust toward the same hut Ramp was now standing on top of.

His hooves were perched right on the very pointiest part of the roof, and he held himself with such perfect balance that he looked much lighter than he should have. (He still looked terrifying. He was *definitely* a crazy monster, but he was a crazy monster who wasn't moving in a scary way.) He cradled the Quantum Kringle in one arm, and it glowed with a soft blue light. There was a rusty metal ladder against the back of the hut, so I climbed up it and sat down on the roof next to him.

"That's Earth." Ramp lifted his finger and pointed up past the swirling snow into the sky. The sun was setting off to one side, and

I could just barely make out a blue spot all the way near the other horizon.

"Oh," I said, like it was a totally casual and normal thing for someone to tell me. Like it was *one-hundred-percent not a crazy scary big deal that I guess we were in space or whatever.* "Cool."

"Yeah, it is pretty cool." He slid his legs down the roof and sat down next to me. "Kris Kringle made it."

"Your lisp is gone." I looked at his mouth, and his tongue was shrinking back down to normal size. His horns looked just a little smaller, too, and his fur just a little shorter. He didn't offer an explanation. "Are you . . . OK, Ramp?"

"My name is Krampus. And also, no."

Krampus flicked his eyes to me and scowled, then flicked his eyes back to the sky.

"The computer said you were Kris Kringle. And you kind of look like him."

"I'm not Kris Kringle," he growled. "But he made me."

"*Made* you?"

My question hung in the air for a moment. Krampus looked down at the dusty red ground, then back at the sky. He took a deep breath.

"Kris Kringle didn't build the Quantum Kringle, Ollie. He found it. He found it, and he used it to make all the other inventions. He used it to build *everything* – the North Pole, The Workshop, Christmas as you know it was all made by this . . . thing." Krampus threw the Kringle at the ground, where it bounced harmlessly in the red dust and rolled to a stop.

"He didn't trust anyone else with it. Not even his son. So he made me, a perfect copy of a perfect man. You can see how that turned out." He gestured to his horns. "I got these. And the legs. So I wasn't what he hoped for. I wasn't *perfect*. He tried to teach me anyway, tried to turn me into a Santa worthy of his legacy, but every mistake I made was another reason I wasn't right. I was broken."

I wasn't sure what to do – I didn't really have a rule book on what to do when someone told you they were a disappointing clone of the creator of Christmas – so I just reached over and patted his furry leg a few times. He scowled at me again.

"So he lied. He left me on an island alone with no map and no way out and told no one else I even *existed*. Kris Kringle – the man your whole city worships – didn't know I couldn't die. *I* didn't even know yet. He probably thought I would. He lied about me, he lied about his inventions, and now this disgusting holiday celebrates him."

"That's why the plans for his inventions aren't complete," I realized. "*He* didn't even know how to make them. Not really." I could freak out about all the ridiculous, insane things that were happening to me later. For now I just wanted to make sure I understood everything. "And you hate Christmas because you think it's about him."

"It *is* about him. Santa parades around in that same hideous outfit to this day. The same thing we're both wearing." He gestured between the two of us.

"Hideous? Really?" I made a pouty face at him. "I thought I looked adorable!"

Krampus laughed, and his horns and hair receded even further – his eyes were clearing up, too, and he almost looked like the frail old man I met before the first trial.

I went on. "That's not what Christmas is about, though." I took my hat off and scratched an itch in my hair. "Kris Kringle was just one of a lot of Santas, and Christmas isn't even *about* Santa, you know? Or it's not supposed to be. It's about . . . hm." I thought for a second. "It's about, like, when two people help another person run farther than he could have run on his own. It's, like, when you're competing with your friends and everybody's trying to win, but they're also having fun and you don't mind sharing your popcorn balls with the competition." I tugged at the fur ball at the end of my hat because looking people in the eye is hard when you're telling the truth and also because I didn't know I knew what to say until I said it. "It's, like, when everybody's tired from competing for a whole week, so they lean on each other to keep each other going. Or when all your friends come to your birthday party, or when those same friends all dress up in the same outfit and try to save the world."

I sniffled and started tearing up. "You didn't get a real Christmas, I guess, since your gene-dad invented it and then didn't really give you a chance to celebrate it, but that's the kind of stuff that it's about. It's about everybody getting together and doing something kind and also doing something fun." Now the tears were definitely coming down my face, and I glanced up at Krampus to see if he was crying, too. He wasn't, but his frown seemed softer than normal.

He cleared his throat and spoke softly. "Then why do we need Santa? Why do we need the North Pole?"

"We don't, I guess." I dried my eyes with my sleeve. "But it's a place where a lot of people live, and what we do makes a lot of people happy. We give people a reason to get in the same room and open presents, and run, and race, and dance, and save the world. Mostly with toys, but same thing, I think."

I took a deep breath and nodded. *I'm right*, I thought. *I didn't know for sure I would be right when I started talking, but now I think I am.*

"Kris Kringle sounds like he did some stuff wrong. Some big stuff. But he also used the Quantum Kringle to do really beautiful things, like this . . . Christmas on Mars." I looked at Krampus for real this time; a serious look. "He might not have been a good person, but he made a good thing. Christmas isn't perfect yet, but Santa thought it could be better. Now I think so, too. If you keep trying to ruin it, though, we might never find out."

We sat in silence again, this time for a long time. Fake snow danced around red dirt, mirroring the colours of our outfits.

"How'd you get so smart, when you're just a kid?" Krampus asked.

"I'm not a kid any more," I reminded him. "I'm twelve."

He laughed again. I'd never heard him laugh this much before – I'm not sure I'd ever even seen him *smile*. It made him look even more like Kris Kringle, which made me feel bad again, so I scooted over and gave him a big hug.

"Fine." Krampus wrapped one arm around me and lifted up to a standing position, leaving me clinging to his side. He jumped to the ground and grabbed the Quantum Kringle, then jumped back to the sleigh in four huge bounds.

"Hey – OOF – this is – *whoa*—"

He tossed me down on the sleigh and twisted the Kringle. The reindeer tilted up and shot out into the sky. Within a moment we were back in the colourful tunnel.

"Wait, what are we doing? Because if you're going to try to ruin Christmas again, I really think we should talk for a little bit longer—"

"I said *fine*."

"Meaning?"

"I'll stop trying to 'ruin Christmas,'" he grumbled, and waggled his fingers into air quotes. "I was getting hungry anyway."

Chapter 24

We rode back to Earth in silence. When Krampus slowed us out of the tunnel, we were sliding to a stop in front of Claus Castle. My headset chirped.

"Ollie! You're back!" Bertrand sounded surprised. "Where did you go?"

"Space," I said, like it was an everyday A-OK thing to say and not something really amazing and also kind of a brag. "Where is everybody?"

"Celia picked everyone up and brought them back here to get their sleighs and split the remaining gifts. There are still a lot of presents to distribute and not a lot of time left in Christmas Eve. Not that those rules really matter any more, I guess. Usually Santa tries to follow the night across the world, but . . . Krampus kind of threw that out the window."

The side door creaked, and Santa stumbled out, rubbing his eyes and yawning. "Ollie Gnome!" he boomed, smiling and spreading his arms wide. "My kids explained everything. I'm so, so sorry for the mix-up." He lifted me off the ground into a very tight hug.

"That's OK, sir." I struggled to breathe. "You didn't know."

"I suspected. You always seemed like the trustworthy type."

"Thanks." I pointed my thumb back toward the sleigh. "I should maybe introduce you to Krampus. He's kind of your grandpa, or something."

Santa gasped. "What happened to these reindeer?!"

Krampus glanced over at them. "Oh. Sorry about that." He raised up the Kringle and released the snow, which wrapped around the reindeer and returned them to normal.

"Oh. My. Gosh. We went to *space*." The newly single-headed leader of the three unhooked from the sleigh and bounded around, excited. "I mean, we went as disgusting monster versions of ourselves, and we were trapped in our bodies unable to speak or move of our own free will, but weweretrappedinourbodiesunableto-speakormoveofourownfreewill *on Mars*."

"Ugh, there she goes again." The other two reindeer both rolled their eyes. "Stargazer's never going to shut up about this."

The third reindeer turned on Krampus and lifted on to his hind legs, jabbing a hoof at Krampus's chest. "You're lucky we're reasonable reindeer who get that you were going through some messed up stuff, 'cause that was *way not cool, bro*."

"You are right." Krampus nodded and scratched his beard. "It was 'way not cool.' I apologize." He handed the Quantum Kringle to Santa.

Santa clapped his arm around Krampus's shoulder, and Krampus scowled. "Seems like we've got a lot to talk about!"

The air cracked and sizzled, and Celia dropped out of nothingness on to the ground in front of us. All nine of her reindeer immediately unhitched and collapsed to the ground, groaning in relief.

"Ollie!" she yelled, pushing her goggles up on to her forehead

and running over to me for a hug. "I was so worried! I did, like"
– she looked up at the sky and made the scrunched-up face she
used for mental calculations – "four hundred laps around the
world or something, looking for you. And it only took like a
minute!"

"You only looked for me for *one minute*?"

"Well, I wasn't going to waste time when there was work
to do." She gave me another hug squeeze. "I trusted you to figure
it out."

I brought my voice down to a whisper. "I actually don't think
I really did anything? But I totally went to space."

Celia slapped both of her own cheeks with her hands and
gasped. "What?! I want to go to space! You have to show me where
you went *right now*." She started climbing back on to our sleigh.

"*YES!*" Stargazer yelled, and did a flip in the air. "I AM SO
PUMPED TO GO BACK TO SPACE WITH FULL CONTROL
OF MY BODY AND MIND."

"Now, wait a minute," Santa interjected. "There will be plenty
of time to go to space after we get everything sorted."

"I agree," I agreed. "Plus, I haven't eaten or slept in almost an
entire day, and that's not a good idea because I'm a growing boy."

"We're all growing boys!" Celia yelled, frustrated. "Why can't
we go grow in space?"

A flock of sleighs interrupted us by flying up and landing in
the snow around us – all our friends were returning together from
their parts of the world.

"The presents are all done." Sally led the group over to us. "We
didn't have time to fix *all* the weird things Krampus did around

the world, and there are still going to be a lot of questions from . . . well, everyone, but at least we did what we set out to do."

"So you could say you . . . saved Christmas?" Santa beamed big at all of us, with all of his bright white teeth.

"That's kind of a simplistic way to put it, Dad. I don't even know right now if 'Christmas' is going to be the same thing any more. There's so much to talk ab—"

She was cut short by Santa scooping her into another big hug. That's when it hit me.

We did it.

Christmas happened.

The North Pole was going to be fine. Different, maybe. *Better*, maybe. Kids were opening their bird-delivered presents all over the world. Parents were taking a break from their worries to buy last-minute batteries and pretend to lose at board games. Snow fell and grandmas smiled and bells jingled and everybody ate too much.

We'd given people a reason to get in the same room to run, and race, and dance, and save the world. With toys, mostly, but that's the way it should be. (Reporters were really, *really* concerned about the whole "evil Santa" thing, but we'd worry about that later.)

In this moment, Santa was happy. We were happy. Everything felt *right*, and *good*, and *one-hundred-percent Christmas-y*.

The group around us got a little bigger as the North Pole realized we were home. A few elves brought their trumpets and played. A couple of others popped confetti into our faces. Somebody started singing "Deck the Halls" and a little kid who should have been in bed asked for my autograph.

"I'm so proud that all of you saved Christmas!" Santa spun Sally around while she laughed. Celia and I did a complicated series of high fives. "I just can't contain it!"

"Yeah, thanks for that." Klaus walked out of Claus Castle and leaned against the stone wall. "Otherwise it wouldn't have mattered that I won."

The whole crowd went totally silent. Santa cleared his throat and looked down at the ground uncomfortably.

"Now, Klaus, I don't know about—"

"What? What don't you know?" Klaus advanced on his dad, already yelling again. "I was the only one who even *showed up* for the challenge. I won. Those were the rules."

Celia made eye contact with me and heaved a sigh that puffed up her cheeks. Her look said, *Sheesh. Not this again.*

I dragged my face down with both hands, making my eyes look scary and weird. I stuck out my tongue and wiggled it like I was saying *bleeeehhhhhchchhhh.* Celia snorted, but covered her mouth so as to not interrupt the moment.

"Things changed, son. I was unconscious. The trial couldn't have happened anyway."

"Fine, then let's do the trial right now. I'm ready."

Celia hasn't slept in almost two days, I thought. *PLUS, she saved the world. That's not fair.*

"Klaus, *no.*" Santa raised his voice just a little, and it sent a shiver down my spine. "Celia and Ollie saw a crisis, and they dealt with it. You didn't even help them, Klaus. You put yourself before everything, and that proves to me that you're not ready."

"I was following the rules!" he argued. "You said that if we didn't show up, we'd be disqualified!"

"Which wouldn't have mattered if no one had shown up," I pointed out.

Klaus glared at me with an anger I'd never seen from anyone before. "They didn't even ask me to help!" Klaus was tearing up now, and his face was bright red.

"Yeah, we did." Kurt crossed his arms. "Ollie called you just like he called us. And then Sally and I both left messages on your phone."

"My . . . uh . . . phone was off because I was studying!"

"You texted me back and said, 'I don't care, leave me alone.'" Sally held up her phone.

"It was an auto-response text!"

"That's such a lie!" Buzz yelled.

I don't care any more, I thought. *I just need to take a nap.*

Santa clapped his hands loudly, silencing everybody.

"I've made my decision. Ollie, Celia, your bravery is the only reason we're even able to have this conversation. One of you is Santa."

"Celia," I said.

"Ollie," Celia said at the exact same time.

We looked at each other and frowned.

"It should *obviously* be you," we both said.

"No, *you!*" we argued.

"Don't argue with me!" we chided each other. And then we both laughed.

Klaus clenched and unclenched his fists and breathed heavy out of his nose. "I'm leaving." He said it forcefully, almost a yell. There was no doubt he meant it. "If you do this, Dad, I'm leaving. *And I'm not coming back.*"

Santa swallowed, but didn't look at Klaus. He took a deep breath. "I don't think it's fair for me to decide which. You two work it out. We'll make the announcement when you're ready."

Klaus screamed something that didn't sound like words. He ran inside and slammed the door. Santa winced.

"Go get some rest." Santa started walking to the door to follow after Klaus. "You can explain everything after."

The door shut, and the rest of us collectively yawned.

"Do you really think Klaus is going to leave?" I asked.

"I hope so," Buzz said. "What a jerk."

I didn't hope so. I glanced at Krampus, who sighed.

"I know how he feels." He scratched at the base of one of his horns. "But Santa made the right call."

"Wait, why is *he* here?" Andrea whirled on Krampus. "Wasn't this all his fault?"

"Yes," Krampus retorted. "And don't talk to your elders that way."

Celia spread her hands out and made shushing noises. Everybody waited for her to say something, but she didn't, and everyone understood. Silently, we drifted away. Celia and I hugged and agreed to meet up to talk after a nap.

Krampus awkwardly bounced from hoof to hoof like he wasn't sure what to do. I took his hand and led him through the sleepy town to my house. We looked ridiculous – a grumpy old man and a sleepy elf covered in red dirt and snow walking down the street in ragged Big Red suits.

"I'm sorry," he mumbled as we crunched through the snow.

I nodded and squeezed his hand. "I know."

❄ ❄ ❄

The very last day of the year was a lot like the middlest. But on this particular December 31st, as we waited for Santa's Big Speech, nothing felt normal. Everyone at the North Pole crammed into Peppermint Square, just like they always did on December 31st. Claus Castle also looked like it always did on December 31st, its balcony decorated with bright, colourful flags and a candy-striped carpet just for the occasion.

There was only one big difference this year:

Celia and I were *backstage*.

Celia was pretty sure this was a HUGE PROBLEM.

"What if they hate me?" Celia panicked to her best friend, me. "What if this is a really bad idea?"

"You're just being paranoid," I told her, and adjusted the collar on her Big Red Suit. "Think about it like another game. We're making the best move."

"This isn't a game, Ollie. This is *Serious Christmas Business*." Celia flapped her hands in the air and took deep breaths.

Trumpets sounded out on the balcony, and Celia's eyes widened. "What if I fall asleep at the computer and switch all the naughty and nice kids?" she asked me. "What if my beard gets stuck in a door? *What if I put every nice kid on the naughty list AND my beard gets stuck in a door?*"

I looked at her like her noggin was full of eggnog.

"You probably won't grow a beard," I explained. "I don't think that comes with the job. You're just nervous because it's your first speech."

"It's a good idea." Krampus crossed his arms and frowned at us supportively. "So quit yer whining."

Celia and I turned around and looked at all our other friends, all dressed in their Big Red Suits and just as nervous as we were. Buzz and Gadzooks, Kurt and Sally, Bertrand and Krampus, Andrea and Karl, and – I could have sworn there was someone else. I looked around the room and didn't see anyone, though. *Oh well.* Klaus had really disappeared, and no one knew where he was.

We heard the tail end of Santa Claus's speech. "And now I'm proud to introduce to all of you my successor in just a few years' time: *Santa Pixie!*"

The doors to the balcony opened, and our friends paraded out in front of us and took their positions along the edge of the balcony. Celia and I squeezed hands for support one last time, then I walked out alone, waving, and took my place next to a centre podium with steps in front of it so Celia could see out over the top.

Celia came out of the doors, and the whole North Pole cheered. Even the elves and Clauses who had supported Klaus before knew her plan was what had saved Christmas, so they joined in, too. It was the loudest cheer I'd ever heard, and *trust me*, I'd heard a lot of Christmas cheers.

Celia cleared her throat and adjusted the papers with our planned speech on the podium. She wiped some sweat from her brow and glanced down at me. I smiled up at her, which wasn't new; she's always been taller.

" 'Santa' is a name I never even imagined I would have. None of us did." She swallowed heavily. I tried to project positive vibes by focusing really hard on good, confident things, like unicorns and dragons.

"My parents, like probably a lot of yours, told me since I was a baby that I could grow up to be anything I wanted. That wasn't

274

really true, though, until Santa Claus decided to institute the Santa Trials and give us all an opportunity to become something we thought we weren't born to do."

I saw her mum out in the front of the crowd, crying. Her dad was crying, too, and so were both of my parents. *Come on, guys,* I thought, and then I realized that I was also crying.

"Santa Matthew Claus has given us the chance to change Christmas for the better. He told us that it would be a tough job, that sometimes it was too much for one person. We knew we'd have to be everything Kris Kringle was: an inventor, a leader, a lover of toys. Kind to everyone. Never made a bad decision. Never got angry. Never had any trouble. Everything worked out perfectly for him his whole life." She grinned at the crowd. She was finding her groove. "If that sounds impossible, it should. It was. Kris Kringle made mistakes, just like all of us. Mistakes that we're still learning from today."

I glanced over at Krampus, who was scowling out at the audience next to Bertrand. Bertrand patted him on the back, which he had to reach up really high to do. It was *adorable.*

"The group of kids – and one old man – that you see onstage today decided that it *is* too much for one person. Christmas would be over if it weren't for everybody here. We'd all be moving out of the North Pole if every single person you see hadn't stepped up to save the day. Because of that, I have a few announcements to make."

This was the fun part. I stood up straighter and saw that everyone else was doing the same.

"After the events of Christmas Eve, the world has a lot of questions. While I am training to be Santa, Andrea Claus will be preparing to become the leader of my new World Relations team . . ." Celia narrowed her eyes at her paper. I nudged her. ". . . with help from Maria Duende."

Andrea whipped out a sign that said *BREAKING NEWS: SANTA PIXIE IS THE GREATEST!* The crowd – even Maria Duende – clapped and cheered.

"For the same reason, more people from the outside world will be trying to find us and visit the North Pole. This could be an amazing opportunity, but it could also put us in danger. That's why Buzz Brownie and Karl Kobold will take charge of the Secret Helpers and form our new North Pole Defence team."

Buzz stepped forward and flexed with Karl standing on his bicep, posing. Two Secret Helpers he had brought with him crouched on either side and made finger guns to complete the picture. The crowd laughed.

"As some of you know, Bertrand Claus has finally replicated one of Kris Kringle's original inventions. Because of his breakthrough, and because of Krampus Claus's unique knowledge and experience with the Quantum Kringle and Kris Kringle himself, the two of them will now work together to head our Research and Development team."

Bertrand twirled his bow tie and little fireworks flew from it and into the air, spelling out *LET'S DO SOME SCIENCE!!!!* Krampus did some lazy jazz hands.

"Kurt and Sally will become head of The Workshop; Kurt will help us make a plan to keep older kids and teenagers interested in Christmas, and Sally will have final say before me on all toy-related matters." Sally waved with a few fingers and then used those same fingers to flip the page in her book. Kurt did a riff on an air guitar but real noise blasted out over the crowd. I was surprised enough that I jumped, which the crowd saw and laughed.

"Gadzooks will remain in charge of birds and will continue to help us understand the things that science can't explain."

Gadzooks threw her top hat out over the crowd and doves streamed out of it, dropping a piece of candy to everyone in the audience, who didn't cheer because it was butterscotch and butterscotch is so good that they all ate theirs immediately.

"We also have . . . a friend . . . in charge of finance and espionage, but it seems like he might not have been able to make it today—"

"I'm here!" The boy in the beige sweater waved from the far end of the balcony. "And I've been thinking of calling my job 'spynance.'"

I still don't know who he is, I thought, *or how he got out here without me noticing him, but that is a very good pun.*

"I really appreciate the opportunity," he continued. "You guys are really just the best friends I could ask for."

"Alright, enough of this," Krampus grumbled. "Kid, *what is your name?*"

The boy in the beige sweater blinked. "Uh, it's . . . uh . . ." He grinned and shrugged. "I guess I've forgotten! Whoops!"

Oh my actual gosh.

"Finally," Celia continued, "Ollie Gnome will be my Second Santa, and will be in charge of the council made up of all these people to advise me in the decisions I make going forward." She grinned at me, and I jumped up and down and waved at the crowd.

"He will make sure we always keep the spirit of Christmas in our hearts and minds while we make our decisions."

Celia pulled me up the stairs of the podium so we could say the last part together. "We have a wish: We wish for a new Christmas. A better Christmas. I hope all of you will support us in making it come true."

Celia and I pulled goggles out of our pockets and popped them on. "Now if you'll excuse us . . ."

Right on cue, Crasher led our team of reindeer in pulling our brand-new, built-for-everybody sleigh up in front of the balcony. Celia and I jumped on together, and then the rest of our friends jumped on with us. Even Santa jumped on.

Celia clicked some buttons. "How's the engine, Bertrand?"

"Engine's good. Quantum Kringle installed and ready for action."

"You ready, Little Nine?"

Crasher snorted. "Ready as we'll ever be, Cap'n!"

"Krampus, you put in the coordinates?"

"Yeah, yeah, yeah." He rolled his eyes. "Let's get this over with."

"Wait, let me get the camera ready." I turned on a handheld camera and pointed it down at the crowd as we adjusted and flew over them. We waved, and they waved back. "OK, it's ready."

"WE'LL BE RIGHT BACK, GUYS!" I yelled.

"We need some tunes!" Kurt exclaimed. He clicked his music box and put on something exciting, with a good build.

"You want to do the thing?" Santa asked us.

Celia and I looked at him. "The thing?"

"Yeah, you know." He winked. "The thing."

"We can?"

"You can."

Celia and I cleared our throats.

"ON CRASHER! ON ROCKER! ON SLAMMER AND JAMMER! ON SNOOZER! ON TRUTHER! ON TREASON AND SEASON!"

"AND STARGAZER!" Stargazer yelled. "I WASN'T GOING TO MISS THIS ONE!"

Then:

Over the rush of the engine, the crowd, and their roar
(Even Krampus himself couldn't manage to snore),
They all heard us exclaim, with a grin on our face:
"MERRY CHRISTMAS TO ALL! NOW WE'RE GOING TO SPACE!"

Acknowledgements

Thanks to my parents (Jason, Connie, Kim) for their incredible support from the babytimes onward. This book exists because a little kid spent too much time on a computer playing games, and you're the ones who made that possible. In that, I must also thank my huge network of grandparents and aunts and uncles and greats for encouraging me to speak up and believe that my words were worth hearing.

Andy Carter: Time flies inside a locker. You have been there for me every second for years and I don't know what I would have done without you. Words absolutely cannot do it justice. Thank you.

Connor Ratchford sat on our couch and listened to me read the first chapters of this book as soon as I had finished them because I was too excited to contain it. Thanks for laughing at the jokes, and for growing into an adult with me.

Some people read parts of this book before it was even good. Thanks to Austin Jenkins for asking the right questions, Nick Splendorr for always having a joke ready when I needed one, and Will Walton for being one of the most amazing listeners I've ever met.

Janet and everybody at Avid Bookshop are owed my life for their support and love. I wake up every day because of you guys.

Thanks to Justin, Travis and Griffin McElroy for always having a podcast or video when I needed a laugh, a story, or a lovable monster to lead me out of a dark place. Magic is easy, thanks to y'all.

More thanks to: Alexandra Martin, Aliza Goldstein, my parents again just in case, Team Lunch, Amber Bradshaw, Peter Reitz, Hendershot's Coffee, and everybody at Scholastic for their incredible energy and kindness.

Unending gratitude to my editor, David Levithan, for guiding me through this entire process, and being my hero. You taught me so much, and showed me how much more I have to learn. You listened and understood in ways I never expected. You did more than you ever had to, and I will always be thankful for that.

Oh, and thanks to Saint Nick for being a pretty cool guy.